J.w.a.
8/4/85

I0617579

Longarm stepped from cover and drew.

He got a quick glimpse of a woman sitting on the floor inside the cabin, her arms bound behind her back, and Snake Trague standing over her.

"Freeze, Trague!" Longarm called, leveling his Colt as he spoke.

Trague whirled, clawing his revolver. Longarm triggered his Colt as Trague's weapon cleared its holster. Longarm's gun hand flew up and back, and a searing pain ripped up his arm as the Colt flew from his hand. Before the Colt reached the floor, though, Trague was crumpling.

Reaching for the derringer, Longarm didn't bother to finish drawing it. He'd seen dead men fall before...

TABOR EVANS

LONGARM

ON THE GOODNIGHT TRAIL

A JOVE BOOK

LONGARM ON THE GOODNIGHT TRAIL

A Jove Book/published by arrangement with
Context, Inc.

PRINTING HISTORY
Jove edition/August 1985

All rights reserved.
Copyright © 1985 by Jove Publications, Inc.
This book may not be reproduced in whole or in part,
by mimeograph or any other means, without permission.
For information address: The Berkley Publishing Group,
200 Madison Avenue, New York, N.Y. 10016.

ISBN: 0-515-08331-3

Jove books are published by The Berkley Publishing Group,
200 Madison Avenue, New York, N.Y. 10016. The words
"A JOVE BOOK" and the "J" with sunburst are trademarks
belonging to Jove Publications, Inc.

PRINTED IN THE UNITED STATES OF AMERICA

Chapter 1

Longarm's cold anger matched the chill of the little room in the Rock Springs undertaking parlor where he stood looking down at the body of Deputy U. S. Marshal Les McWhorter. The dead deputy was younger than Longarm and had been assigned to the Denver office less than a year before, too short a time for a close friendship to develop between them. But they had worked together on a few cases, enough to create the bond of danger shared in a common effort.

Like most men who wore a lawman's badge in the West, Longarm looked at an attack on a fellow lawman as being an attack on himself. The undertaker had just started to undress the dead man, and Longarm's eyes grew cold when he saw the wound left by the bullet that had killed McWhorter. It had been a rifle slug, and had entered the young deputy's body from the back, a few inches to one side of his spine. There was a gaping cavity in his chest where the bullet, exiting, had torn away flesh and skin, leaving a gaping, raw red crater that was ugly in the lamplight flooding the windowless room.

"How long you figure it was since he got killed?" Longarm asked the undertaker.

"Not more than about four hours," the man replied without looking up from his job of stripping the body. "He was still warm when I got there, and that was more than two hours ago. I'd say he died about an hour before the miner came in to report the shooting. Dan Ogilvy—he's our police chief—had to go to Cheyenne to testify in a state case, so I sent that telegram to the U. S. marshal in Denver as soon as the miner showed me the badge he found on the corpse."

"Then you'd've got to where he was shot after the snow began, wouldn't you?" Longarm frowned thoughtfully.

"A little while after," the mortician agreed. "But there wasn't enough snow on the ground then to hold tracks."

"They flagged that train I was on and gave me the telegram

1

from my chief about an hour west of here, at that little whistle stop named Opal," Longarm said. He was thinking aloud rather than talking to the undertaker. "And I saw the first snowflakes from the train window about the time we crossed Green River." He paused for a few moments of mental calculation, then went on, "So the killer ain't got too much of a start on me, and I'd imagine the snow's going to slow him down some. You're sure he's headed north, are you?"

"Marshal, I don't rightly know. I've already told you all I'm sure about. The miner who found the body was going home from the Staghorn, and that's the last saloon on the north side of town. He swears he didn't pass anybody on the road before he stumbled onto the body."

"What is there to the north? I'd guess it's mines, and maybe some shanties. I don't recall another town up that way," Longarm went on.

"No," the undertaker replied. "The first town's Farson, and it's right at fifty miles away. There's a few cabins along the road. There's what's left of some buildings at the shafts of some worked-out mines, but they're not more than piles of boards. Still, I guess they'd do for a man to hide in, or shelter in from the snow."

"Well, I appreciate your help," Longarm said. "I'll get on over to the livery stable and rent me a horse. You'll take care of sending that wire I wrote out a minute ago?"

"Just as soon as I finish here, I'll head for the depot and send it," the man promised. "And I'm sorry about your friend. Hope you find whoever it was that killed him."

Longarm wasted no time at the livery stable. He fended off the questions of the curious hangers-on who'd heard of the shooting. Less than a quarter of an hour after he'd left the undertaking parlor, he was riding slowly along the stone-studded dirt road—little more than a rutted trail—heading north.

Already the snowfall was beginning to slacken. Longarm knew the weather patterns of the western Rocky Mountain slopes well enough to realize that what he was seeing now, in early April, was winter's final gasp. Almost every year, especially at the more than mile-high country through which he was travelling, there was an early-spring snow or two.

Generally, the springtime snows swirled down in only a few tiny scattered flakes which melted as soon as they touched the ground. Occasionally, however, the fall was blindingly heavy, made up of big, wet flakes that blanketed a dozen or more square miles of the Rockies' slopes to a depth of two feet or more, the flakes packing to slick mushy ice under the feet of men and horses and bringing to a halt not only the travellers on the roads, but those on trains as well.

It was a raw, barren country through which Longarm rode. Years of coal mining had seen the pines chopped down for shoring timbers, and without the shelter of the big trees the thin soil leached into sterility as its surface was washed away during the spring snow-melt.

Everywhere Longarm looked he saw rising above the snow the tops of house-sized boulders as well as long-stretching red-brown ledges of raw shale. The snowfall had begun to slacken only a short time after he'd left Rock Springs, as the freak spring storm moved on across the mountains. Now, a ray or two of pale pre-sunset sun showed around the edges of the scudding clouds.

As he pushed his horse ahead, keeping an eye on the surface of the snow that lay deeper on the ground as the rough road shelved upward, Longarm took out the telegram that Billy Vail had sent to intercept the eastbound Union Pacific train on which he'd known Longarm would be riding on his return to Denver after having closed the case he was on in Utah.

WIRE JUST IN FROM UNDERTAKER ROCK SPRINGS STOP MCWHORTER MURDERED THERE STOP MCWHORTER TRAILING TRAGUE WHO BROKE PRISON MONTH AGO STOP STOP AND TAKE OVER CASE.

Billy Vail sure don't waste no words when he's mad, old son, Longarm told himself as he tucked the flimsy back in the pocket of his long black coat. He brushed his forefinger thoughtfully along the edge of his flaring longhorn-swept moustache as he rode slowly, keeping his eyes on the trail, continuing his silent monologue with himself. *Billy didn't need to say much this time, seeing as he knows it was me that taken Snake Trague in the first place, after he killed that purty little Cora girl that was laying up with Ace Glass.*

Longarm's retentive memory needed no jogging to recall his search for Trague and the outlaw's ultimate capture. The scene in the isolated shack where he'd at last run Trague to earth had burst on his eyes in shades of red and with the impact of a scene in a slaughterhouse.

When Longarm kicked in the door, the floor and walls of the shack were smeared with blood, and drops of crimson were running from the edges of the table where Trague stood. The outlaw held a ten-inch Bowie knife in his hand and was still hacking at the body of the girl who'd been Glass's mistress.

Engrossed in his grisly butchery, Trague had been slow in dropping the knife to reach for his gun. When he did swivel to grab at his revolver butt, his boots slipped on the weltered floor and he fell heavily, squirming to reach his pistol.

Longarm was not a killer of unarmed men, even when they were on the borderline between men and animals. He'd reached Trague's side before the outlaw could make a second grab at his gun butt, and kicked the killer's hand away from the revolver. Then he'd planted his foot firmly on Trague's wrist, pinning his gun hand to the blood-slick floor.

Only after he'd yanked the murderer to his feet and clamped handcuffs around Trague's wrists did Longarm get a clear look at the naked body of the girl, slashed almost beyond recognition as being human. Holding his surging anger in check, Longarm had hauled Trague to jail. Later, testifying at the outlaw's trial, he'd painted a graphic verbal picture of the scene, and had sat in jaw-gritting silence when he heard the judge impose the death penalty on the killer.

Now, riding through the lengthening shadows, searching the snow's surface for tracks of the fugitive, but finding none, Longarm wondered how it had been possible for Trague to be free, how Les McWhorter had found his trail, and how his fellow deputy had come to join the list of Snake Trague's victims.

That wire Billy Vail sent sure didn't give you many answers, old son, he told himself as he fished a cheroot from his pocket and flicked his thumbnail across a match-head to light it with. *Not that you'd need a lot of palaver. Billy'd know that. So what you better do now is forget about how you feel about that son of a bitch Trague, and keep your mind on your job.*

He was reaching the end of the area over which the little snow cloud had passed. Dark patches of soil were already beginning to show on the road ahead and on the slopes beside it. Longarm was scanning those slopes with watchful eyes when he saw the cabin ahead.

It stood off the road a dozen yards, its roof-peak sagging, the rough-sawn boards that formed its sides warped and bent. In an instant reaction, Longarm reined his horse off the road. He turned the animal's head sharply and rode a few yards at a slant that took him far enough downslope to avoid being seen by anyone in the cabin—if it was indeed occupied, which he thought wasn't likely, considering its dilapidated condition. He slid out of the saddle and looped the horse's reins around a taller than usual stump, then moved forward on foot to investigate.

Advancing stealthily, taking advantage of every bit of the scant cover provided by the stumps, Longarm worked his way toward the cabin. He heard the voices inside when he was still too far away to make out what was being said.

Moving even more slowly to be sure his approach stayed noiseless, Longarm started across the short stretch of rock-studded soil that separated him from the cabin. As he drew closer, he saw a movement on the stump-studded slope beyond the shanty, and froze for a moment. Then he could see the horse tethered a short distance from the back of the dilapidated structure, and knew his search had come to an end.

Holding his position, he studied the cabin for a moment. He was directly in line with one of its corners, and was close enough to see that the cracks between the boards where the side and end walls joined were smaller than those along the walls. A doorway without a door opened in the end, and a window without panes was set high in the side.

Gambling that he'd be able to finish his approach without being seen, Longarm moved ahead. He was within a few feet of the shanty's corner when he heard a woman's voice inside, and he quickly covered the remaining distance. Shielded now from being seen, he stopped for a moment to listen.

"But I don't know, I tell you!" the woman was protesting. "Even if Cora was my half-sister, she never told me anything about Ace Glass!"

"Damn you, don't lie to me!" a man said. Longarm recognized Snake Trague's rasping, nasal snarl. Trague went on, "And if you wanta stay alive, don't play me for a fool!"

"I don't know what you're talking about," she said.

"Like hell you don't!" Trague replied. "You taken up with Ace after I killed Cora. I heard that while I was waiting in the pen for 'em to hang me. Stands to reason he must've told you something about where he had his big bankroll stashed!"

"Cora was with Ace two years," the woman said. Her voice was a bit calmer now. "I only spent about two months with him. Do you think Ace would've trusted me enough in two months to tell me anything as important as that?"

"How in hell would I know what Ace'd do?" Trague retorted. "He was crazy as a loon. That's why me and him split up."

"Ace may have been crazy, but he wasn't crazy enough to tell me any of his secrets," she retorted. "And he was as good to me as he could be, for the kind of man he was. I don't see why you had to kill him!"

"If I hadn't shot first, he'd've cut me down," Trague said quickly. Then his voice grew harsh and threatening as he went on, "Now, I've heard all I wanta hear about Ace! You better start talking, woman, or I'll give you what I did Cora!"

"You'll probably do that anyhow, whether or not I tell you anything," the woman retorted. "And since I don't know where Ace kept his money, I can't tell you that, even if I wanted to."

Longarm decided it was time for him to move. He started toward the door. Two long strides took him to the edge of the opening. As he stepped from cover he drew. He got a quick glimpse of a woman sitting on the floor inside the cabin, her arms bound behind her back, and Snake Trague standing over her. Trague's back was to the door.

"Freeze, Trague!" Longarm called, leveling his Colt as he spoke.

Trague whirled, clawing his revolver from its holster. The outlaw had not earned his nickname for nothing. He drew with a speed Longarm had not suspected he possessed. Longarm triggered his Colt as Trague's weapon cleared its holster. The heavy slug from the Colt found its mark in the split second before Trague's finger closed down on the trigger of his own gun.

Longarm's gun hand flew up and back, and a searing pain ripped up his arm as the bullet from the outlaw's pistol struck Longarm's Colt. The Colt flew from his hand, hitting the inside wall of the cabin with a clatter and falling to the floor. Before the Colt reached the floor, though, Trague was crumpling, the weight of his pistol dragging his gun hand down.

Longarm was already reaching for the derringer that he carried attached to his watch chain, but he didn't bother to

6

finish drawing it. He'd seen dead men fall before. He knew Trague was dead even while the murdering outlaw sagged to the floor.

There was a moment of stillness as the echoes of the pistol shots faded. Then the woman on the floor spoke.

"I don't know who you are, but you got here just in time," she said, exhaling a deep sigh of relief. Her eyes moved from Longarm to the motionless body of Trague on the floor. "Another few minutes, and Snake would've been mad enough to kill me the way he did Cora."

"I listened to part of what you and him was talking about while I was moving up. I had a pretty good idea of what was going on in here," Longarm said.

Before he moved closer to the woman, Longarm took the long step necessary to reach his Colt and pick it up. He was surprised by the pain that shot up his arm when he closed his hand over the Colt, but ignored it while he returned the gun to its holster.

Turning back to the woman on the floor, he said, "My name's Long, ma'am. Deputy U. S. Marshal out of the Denver office."

"You'd be the one they call Longarm?"

"Some folks call me that," Longarm nodded.

"You're the one that arrested Snake after he'd killed Cora," she said. "But from what I heard, she was already dead before you caught up with him."

"That's right," Longarm said. "There wasn't anything I could do for her by then."

"I'm Cora's half-sister, Suzanne. And I don't know how you found me in this Godforsaken place, but I'm sure glad you got here when you did. Now, if you'll just untie me—"

"Sure. I guess I should've done that first."

Longarm reached into the pocket of his covert-cloth trousers and took out his knife. He started to open the blade, but when he closed his fingers to do so the sharp pain that he'd felt before shot up his arm again.

He glanced down and saw that the forefinger of his right hand was skinned. Blood was oozing from it all along the back of his hand. Ignoring the pain, he opened the blade and bent over the woman. When he took the knife in his right hand to saw at the rope that bound her wrists, he had to set his jaw as the sharp pangs caused his usually steady hand to tremble.

7

"There you are," he told her, as the last coil of rope fell away from her wrists. He extended his left hand and she grasped it while she got to her feet.

Suzanne looked down at Trague's crumpled body, shuddered, and turned her eyes away. She said, "I think I'd like to get out of here, if it's all right with you."

"Sure," Longarm replied. "I wasn't planning to stay any longer than we got to. Maybe you better step outside in the fresh air." He gestured at the corpse and added, "I got to go through his pockets. Then I aim to let him lay here till the undertaker down at Rock Springs can pick him up."

Suzanne went out and Longarm dropped to one knee beside the outlaw's corpse. He made a quick search of Trague's pockets, but found nothing except a purse containing half a dozen gold double eagles and some other coins of smaller denomination. He closed the purse, picked up the dead man's gun, and dropped both purse and gun into his capacious coat pocket, then joined Suzanne outside the door.

For a moment they studied one another in silence. Suzanne was past her twenties, he guessed. The loose bodice of the brown chambray dress she wore did not hide her full breasts and wide womanly hips. She was a tall girl; her eyes were almost level with Longarm's chin as she looked at him.

Her nose was aquiline, her cheekbones high, her chin rounded and firm. He read the evidence of the strain she'd been under by the ripple of anxiety wrinkles on her brow and the way she kept her lips pressed into a straight line. Her eyes were a deep blue under light brown eyebrows that matched her hair, which was gathered into a twist at the back of her neck.

Longarm slid a cheroot out of his pocket and took out a match. Forgetful of his skinned forefinger, he started to flick his thumbnail across its head, but his hand jerked open in a reflex of sudden pain, and the match fell to the ground. He picked it up and struck it on his boot sole and held the flame to the tip of the long slim cigar, the matchstick grasped between his thumb and second finger, his forefinger extended stiffly.

"You've hurt your hand," Suzanne said.

"It ain't such a much. Just a skinned finger."

"Just the same, it ought to be wrapped up," she told him. "Give me your handkerchief."

Longarm reached into his hip pocket, instinctively using his right hand. As he straightened out his fingers, the pain of moving them struck again. Suzanne put her hand on his arm.

"Your finger's getting stiff and I know it must be sore," she said. "That's a terrible scrape, and it's starting to dry up. Would you mind if I get the handkerchief for you?"

"Why, no, it wouldn't bother me."

Longarm twisted to bring his hip pocket into easier reach for her. Suzanne fumbled at his back for a moment before finding the pocket, then her fingers snaked out the folded bandanna. She shook it to break the folds, and spread it across her arm. Then she took Longarm's callused hand between the palms of both her hands and looked closely at the raw flesh where the scraping of the Colt's trigger guard had removed the skin as cleanly as though it had been shaved off by a razor or a surgeon's scalpel.

"I don't like the way this place looks," she frowned. "It's drying up too fast, and starting to pucker up. There's only one thing I know to do that might keep it from shrinking so fast. Now, just keep your hand still and let me take care of it for you."

Longarm was totally unprepared for Suzanne's next move. She bent her head and took his forefinger into her mouth. He moved instinctively, but she grasped his wrist firmly and held his hand motionless. He felt the tip of her tongue travelling along the edges of the raw flesh, and after a few moments the warmth and moisture began to ease the stiffness that had been setting in.

For what seemed to be a long time, Longarm stood without moving while Suzanne held his finger engulfed, tracing her tongue along the edges of the wound now and then. At last she released his hand and quickly folded the bandanna into a triangle. Wrapping his finger in the broad vee of the kerchief, she pulled the points below Longarm's wrist and tied them together around the folded portion of the triangle.

"Try not to move it too much," she said. "And when we get back to Rock Springs, maybe we can get some cloth to make a proper bandage."

"Well, I do thank you," Longarm said. "I never had any doctoring like that before."

"It's an old grandmother's trick," Suzanne told him. Then she went on, "Now, can we start back to town right away? I keep thinking about Snake Trague's body in that cabin, even if I try not to, and it's making me feel spooky."

9

"There's sure not any reason for us to stay here," Longarm replied. "You ride Trague's horse, and I'll ride my livery nag. The sooner we get back to Rock Springs, the quicker I can get this case closed."

Chapter 2

"Looks like all we got to do now is wait for the morning eastbound train," Longarm said.

"Yes. And I'll be very glad to step off that train at Laramie," Suzanne told him. She smiled a bit sadly and added, "At least, I suppose I will. I don't have much there to call home, but what I do have looks real good to me right now."

Longarm and Suzanne were finishing their after-dinner coffee in the dining room of the Northern Pacific depot. During the two hours that had passed since their return to Rock Springs from the shanty, Longarm had moved quickly to tie up the loose ends of the case; as far as he was concerned, it could now be marked close.

He'd wired Billy Vail to report the death of Snake Trague. The casket containing McWhorter's body was in the depot's baggage room, waiting to start its trip to Denver. Since no one was even sure that Trague was the real name of the dead outlaw, the undertaker had agreed to bury him as a county pauper. Suzanne had sworn to a statement before the local justice of the peace, and Longarm had it folded in his coat pocket to add to his report when he wrote it up.

For a few moments they sat silently, then Suzanne said, "I suppose we'd better go back to the hotel now. I've had too much excitement today. All I can think of is bed."

"I'm about ready to turn in, myself," Longarm agreed. "I'll walk across the street with you and have a nightcap in the hotel barroom. Then I'll be ready to hit the hay."

"I hope your hand feels better," Suzanne said as they stood up and started out of the restaurant. "I still think you should've found a doctor and had him look at it."

"I've been hurt a lot worse and got over it," Longarm told her. "Don't go fretting on my account."

"If you're sure it's all right—"

"I'm sure," he replied firmly. They reached the hotel and

11

stopped for a moment in the small bare lobby.

Suzanne said, "Well, good night, Longarm. I'll see you at the station in the morning."

"Sure." He nodded. "Good night."

Longarm had discovered before supper that the barroom in the hotel did not stock Tom Moore, or any other Maryland rye. The Pennsylvania rye the barkeeper poured him was as flat and insipid to his taste as it had been when he'd had a drink before supper. He downed it at a gulp, got his key from the desk, and went upstairs to his room.

In spite of his assurances to Suzanne, Longarm's hand was bothering him. When he began undressing he grew impatient with the clumsy business of using his left hand to unbutton his shirt and fly. He tried to use his right hand, but its throbbing, swollen forefinger was even clumsier. When he'd finally stripped down to his balbriggans, his finger was puffier than before, and pulsing painfully, the skin around its base angry and red.

You know, old son, he told himself as he arranged his vest over the back of the chair where the derringer in its pocket would be in easy reach, *you been hurt a lot worse without it bothering you a bit. Maybe what makes this little scratch feel so bad is because it's crippled up your trigger finger. But it ain't really such a much, so the best thing for you to do is just figure to use your Colt with your left hand till that finger's well again.*

Thinking of his Colt reminded Longarm that the weapon still had a spent shell in one chamber. He hadn't yet replaced the one he'd use to drop Trague. He slid the Colt from its holster and took a fresh cartridge from his coat pocket, but when he opened the loading gate he could see that the cylinder hadn't made a full revolution.

Holding the weapon in his injured hand, he tried to turn the cylinder into proper alignment, but it did not move. Neither did the ejector rod when he pressed its tip. Frowning, Longarm padded on bare feet to the dresser and held the Colt in the light of the lamp. He examined the gun while he tried again to move the ejector rod. Even then he could see nothing wrong, but he had no better success than before when he tried to rotate the cylinder and bring the chamber with the spent shell in line with the ejector. He thumbed the hammer experimentally. Like the ejector rod and cylinder, it refused to move.

"Damn it, it just ain't right for this Colt to act the way it is," he muttered under his breath. "It never jammed up this way before."

Stepping to the window, Longarm raised the sash and looked down at the street. Across the street, a flare of blue-white light from an acetylene lantern beckoned patrons to a saloon and gambling house; the light brightened the sky as well as the street. The dusty thoroughfare was deserted. Longarm thrust the revolver out of the window, its barrel slanted down to the middle of the street, and tried to fire it. Nothing happened.

For a moment Longarm stared at the useless Colt, then told himself, *It's a good thing you got your case closed when you did, old son. Likely you won't be needing this before you get back to Denver. Quit fretting now, and hop in bed.*

Matching his actions to his words, Longarm holstered the Colt. He went to the bureau and blew out the lamp, moved the chair closer to the bed to bring his derringer within easier reach, and stretched out with a contented sigh.

Though the room was quiet in the darkness, sleep eluded him. He lay staring at the shadowed ceiling, closing his eyes from time to time, but opening them again almost at once. After his third effort at summoning sleep failed, he reached across to the chair, groped clumsily through his coat pockets for a cigar and matches, and lighted the long, slim cheroot. Flushing thoughts of the day from his mind, he lay watching the smoke from the cigar float through the dimness until it vanished.

When he heard the first faint scratching on the door, it was so faint and tentative that Longarm thought it was nothing more than the sort of indeterminate sound that might be heard in any hotel corridor. Then it was repeated, a bit louder.

Though he was sure he knew who was signalling him, Longarm had learned from experience to be cautious. He reached to the chair and slid the derringer from his vest pocket. Ignoring the watch dangling from the end of its chain, he padded on bare feet to the door. The scratching was repeated just as he reached it. He turned the key silently and cracked the door open.

"Can I come in, Longarm?" Suzanne whispered softly.

Longarm swung the door wider and she slipped into the room. She still wore the dress that she'd had on that afternoon. She saw the derringer in his hand and her eyes widened.

"You don't take any chances, do you?" she asked.

13

"In my business a man's liable to be real sorry if he ain't careful," Longarm replied, closing the door.

"You're no fool, Longarm," she said. "You must've known it was me at the door."

"I figured it might be," he replied, replacing the little snub-nosed gun in his vest pocket.

"I waited for you to come across the hall to me," Suzanne went on. "Then when I decided you weren't going to, I..." She shrugged and concluded, "Well, here I am."

"I didn't have much luck going to sleep, either," Longarm admitted.

"Is your hand bothering you?"

"Oh, a mite. Nothing I can't put up with."

"Come over to the window where I can see it," Suzanne said. She took his hand and led him to the window, into the square of brightness created by the acetylene lantern across the street. Lifting his hand, she peered at the swollen finger and the puffy, reddened area that surrounded it.

Shaking her head, she said, "You've been using your hand too much and irritated it. I'd better soften it again."

Without hesitating, she raised Longarm's hand and took the injured finger into her mouth, as she'd done earlier at the cabin. After a moment or so she raised her eyes and looked at Longarm. He met her gaze, but kept his face expressionless. He felt the gentle pressure of Suzanne's tongue as she moved it over the tender flesh where the Colt's trigger guard had scraped away the skin. For several minutes they stood motionless, Suzanne keeping a firm grip on Longarm's wrist. Then she lifted her head and freed his finger, but still gripped his wrist.

"I'm not fooling you a bit, am I?" she asked.

"Now, that depends on what you mean, Suzanne," he replied.

"I mean that you know quite well why I came in here. I can't be the first woman who's gotten so worked up by something like what happened this afternoon that she came looking for you."

"Well, now..." he began.

"You don't have to answer me, Longarm," Suzanne said. "I could tell you knew this afternoon."

Her hands were busy at the neck of her dress. She shrugged her shoulders and the dress slid down her body. The glow from the window flooded her body, bringing into sharp relief the

14

pebbled rosettes and jutting tips of her full breasts. She drew back her shoulders, lifting the creamy globes still higher, and leaned forward, offering them to him.

"Go on, Longarm!" she urged. "I'm aching to feel your lips on me! Now!"

Longarm bent to caress the budded spheres. He brushed his lips across their tips, moving from one to the other. Suzanne's body twitched and he felt her muscles grow taut. She brought her hands up to cradle his chin and guide him from side to side. Then, as he continued his caresses, her fingers moved to the buttons of his balbriggans, undoing them, then pushing the underwear down his body to the floor.

Longarm felt Suzanne's hands on his swelling shaft. For a moment she seemed satisfied to cradle it softly between her palms, but in a few moments her fingers closed convulsively and she began to squeeze and knead the fleshy cylinder.

Wrapping his muscular arms around Suzanne, he lifted her and carried her the few steps to the bed, but when he started to lower her on her back she twisted from his grasp. Longarm dropped his arms and Suzanne grasped his shoulders and pushed him down on the bed, then quickly fell forward, the weight of her body pushing him down until he lay on his back, his erection trapped between his body and Suzanne's.

They lay quietly for a moment. Then Longarm sought Suzanne's lips. She opened them to his tongue and her hand moved down his side while she raised her hips and slid it between their bodies. Longarm felt her hand close around his jutting shaft, but contented himself with stroking the smooth skin of Suzanne's back. Suddenly she raised her shoulders and pushed herself down his body until her knees slipped from the bed and came to rest on the floor.

"You're man enough not to mind," she gasped, raising her head to look up at him, her hands closed around his swollen sex. "I like to start this way."

She dropped her head and Longarm felt her lips on his shaft; then her moist, warm mouth engulfed him. He lay motionless, letting Suzanne have her way, watching the changing nimbus of light created in the waving tendrils of her golden-brown hair as she slowly raised and lowered her head. When the soft rasping of her agile tongue began to bring him close, Longarm stirred and clasped her cheeks gently between his hands. Suzanne raised her head, and now his night vision enabled him to

15

see the puzzled look on her face.

"Don't you enjoy what I'm doing?" she asked.

"Sure I do, Suzanne. But you said you just wanted to start off this way, and I figure when a man and a woman's in bed together, they both oughta enjoy it. Come up on the bed with me now."

Obediently, she rose and lay down beside Longarm. He bent his head to caress her breasts with the tip of his tongue for a moment or two, while her hand stroked his engorged shaft. Longarm recognized the urgent message that her hands conveyed and rose above her. She guided him as he lowered his body and with a single quick drive he went into her moist warmth.

"Ahh!" Suzanne moaned softly. "Oh, Longarm! Stay there as long as you can!"

Longarm did not reply, but began stroking slowly, long deliberate thrusts that he held at their conclusion while Suzanne arched her back as though trying to bring him deeper into her. She clamped her legs around his hips and clung to him as he rose and fell, and each time he reached the end of one of his downward strokes she sighed with a gusty groan that was like the purr of some great kitten.

Longarm did not hurry. He stayed with his steady pace until Suzanne's moans became short, panting sighs, then speeded up the tempo of his strokes. They were no longer deliberate now, but hard, quick, piston-like drives that soon brought Suzanne from slow groans of purring pleasure to short, sharp cries that burst from her throat at shorter and shorter intervals as Longarm's strokes grew closer together.

He was driving fast when Suzanne cried, "Oh, yes, Longarm, yes! Hurry now! Oh, hurry! I want you—"

Her words were lost then in a keening sob that burst from her throat in a single column of sound that rose and fell as she writhed and moaned. Her eyes crimped shut while she shuddered into a spasm of ecstasy that kept her body quivering long after the sighs faded to long, quiet exhalations. Then the quivering subsided, too, and she lay silent.

Longarm had stopped his lusty thrusting as Suzanne entered her climax. He did not move now, either, and when she realized that she was still filled by his erect shaft Suzanne opened her eyes and gazed up at him questioningly.

"Didn't you—" she began.

Longarm broke in to say, "Not yet, Suzanne. But don't let that bother you. I still got a full head of steam, and we'll start off fresh soon as you've rested a minute or two."

"I don't need to rest," she replied. "I'd like to start again right this minute."

Longarm recognized the urgency in her tone. He began thrusting once more. This time he did not start slowly and build to a greater spead, but pounded with the full force of his muscular body. Suzanne lay supine for only a few moments before she was once more thrashing beneath him and clinging to his hips with her entwined legs, bringing up her hips to meet his downward strokes.

Her cries of ecstasy began almost at once, and Longarm no longer held himself in check. He drove on lustily, racing to his own climax now. As Suzanne's final small, smothered screams rose from her trembling throat, Longarm reached his peak. He fell forward on Suzanne's soft warm body and joined her in a final trembling moment as he jetted and drained and let his muscles go limp while her final throaty sighs of satisfaction sounded softly in his ears.

Suzanne lay quietly for a moment or two, and Longarm felt her hands on his back, stroking his still-quivering muscles. After a while she said, "I like the way I feel now, Longarm. But I liked what made me feel so good even better, if that makes any kind of sense."

"I'm glad," he said. "I feel pretty good, too, right now."

"If we rest a while, can we do it again?"

"Sure. And another time or two after that, if you want to."

"I don't know how much I can stand, but I'm willing to try," Suzanne said. She was silent for a few moments, then she went on, "I wish I'd met you a long time ago, before I got into such a mess with Ace Glass and Trague."

Longarm said, "It ain't none of my business, Suzanne, but I been wondering how you got wound up in all this in the first place."

"Ever since Trague shot Ace Glass and kidnapped me, I've been wondering that myself," she replied. "And I guess the only answer is a little bit at a time."

"If you don't mind me saying so, that don't make much sense," Longarm said. "Unless you mean you just done what was easiest at some time along the way."

"You put it better than I could," she said. "Our family life

17

wasn't very happy. My father resented Cora, because she reminded him that Mother'd loved another man before she met him. So Cora got away from home as soon as she was old enough by taking up with Ace Glass. Mother seemed to blame me for the way Cora felt, and I was always uncomfortable."

"Maybe things will be better for you at home now that Glass ain't around any more," Longarm suggested.

Suzanne shook her head. "No. She didn't like Ace because she always claimed he stole Cora from her. Then, after Cora was killed, Ace started paying attention to me. Of course, I knew Trague was in jail, and even if Ace was so much older than me, he had a lot of money, so—"

"You went off with him, just like your sister had," Longarm finished for her.

After a moment she picked up their talk where unpleasant memories had interrupted it. "I liked Ace, but I didn't feel anything like love for him," she said thoughtfully. Then, with bitterness creeping into her voice again, she added, "I guess it's just always going to be a general mess, even if I find where Ace kept his money and give it all to Mother."

"That's what you figure to do, is it?"

"I've thought about it," Suzanne replied. "Or most of it. Because, as anxious as I am to go home right now, I can see it's just a question of time before I'll get restless again."

"Just take things easy," Longarm advised. "See if they don't settle down after a while."

Suzanne sat up suddenly and said, "Longarm, Ace had a whole lot of money put away, I know that. It's going to be mine now. Instead of risking your life all the time for people you don't even know, how'd you like to have a rich wife who could give you whatever you wanted?"

Longarm shook his head. "I'm right flattered to have you ask me, Suzanne. Trouble is, I don't want a thing that I ain't got right now."

"Meaning you don't want me, or that you just don't want any woman interfering in what you feel like doing?"

"Well, it sure ain't anything against you. But I just don't feel like I'd fit into a double harness."

Suzanne sighed. "I was afraid you'd say that. Well, I'll settle for what I've got right now." Turning to him, she held

18

out her arms and added, "If you're not too tired, that is. The night's going to be too short for me, and I don't want to miss enjoying a minute of it."

Chapter 3

Midnight was only a few quick clock ticks away when Longarm glanced out the window of the hackney cab he'd hailed at the Denver depot to take him home. In the flickering light of the gas lamp of the intersection he saw the street sign: Twelfth and Champa. Making a sudden decision, he leaned forward and called for the driver to rein in.

"I changed my mind about going out to Cherry Creek," he told the driver as he stepped out of the cab. He reached into his pocket for money to pay the driver, but when he tried to move his fingers a sharp pang shot up his arm. Ignoring the pain, Longarm fumbled clumsily in the pocket until he found a half-dollar and handed it to the cabbie, adding, "There's a little business out in this part of town I better tend to right now."

"It's getting on for late, mister," the hackman observed. "If your business ain't going to hold you up too long, I'll just take you right to where you're heading and wait for you. I won't charge nothing extra. We're pretty far out, and you'd likely have to walk all the way to town before you'd find another hack at this time of night."

"Walking won't bother me a bit," Longarm replied. "Matter of fact, it'd do me good to stretch my legs after setting in that chair car all day and half the night."

Waiting until the hackney had vanished into the gloom beyond the streetlight's feeble glow, Longarm started walking up Champa Street. The night in mile-high Denver was cool and crisp, not bone-chilling as it had been when the train pulled out of Rock Springs that morning, or with a high wind whipping up the tracks as it had been at Laramie where he'd said goodbye to Suzanne, or moist with a threat of rain as it had been when he'd paced the platform at Cheyenne, waiting for the connecting train which had finally deposited him in Denver.

Whistling tunelessly as he walked, Longarm covered the

block and a half to his destination. He smiled to himself in the darkness when he saw lamplight shining from the single high window of the building for which he was heading.

There was no sign in front of the narrow cut-stone building, and its entryway was a step below the sidewalk. Longarm stepped down, ducking as tall men have a habit of doing when they make a downward step over a projection designed to clear the heads of shorter individuals, and tugged the bell-pull.

Knowing he would have to wait, Longarm fished a long, slim cigar from his vest pocket, clinching his jaw again as the pain shot up his arm once more. When his stiff fingers brought out a match, instead of flicking it into flame with his thumbnail, he drew the head across the sole of his boot.

In the glare of the match while he puffed his cheroot alight, Longarm glanced at the familiar name that was inscribed on the modestly small gilt door-plate: "Theo Bryson, Gunsmith." He heard the metallic clink of a door-chain being unlatched as he blew out the match with a puff of exhaled smoke. Then the door swung open and the light from inside flooded the entry.

"Ah, weel, Longarm," said the man who had opened the door. He had a thatch of wiry, snow-white hair that ran down his jaws into wide, fluffy sideburns, but his chin and upper lip were clean-shaven. Thick-lensed, gold-rimmed spectacles were pushed high on his forehead, and he looked at Longarm with twinkling blue eyes set in a network of wrinkles. He went on, "I've nae seen ye for a while."

Longarm would have been disappointed if Bryson had greeted him any other way. He replied, "I take care of my guns, Theo, or you'd see me a lot more often."

"Then I misdoot ye've trouble, or you wouldna be here," the gunsmith said. "Weel, come along inside, and I'll see wha' can be done tae set things richt for ye."

Longarm entered the long narrow room and looked idly around while he waited for Bryson to secure the door. There were no counters or racks of weapons on display. The side walls were lined with wooden cabinets, their doors closed, and except for a wide deep desk shaped like a cube that stood in the center of the room, there was no furniture. A high workbench stretched across the back of the room, a pair of carbide reflector lamps at each end concentrating their beams on its surface. A rifle barrel and action were clamped in a vise on the bench.

21

"You're keeping busy, I see," Longarm remarked through tightened lips as he slid his Colt from its cross-draw holster and handed it to Bryson.

"Och, aye," the gunsmith nodded. "Even the way Denver's grown there's ne'er enough of us smiths tae keep up wi' the work."

While he talked, Bryson began his examination of the Colt. Holding it by the butt, his fingers well away from the trigger, he raised it with the barrel parallel to his eyes. Squinting, he peered into the narrow space between the hammer and the rear end of the cylinder. Even standing a bit away from him, Longarm saw the brass bases of the chambered cartridges in the open slit. He watched the old gunsmith's eyes as they moved slowly over the bulge of the ejector rod housing.

Shaking his head, the crinkle of a beginning frown forming on his high forehead, Bryson upended the weapon and examined the side-plates and, finally, the trigger and its curved guard. The frown of puzzlement took in his entire face now as the gunsmith looked from the gun to Longarm.

"I canna see anything wrong wi' the weapon," he said. "Oh, aye, it shows it's been used. The blue's thin from holster-rub, and the grips are beginning tae look worn, but I see nae muir than that."

"Try to fire it," Longarm told him.

" 'Tis nae like you tae make such a suggestion," Bryson said, looking up at Longarm in surprise. "If I'm tae fire the gun, 'twill be downstairs, where 'tis safe."

"Don't worry, Theo," Longarm said. "If it'd fire, I never would've suggested you touch the trigger."

Gingerly, holding the gun at a low angle with its muzzle pointing to the polished flagstone floor, the gunsmith tested the trigger. When it did not yield to his finger's pressure, he brought his thumb up and tried to pull the hammer back to cock. The hammer resisted him as stubbornly as the trigger had.

"Weel, now," he said slowly, "I've nae seen ane of Sam Colt's revolvers freeze up before. What's happened tae it?"

"A damned murdering outlaw skunk shot it outa my hand, is what happened, Theo," Longarm replied. "I drew a mite faster than he did, so I'd already got off my shot at him. I got to admit he wasn't all that much behind me. It was so close that his slug hit the Colt and knocked it outa my hand. By that

22

time it didn't matter much, because my aim was better than his, and he was dead."

"And ye came out wi' a whole skin?"

Instead of answering, Longarm extended his right hand for Bryson to look at. The web of his thumb was still swollen and red, and in addition to being swollen like the surrounding area, his forefinger was now scabbed over from the back knuckle almost to the fingernail.

"I figure I come out pretty good," he said.

"A muckle better than good," Bryson agreed. "Twa men I know had their fingers cut awa' by the trigger guard when their guns were shot fra' their hand."

"I saw that one time, myself," Longarm nodded. "But this ain't getting my Colt fixed, Theo. What in tunket's got it jammed up so it won't fire?"

"A weel, let's have a look," the gunsmith said.

He started back to his workbench, Longarm following. Fixing a jeweller's loupe in one eye, Bryson held the Colt where the brilliant rays from the carbide lamps overlapped to give the brightest light. Bending close to the gun, he revolved it slowly. He'd turned the weapon almost a complete revolution when he stopped and nodded. For a moment he peered at the ejector rod housing, then he nodded and looked up, removing the loupe as he raised his head.

" 'Tis saething I've nae run into before," he told Longarm. "Ye canna see it wi' just the naked eye, but there's a bit of lead fra' the slug that struck the Colt lodged back inside, against the ejector rod. I'm thinking it's pushed the rod back tae wedge the cylinder tight."

"No wonder I couldn't pull the trigger, then," Longarm nodded. "I reckon you can fix it?"

"Och, aye, Longarm. Sam Colt's revolvers need sae little fixing that I've new parts in stock I bought ten years ago. The job will take only a wee bit o' time. D'ye want tae leave the gun wi' me the nicht? If y'd like, I've a Colt this model in my stock that I can lend you till the morrow."

"If you're not too busy with that rifle you was working on when I come in, I'd rather wait while you get it back in shape, Theo. Billy Vail might send me out on a new case when I report in at the office tomorrow morning, and a man in my business is a plain damn fool if he lets himself get caught in a tight spot with a gun he's never triggered before."

"Aye," Bryson nodded. "Well, if you've a mind tae sit a spell, I'll see to it richt now."

Longarm looked around the bare room and grinned. "Even if I was of a mind to set, I don't see anything to set on," he said. "But I'd just as soon stand up and walk around while you're doing the job. I been setting on a day coach seat all day, and my butt's damn near raw. It'll do me good to stretch my legs a little while."

Bryson nodded and turned back to his workbench. Longarm watched while the gunsmith removed the single screw that held the ejector housing in place and revolved the shield to remove it from the frame. Bryson held the assembly for Longarm to look at. Freed from the frame, the chunk of lead that had locked the spring and ejector rod was plainly visible. So was the slight curve near the rear end of the rod, where it had been jammed against the cylinder.

"Y're a lucky man, Longarm," the old gunsmith said. "If ye'd needed tae fire another shot, you'd nae be here the noo."

Longarm nodded through a veil of smoke from his cheroot. Bryson opened a drawer of the workbench and began taking out small wooden boxes. He'd piled half a dozen on the workbench before he found the one he was after. Opening it, he took out a duplicate of the bent ejector rod that lay on the bench. He took a spring from another box and placed it beside the rod.

With fingers as sensitive as those of a violinist adjusting the tension of his bowstrings, Theo checked the resistance of the new spring against the old one. Satisfied, he slipped the spring over the rod and inserted the new assembly in the housing. Then he laid the housing aside and picked up the Colt again.

" 'Tis nae likely the rachet's marred," he frowned as he began to remove the revolver's cylinder. "But sin' I've got the gun stripped this far, 'tis best tae take a look."

Longarm moved up to the bench and watched over Bryson's shoulder as the old gunsmith subjected the cylinder to a close scrutiny through his loupe. After he'd revolved the cylinder twice, concentrating his attention on the rachet, Bryson nodded and began reassembling the piece.

"Ye'll want tae test it, I misdoot?" he asked Longarm as he handed him the assembled weapon. "Though 'tis nae as though I'd changed the trigger-pull."

"Just to be safe, Theo," Longarm nodded.

Bryson opened another drawer and scooped up a handful of cartridges, then lifted one of the carbide lamps from its hanger. Longarm followed him down a flight of steep, narrow stairs to a basement that extended the full length of the shop. The walls and floor of the underground chamber had not been bricked up, and a rich smell of loam mixed with the faint acrid scent of burned gunpowder filled the long room.

Bryson hung the light on a scantling that had been driven into the earthen wall beyond the foot of the stairs. He handed Longarm the cartridges and said, "I'll set the mark while you load. They're cut cartridges, but ye're nae concerned wi' sights and range."

While Longarm thumbed shells into the Colt's cylinder, Theo went to the far end of the basement and picked up a six-foot length of pine board from a stack that stood by the wall. He upended the board and leaned it against the back wall, then returned to the end where Longarm stood waiting. Longarm had not yet moved the Colt to his right hand. He did so now, but when he started to curl his forefinger into the trigger guard he stopped and shook his head.

"My damn trigger finger's stiff," he said. "But I'll try the next one."

With his second finger on the trigger, his swollen forefinger extended below the cylinder, Longarm raised the Colt and triggered off three quick shots. The first two spattered into the earthen wall beside the board; the third took a chip off its edge. Longarm shook his head.

"Damn poor shooting," he commented, as much to himself as to the gunsmith, as he ejected the three spent cartridges and replaced them with fresh loads. "But I don't guess I'll do much better till that finger gets the soreness out. The gun's all right, though."

"Try wi' your left hand," Bryson suggested. "Ye'll be better using it than y'r right until that finger's healed."

Shifting the Colt and shuffling in a quarter-turn, Longarm fired three more rounds with his left hand. The first slug missed the board; the next two drilled neat black holes no more than an inch on either side of its center.

"I'll get by," Longarm nodded. He reloaded as he spoke, and reholstered the Colt. "Thanks for the quick repair job, Theo. Let's go back upstairs and I'll settle up. Then I'll be on my way and let you go back to fixing that rifle."

Ten minutes later, Longarm was walking leisurely down Champa Street. He turned at the corner of Eighteenth and started toward Larimer. The Windsor Hotel's barroom was open all night, and he knew that they always kept Tom Moore on hand.

When Longarm arrived at the U. S. marshal's office in the federal building the next day, morning was well along toward noon. The young pink-cheeked clerk in the outer room looked up and, when he saw Longarm, his eyes widened and he tried to keep a smug grin from showing on his face.

"Maybe you'd better throw your hat in first, if you're going into Chief Marshal Vail's office," he said. "Ever since he got here at eight o'clock he's been expecting you to show up."

Longarm gave the young fellow no reply except an absent-minded nod as he crossed to the door to Vail's private office. The door was ajar and he pushed it open. Vail looked up from the heap of papers that lay in front of him on his piled-up desk.

"What kept you so long?" he asked, looking pointedly at the Vienna Regulator clock that hung on the wall. Its hands were indicating ten o'clock. Vail went on, "I've been expecting you for the last two hours."

"Now, Billy, you know that train down here from Wyoming don't move as fast as a snail can trot," Longarm said mildly.

"Well, now that you've finally shown up, come in," Vail said, putting down the letter he was holding. "I want to know what happened up there in Rock Springs. Les McWhorter was a good man. I hate to lose him."

"He didn't have a chance, Billy," Longarm said soberly as he settled into the red morocco-upholstered chair at the end of the chief marshal's desk. "He was trailing Snake Trague and the son of a bitch bushwhacked him. One shot in the back with a rifle. Les never knew what hit him."

Vail nodded, and sat silently for a moment. Then he said, "We're burying Les today, of course. The funeral will be at noon, and I'm closing the office at eleven. But we'll be back on the job at two, and I'll want to talk to you then about your new case. There's not enough time to fill you in on it now."

"Two o'clock will be fine," Longarm said.

Vail made no reply, but sat with his face sober, staring at the paper in his hand without really seeing it. Longarm started to get up, but thought better of it, not wanting to break in on

26

his chief's silence. He'd exhausted his own supply of silence during the long slow train ride down from Cheyenne. He fished a cigar from his pocket and bent forward to strike a match on his boot sole. Vail looked up at him and watched while he lighted the cheroot and blew out the match.

"Maybe you'd better tell me how you got your hand bunged up the way it is," the chief marshal suggested. "Trague again?"

Longarm nodded. "He was faster on the draw than I'd give him credit for. His slug hit my Colt and knocked it outa my hand right after I'd got in the first shot."

"You're lucky it didn't break your trigger finger," Vail said. When Longarm made no reply, he went on, "I think we both need a drink, Long. Let's get out of here and drop in at that fancy new hotel of Haw Tabor's. It's not likely we'll see anybody in the barroom there who'll want to talk to us, and if you feel the way I do, we won't have much to say to each other."

Neither Longarm nor Vail had spoken during their long ride from the cemetery back to the federal building after Mc-Whorter's funeral. They walked up the wide flight of marble stairs in silence. Longarm waited for Vail to unlock the office door, then followed him inside. The chief marshal led the way to his private office and hung his hat and coat on the clothes tree in the corner, then settled down behind his desk. Longarm, equally silent, sat in the red morocco-upholstered chair and waited for Vail to begin.

"I didn't think you'd mind coming back here, even if I did give everybody else the rest of the day off," Vail said at last. "If you'd rather wait until tomorrow to talk about that new case you're going on..." His voice trailed into silence, and he looked searchingly at Longarm.

Longarm had seen a new side to his chief that afternoon, and realized that now Vail needed something to keep him busy, to get back to an established routine, to take his mind off the funeral.

"Don't worry a bit about that, Billy," he said. "It don't make no difference to me. I'd as soon find out about it today as tomorrow."

"Good," Vail nodded. "Just as long as you don't think I'm pushing you and going easy on the others." Hunching forward in his chair, the chief marshal went on, "I don't usually play hunches in my job, Long, you know that. The cases I hand

27

out to you and the other deputies are the routine ones we get from the district or from Washington. But this time I'm going to poke my neck out a country mile, and I just might get it chopped off for exceeding my authority."

Until now, Longarm had given no real thought to the new case Vail had mentioned that morning. Now, hearing him make such an unusual statement, his interest perked up. He sat up a bit straighter and inched his chair closer to Vail's desk.

"I guess you've heard me mention Travis Morrison?" the chief marshal asked.

"Sure. Your old friend from the time when you was a Texas Ranger, ain't he?"

"That's Trav," Vail nodded. "He left the Rangers a good while after I did, of course. Now, he's got some kind of bee in his bonnet and he wants me to send a man to look into it."

"Seems like the Rangers oughta be the ones to do that, if it's down in Texas," Longarm frowned.

"Morrison says it's not the kind of case for the Rangers. But if it's a federal case, I don't know why he picked me out, when there's a district marshal's office in Austin that's a lot closer to him. But he did and, knowing Trav the way I do, he's bound to've had a reason."

"It sounds to me like you got a feeling this case might turn out to be a hot potato, Billy," Longarm suggested.

"If it does, all they can do to me in Washington is issue a reprimand for exceeding my authority," the chief marshal said.

Longarm's interest increased. For a man in Vail's position to be reprimanded meant a permanent black mark on his record, and virtually barred the way to any further advancement. He took a cigar from his pocket and lighted it, waiting for Vail to go on.

"Damn it, I'm beating around a bush!" Vail snapped angrily as he straightened up in his chair. "Travis Morrison was a damned good Ranger, and he's still my friend! Long, I'm going to ask you right straight out: are you willing to risk the chance of getting a black mark on your record along with mine, if I send you on this damn fool case without any authorization from Washington?"

Longarm started to speak, but before he could open his mouth Vail went on, and for the first time he could remember, Longarm heard a genuine tone of worry in his chief's voice.

"Now, think twice before you answer me," Vail urged. "Because if this case turns out to be a wild goose chase, you could be in damned near as much trouble as I will. In fact, it might cost both of us our badges!"

Chapter 4

Longarm did not hesitate, but said, "You didn't need to ask me that, Billy. You know damn well I am."

Visibly relaxing, Vail settled back in his chair. He said, "I guess I did know what you'd say, but I wasn't going to lead you into something blindfolded."

"Well, if I didn't know before, I do now," Longarm told him. "Go ahead and loop it out for me, Billy."

Vail did not reply at once, but busied himself for a moment rearranging the stacks of paper on his desk. At last he settled back into his swivel chair and began.

"First off, you'd better know why I feel the way I do about Travis Morrison," he said. "When I joined the Texas Rangers, all I knew about a lawman's job was what I'd learned when I was a deputy town marshal up in the East Texas sandhill country. That wasn't much, back at the time I'm talking about. But for a long time, I'd wanted to join the Rangers. I guess I wasn't the only young greenhorn who did, because I waited in line for a long time before I got accepted."

Vail paused and Longarm relighted his cigar, which he'd allowed to go out. When the cheroot was going again and Vail still hadn't picked up the thread of his story, Longarm said, "I guess you was sorta like me, when I put in to get on as a deputy marshal, Billy. And I'd say your friend Morrison give you a hand a time or two, like you done for me."

"Something like that," Vail nodded. "But the Rangers in those days were a lot tougher than any U. S. Marshal's outfit I've ever run across. There were only sixty of us in all, to back up a bunch of mostly green county and city law-enforcement men. That wasn't too long after Reconstruction, you know, and half our job was to undo all the damage the Reconstruction Police had done."

When Vail stopped talking, his mind obviously going back to days that were no more, Longarm nodded and said, "Along about then, I was knocking around, drifting from one cow-punching job to the next one. But I sure heard a lot of talk about what the Texas Rangers was doing."

"It wasn't all talk, either," Vail assured him. "One riot, one Ranger, was the way we operated then. And my first case was just exactly that. The lid was about to blow off in a little town down in the Rio Grande Valley where a crooked political ring was bleeding everybody dry, and I was sent to clean it up. I didn't expect to run into a small army of gunfighters that the ring kept on hand, and if it hadn't been for Travis Morrison leaving his post up in the Big Bend when he got word I was in trouble, and coming to help me without waiting for orders, it's likely I wouldn't be sitting at this desk right now."

"You don't need to fill in all the blanks, Billy," Longarm said when his chief paused again. "Hell's bells, you know I'd take your word about this Travis Morrison being a good man. Just go on and tell me what I got to look out for on this new case."

"I wish I could," Vail replied. "And the reason I can't is because Trav himself is just going on a hunch."

"Tell me about the hunch, then," Longarm invited.

Vail frowned as he replied, "There's an outfit nobody's ever heard of before, called the Arapahoe Cattle Syndicate. They're driving a herd of Mexican longhorns up here from the Rio Grande. And Travis Morrison's got a hunch that there's something smells bad about the syndicate and the trail drive, too."

Longarm's jaw had begun dropping when Vail mentioned Mexican longhorns, and it fell open even wider when the chief marshal got to the words "trail drive." He asked incredulously, "Trail driving Mexican longhorns from the Rio Grande plumb up to Denver at this day and age?"

Vail nodded. "That's right. And I felt just about like you look right now when I got to that part of Trav's letter."

"You think they're rustled cattle, Billy?"

"That's what your job is, to find out."

"Hold on there, Billy!" Longarm exclaimed. "If they're rustled cattle stolen in Mexico, finding out'd be a job for the *rurales,* and if they was stolen in Texas, it'd be up to your old outfit, the Rangers. And both of them has got grudges against me that they never have had a chance to settle."

"Oh, they might've been mad at you a long time ago, but neither the *rurales* nor the Rangers carry a grudge forever,"

31

Vail said. "Besides, since you had those dust-ups with the *rurales* and the Rangers, you've had other cases in both Texas and Mexico, and you've come away scot free."

Longarm shook his head. "Seems like I recall hearing a preacher talk about a little pitcher that was took to the well one time too many and got busted to smithereens. Now, I sorta got on the good side of one or two of your old buddies in the Texas Rangers, but a hell of a lot more of 'em holds me a grudge over them run-ins I had when I was cleaning out that rustlers' nest down on the Rio Grande, and when I was dogging after Sim Blount in the Big Thicket."

"Well, I'll have to admit the boys in my old outfit have long memories, but those two cases were a long time ago," Vail said. "They've probably forgotten those old grudges by now."

"Just the same, there's still some of 'em that'd like nothing better'n to even up them old scores. Ain't there a way to handle this case without going down to Texas again?"

"I don't see how. But there's not much of a chance that you'd run into any Rangers at all, because that trail herd was cleared to cross the border," Vail pointed out. "The steers didn't have any hoof-and-mouth disease, and the brands were all according to bills of sale. That'd rule out there being Rangers or *rurales* after them."

"Well, I ain't going to pull in my oars. I guess I can still manage to take care of myself."

"If I didn't think you could, you wouldn't be carrying a federal marshal's badge," Vail assured him. "And if I didn't think that herd needed some looking into, I wouldn't be sending you down to check up on it."

"Oh, I got to agree something smells bad about it, Billy. I can't see any more reason than you or your friend Morrison why anybody'd trail a herd of Mexican longhorns up here to Colorado. They ain't such a much as beef cattle, these days. They're runty and scrawny and mostly bones with a little tough, stringy meat on 'em. Most of the ranchers around here has already shifted over to shorthorns."

"I know that," Vail agreed.

"And there ain't been a trail drive like that made for maybe ten or fifteen years," Longarm went on, frowning thoughtfully. "Ain't this syndicate outfit ever heard about railroads?"

"It doesn't seem they have," Vail said. "And to save you

asking, I haven't been able to find out anything about the syndicate, either."

"I guess they got an office in Denver, seeing as how it's called the Arapahoe Syndicate?"

"Oh, they've got an office, all right. The trouble is, the only one in the office is a young clerk, and all he does is to pick up the mail and pass it on to a fellow by the name of Sterns who comes in once in a while to pick it up."

"And you ain't been able to run Sterns to ground?"

Vail smiled sourly. "You know how much of a job it is to find a man who doesn't want to be found. When I drew a blank at the office, I asked around town a little bit, and nobody's ever heard of him. What I got out of the clerk didn't amount to a hill of beans."

"They'd have to have a certificate or something filed at the Arapahoe County Courthouse, Billy," Longarm frowned.

Vail shook his head. "A syndicate wouldn't. Syndicates are different from other kinds of business under state law. They don't have to file all the papers a corporation does in order to do business in Colorado."

"Arapahoe County's mostly Denver," Longarm said thoughtfully. "Seems to me there's bound to be somebody around town that'd know who's set up this outfit."

"If there is, I haven't been able to find them," Vail replied. "As far as I can tell, nobody in the cattle business or the banking business in Denver's ever heard of a syndicate by that name."

"How'd your old friend Morrison happen to run onto it?"

"He's a brand inspector working down on the Rio Grande, now, at Del Rio. He said in his letter he smelled something fishy in the way the herd was being trailed instead of shipped when it crossed the border. Trav's got a real sensitive nose for things like that."

"Stands to reason he would," Longarm agreed. He was getting an idea of what Vail was taking his time saying, and went on, "Now, if I understand rightly from what you been telling me, it ain't been very long since them Mexican longhorns crossed the Rio Grande."

"A week, ten days, maybe," Vail said.

"Then they'd be someplace southwest of the Colorado along about now, I'd guess?"

"Someplace along the old Western trail drive route across

33

the Edwards Plateau," Vail agreed.

"That ain't going to get 'em to Denver, though." Longarm frowned. "As I recall, the Western Trail branches off someplace in Texas, down around Abilene."

"That's the Porter Trail you're thinking about," Vail told him. "It swings west out of Abilene and crosses the Loving–Goodnight Trail that leads over into New Mexico and north from someplace close to Fort Sumner."

"Now, damn it, Billy, the Loving–Goodnight Trail heads north outa Fort Sumner and crosses Colorado," Longarm insisted.

"Sure it does," Vail agreed. "But it goes west around the Rockies, too, about a hundred miles from the Porter Trail."

"Then how in hell are them yahoos going to drive a herd here to Denver?" Longarm demanded.

"I guess you've forgotten there are two Goodnight Trails, if you ever knew," Vail said.

"Two? I rode for Goodnight a little while when he was on the Cross Timbers, and the only Goodnight Trail I ever heard about is the one we was just talking about, the one they call Loving–Goodnight nowadays."

"That was the first one." Vail nodded. "The new one runs from his place on the Red River up through the Texas Panhandle to Tascosa and swings east to the Western Pacific at Dodge."

"If that's the way of it, the best place I can think of to pick up the herd and keep an eye on it is down in Texas, around Abilene." Longarm frowned.

"That's how I see it, too." Vail nodded.

"Now, it won't be easy to do that, Billy," Longarm said. "How the devil am I going to dog along after a herd of cattle over that bald prairie that lays to the north of Abilene? Why, it wouldn't even take a day for the trail hands to tumble that I was following 'em. Then they'd come asking questions, and—"

Vail broke in to say, "They wouldn't ask any questions if you went along with the drive as a hand."

Longarm had been anticipating this almost from the start of Vail's unusually circuitous approach to his new assignment. He had been thinking much the same thing as soon as he'd listened to Vail's explanation of the case, but in spite of Vail's foreboding and the risk his boss was taking, he had hoped that the methods he would follow in the case could be of his own choosing.

Vail went on, "Now, as slow as that trail herd's moving, I figure that you can beat it to Abilene if you take the first train south. And after crossing the Edwards Plateau, I'll bet dollars to doughnuts there'll be a few hands pulling out at Abilene, so you ought not to have any trouble getting a job."

Because Vail had taken such a serious approach to the case in the beginning, Longarm knew he must agree. He nodded and said, "It wouldn't surprise me a bit, Billy. And I guess that's how I'll do it. But I got one favor to ask you."

"What's that?"

"It'd make this case a lot easier if I knew more about what your friend Travis Morrison found out."

"I've told you everything that was in his letter."

"Sure. But what I got in mind is setting down with him and chinning a while. You know how it is when a man writes a letter, Billy. A lot of the time he don't write as much as he'd say if he was just talking."

"That's right," Vail agreed. "But you won't have time to go to the border and then backtrack to wherever that herd of Mexican longhorns has gotten to by then."

"No. But if you don't mind doing it, you can send him a wire and ask him to catch a train up to Abilene and meet me there for a little talk."

Vail thought for a moment, then nodded. "I don't see any reason why he wouldn't. Trav's job doesn't keep him tied down all that much. He can spare the time, and he might like to get away from the border for a few days."

"You go ahead and send the wire, then," Longarm said. "If I'm going to act like a hungry cowhand that's ready to take on a trail drive job, I got a little bit of juggling to do."

"Such as?" Vail asked.

"Well, now, Billy, if I'm going to act like I'm a cowhand, I got to look like one. And that old McClellan saddle of mine sure ain't something a cowhand'd use, because he couldn't twist a dally-loop without he's got a saddlehorn."

"I'd forgotten your saddle," Vail said. "I guess that's about all you'd have to change, though."

"Just about. I still got some of the duds I used to wear when I was cowhanding, and I guess they'll fit me as good as they ever did. But if I'm gonna put up the right kind of front, I'll have to rent me a horse here, instead of waiting till I get down to Abilene. If I rent one there, somebody with the trail outfit might find out about it."

"That makes sense, too," Vail agreed. "A footloose cowhand wouldn't rent a horse; he'd have one."

"And not much else." Longarm smiled. "There's a few other little bits and pieces I got to take care of, but they won't take much time."

"Maybe you'd better let me in on what you call 'bits and pieces,'" Vail suggested. "When do you think you'll be ready to meet Travis in Abilene?"

"Billy, I ain't laid down a lasso loop in more'n ten years. I can't act like a greenhorn if I'm going to be a cowhand, so I'll need a little bit of practice. And I got to ride the horse I aim to rent, get used to him and my new saddle, let him get used to me at the same time."

"No argument," Vail agreed. "What else?"

"Well, when I go to the chief dispatcher at the Denver & Rio Grande to rent a boxcar, I'll get him to work me out a schedule that'll put me into Abilene as fast as I can get there. He can do it quicker'n I can."

Vail nodded. "Anything more?"

"Nothing that comes to mind right now. I'll need a bale of hay for the horse, and water, of course. But I'll spread out some of the hay to make me a bed, and ride in the boxcar."

"You still haven't answered my question," Vail pointed out. "When I wire Travis, when should I tell him to meet you? And where?"

"I likely won't get outa Denver before some time late tomorrow," Longarm said. "And freights don't run on passenger-train schedules, so I'd oughta be pulling into Abilene in about three days. That'll give your friend Travis plenty of time to get there from the Rio Grande. Matter of fact, he oughta be there about the same time I'll be pulling in."

Vail nodded approval, then said, "I suppose you've got an idea where it'd be safe to meet him?"

"There's a big saloon in Abilene on Cottonwood Street, right in the middle of town. The Delmonico, it was named, but mostly people called it Gus Ackerman's, because he was the fellow that it belonged to. Say I was to wander in there about the middle of the afternoon, when the place ain't likely to be crowded. That sound all right?"

"About as good as I can think of," Vail said. "I'll wire Travis to meet you there if he can, and to let me know right away if he can't. I ought to get an answer before you're ready to leave, so look in at the office here before you go."

"I'd have to do that anyhow, Billy." Longarm grinned. "I sure ain't got the kind of money in my pocket that it takes to hire boxcars and all the rest of it."

"I'll get the clerk to fix up your vouchers first thing in the morning," Vail said. "They'll be ready when you are."

On the street outside the federal building, Longarm hailed the first empty hack that passed. He settled back on the seat after telling the driver to take him to the Diamond K Ranch. The hack turned into Broadway and rolled through the residential area that was spreading slowly south of Denver's heart. The rows of small, neat new houses extended less than half a mile beyond First Street, and the cab was soon rolling across open country. Longarm paid little attention to the lumpy pastureland the dirt road crossed, but spent his time ticking off the matters that he would have to take care of before leaving.

Less than five miles after leaving the houses behind, the road growing progressively narrower and rougher, the hackman turned his cab into an even less inviting road, marked by a wooden arch. The turn was marked by a post topped with a diamond-shaped board on which the letter K had been burned with a hot running-iron. Here the ground was marked by a series of humps, and after topping half a dozen of these rises the cabbie pulled up in front of a cluster of unpainted wooden structures: a long, ramshackle bunkhouse, a two-story dwelling, and a barn which doubled as a stable.

Longarm was out of the cab before the hackman stopped. He handed the driver two silver dollars and started for the house, but before he reached it the door opened and a short, chubby man came out. Longarm had never seen him before.

"You looking for somebody, mister?" the man asked as he came within easy speaking distance.

"I'm looking for your boss," Longarm replied.

"You'll have to look a long ways," the stranger said. "He went down to Manitou Springs to take the water."

"You'd be in charge, then?"

"Sure am. Name's Gibson. What can I do for you?"

Longarm took his wallet from the inside pocket of his coat and flipped it open to show his badge. "Deputy U. S. marshal; name's Long. I need to rent a horse and some saddle gear for a while. Your boss has accommodated me before, so I don't reckon you'd mind doing the same."

"Long?" Gibson frowned. "You'd be the one from Denver? The fellow they call Longarm?"

"That's me."

"Hell, Marshal, I've heard the boss talk about you a lot. Just tell me what you need, and I'll sure be glad to oblige."

"Besides a decent riding nag that's got some range smarts, I'll have to have a stock saddle and a lariat," Longarm replied. "And since I ain't worked cattle for a spell, I'd like to ride out and find me a steer or two that I can practice on."

"Well, I can fix you up with a pretty good nag that's range-broke." Gibson frowned. "And there's all kinda saddle stuff in the barn over there. You just go pick out what strikes your fancy—saddle, saddlebags, lariats, whatever. But you ain't going to find no steers at the Diamond K to practice on. The boss sold off all his cattle before he left."

"Looks like I'll have to make do with a fencepost, then." Longarm shrugged.

"Go ahead and fix yourself up, Marshal," Gibson said. "You'd know what you're after better'n I would."

"Thanks," Longarm said. "I'll saddle up and try a few loops, and then ride on back to town. Tell Jim I'll square up with him when I get back. And tell him not to worry if I don't show up for a few weeks."

After picking over the saddle gear, Longarm selected a well-worn and scarred-up double-rigged saddle with a sparsely padded cantle and a turtlehead horn, and then picked out a narrow bridle with a double-port Shoemaker bit. He sorted the lariats, putting aside those woven from leather and grass, and finally chose a thirty-foot manila-braid rope with a working head that had been worn slick from long use.

Carrying the tack to the corral, he lighted a cigar and stood puffing it thoughtfully while he watched and studied the dozen horses penned inside. There were only two that struck his fancy. One was a buckskin that had the high shoulder formation hinting of a Morgan strain; the other was more quarterhorse in breeding, but with a strong hint of Tennessee in its high hindquarters and flowing mane and tail.

Finally, with a shrug, Longarm went into the corral and led the Tennessee out to try. It stood easily while he saddled it and mounted, and proved to be quick in both starting and stopping when he reined in. He made a few lariat throws at the corral's corner posts, and after the better part of an hour since his arrival, he decided he'd get along all right with his selection of both horse and gear.

Turning the horse toward Denver, Longarm skirted the town's environs as he rode toward the D&RG freight yards to complete his preliminary preparation for what he'd already decided might turn into a long, hard case.

Chapter 5

Outside the cracked-open door of the boxcar where Longarm stood puffing a cheroot, the prairie stretched from the tracks to infinity under a cloudless sky. The land here was not flat tableland, but was broken by low, gentle rises that looked like the swells seen on a quiet ocean. Not a tree, not even a clump of brush, broke the uniformity of the vast expanse of grass. The sun was at high noon, and there were no shadows to break the monotony of the vista.

After two nights and a full day in the boxcar, the part-Tennessee gelding his only company, Longarm was beginning to feel cramped, even though he had most of the boxcar to himself. A barrier of stout slats at one end of the car confined the horse and kept it from moving more than a short distance in either direction, and the animal had proved remarkably adaptable in adjusting its equilibrium to the swaying of the boxcar.

Longarm had found enough to keep him busy during the first part of the trip. He'd adapted the borrowed saddle to his own gear, changing the strings to accommodate his saddlebags, bedroll, and rifle scabbard, so there were no more chores now to occupy him. Except for a wave or two from the yard crews when the car had been switched from the D&RG to the Santa Fe and from the Santa Fe to the C&P, he'd seen nobody.

Damned if this ain't like being in a jail, old son, he told himself as he watched the land flowing slowly past. *Except it ain't got bars or guards. And about now even a prison guard'd be somebody a man could talk to. But this old rattler can't be too far outa Abilene, if that dispatcher in Denver figured it right.*

Longarm's route had been a circuitous one: southeast on the D&RG from Denver to Trinidad, then on the Santa Fe southwest through New Mexico Territory until he was almost at the Territory's southern border, and now he was moving southeast across Texas on C&P rails.

Despite the fact that he was in a string of boxcars and flatcars instead of passenger coaches, the trip had been very little slower, as the freight cars cannonballed over the long hauls with fewer stops and a minimum of delays. There had been plenty of time for him to work flexibility back into his injured hand and to check his Colt with occasional quick snapshots at unwary jackrabbits that hopped along beside the track.

Suddenly Longarm became aware of a change in the rhythm of the boxcar's swaying, the engineer easing up on the throttle and the train beginning to slow down. He leaned out the door to look. Ahead, the tracks curved; he could see the engine and tender, and finally the first cars in the long string. Then the car he was in entered the curve, and now he could see that the character of the land was changing. The vista from the boxcar door was no longer one of flat, uncluttered prairie, but prairie broken by small, raw ledges of gravel and yellow dirt.

Tiny in the distance it stood from the tracks, he noticed a wagon standing, its arched canvas top gleaming white in the high noon sun. The curve of the tracks brought the wagon closer, so that he could see details even across the three or four miles stretching between the train and the wagon. A man was at the horse's head, unhitching it. Beyond the wagon, the sun's rays were caught and thrown back by the rippled surface of a tiny lake, little more than a pond.

Well, there's a fellow in about the same boat you are, old son, all by himself with nothing but a horse to talk to. Longarm's thoughts went on. *Except it's going to take him a longer time than it is you to get where he's headed, because the way that wagon's pointing, he's moving north, and this rattler can't be such a much of a ways outside of Abilene.*

Longarm watched the wagon idly while the long string of boxcars behind him made their way around the curve. Looking at the wagon from the changed angle, he could see that it had the extended tailgate arrangement and possum belly slung below its bed that marked its purpose as plainly as if it had been painted on its sides. No other vehicle in the scanty types of rolling stock used on cattle-country ranches had the features he was looking at except a trail drive's chuck wagon.

You sure cut your cloth close this time, old son, he told himself silently as he watched the chuck wagon and its driver until a rise in the ground hid it from sight. *There ain't no more chance than finding a cross-eyed rattlesnake that there'd be two trail herds in this part of the country. That chuck wagon's got to be the one that's rolling with the herd of Mexican longhorns you're looking for, which means the trail herd oughta be catching up to it sometime around sundown.*

A few minutes after the chuck wagon had been lost to view, the admonitory wail of the locomotive's whistle confirmed Longarm's deduction. He leaned as far as he could from the door of the boxcar, but still saw nothing except the broken prairie bordering the tracks ahead. He held his position, and in a few minutes the train started up another rise and its momentum began to slacken. It moved slowly up the hump, and when Longarm's boxcar reached the crest he could see the roofs of buildings and houses ahead.

This can't be anyplace except Abilene, Texas, old son, he told himself. *And that means it's time to saddle up and get ready to go back to work.*

By the time the engine of the long freight train reached the town, it was moving at a slow crawl. Longarm had his horse saddled by then, and was ready to take down the slats that kept the animal in one end of the car. He stood in the doorway holding the horse's reins until the car creaked to a halt at the freight depot platform. He'd been waiting only a few moments when two railroad workers appeared from the freight depot carrying a loading bridge, which they laid across the gap between the car door and the platform. Longarm led the Tennessee gelding across the bridge and down the ramp. Then he swung into the saddle and rode out onto the streets of Abilene.

During the years that had passed since he'd first seen the town, it had grown from a hidetown occupied by buffalo hunters to a village catering to trail drives, when the saloons and the shanties in the red light district behind them outnumbered the residences. The last time he'd passed through, half the saloons were gone, the red lights diminished to a score or so, and two or three rows of raw wood bungalows fringed the business section.

Now the fringe had become a wide border, most of the bungalows were neatly painted, and a number of more imposing houses, two and even three stories tall, could be seen on the cross streets. Longarm recognized Chestnut Street when he reached it. Like the other streets, it was unpaved, but unlike the others, it was busy.

He twitched the reins to turn the gelding and let the animal set its own pace among the other traffic—buggies, wagons, an occasional surrey, and riders like himself—that moved along the wide, busy thoroughfare. The board sidewalks were as crowded, the saloons were fewer in number and more widely spaced, and the crowds along the walks were quietly decorous instead of being made up of boiling clusters of drunken trail hands. Interested in noting the changes, Longarm almost passed the Delmonico Saloon. He reined across the street, swung out of his saddle, and wrapped the gelding's reins around the hitch rail.

Aside from the fact that it was almost deserted, and quiet enough to hear a pin drop, the Delmonico was much as Longarm remembered it. The windowless building was long and narrow, lighted by coal-oil lamps that hung on silvered chains from the ceiling. Along one wall stood a dozen small tables, only three of them occupied at this early hour of the afternoon.

Dominating the interior was an imposing mahogany bar that ran its full length; the backbar was mirrored, and crowned in the center by a carved and gilded eagle with outspread wings. Fluted columns supported marble shelves that were crowded with bottles, and the marble top itself was a sea of shining, polished glasses. Only four customers stood at the bar, and only two barkeeps were on duty.

In sharp contrast to the busy trail drive days, when men lined up four deep for service and rowdy shouts that too often degenerated into fights or even gunplay, and kept the place in a constant turmoil, the atmosphere was subdued and decorous. The saloon's interior was almost as quiet as that of a church. Longarm stepped up to the mahogany, and before he had quite come to a halt one of the aproned barkeeps moved to serve him.

"What's your pleasure, friend?" the barkeep asked.

"Tom Moore, if you got any," Longarm replied.

Without hesitating, the barkeep turned and picked up a bottle of Moore from the backbar's bewildering array. He wiped dust from the bottle with the small towel stuck into his waistband and put the bottle and a glass in front of Longarm.

"Most of the customers that order rye don't care for a chaser," he observed with a professional smile. "But if you—"

"I don't either," Longarm replied, pulling the cork from the bottle and filling his glass. He fished a silver dollar out of his pocket and laid it on the bar. "I might be here a little while,

43

so let me know when this is used up."

With a small nod of understanding and without touching the coin, the barkeep moved on to serve another customer. Longarm lighted a cheroot and turned to face the barroom, hooking his heel over the brass rail.

Sipping his Maryland rye, Longarm flicked his eyes around the barroom, observing its occupants without appearing to do so. The men at two of the tables wore city clothes, stiff collars and grey derby hats, and kept their heads close together in low-voiced conversation. The man who sat alone at the other occupied table was leaning back against the wall, his wide-brimmed Stetson pulled low on his face, apparently asleep. When he turned his attention to the bar, Longarm placed one of the customers as a teamster by the braided leather whip coiled on one shoulder. Two others were cowhands by their appearance, and the other two were virtual twins to the businessmen at the tables.

None of them fit the description of Travis Morrison that Longarm had been given by Billy Vail, and he decided that Morrison had not yet arrived in Abilene from the border. He refilled his glass and nodded to the barkeep, who moved up to him.

"Maybe you can tell me if there's a train due in from the south later on today," Longarm said.

"Friend, there's not any train that comes into Abilene from the south," the man replied. "If you wanta get here from the Rio Grande country, you've got to go the long way around, through El Paso or San Antone."

"Well, I knew that was the way it used to be, last time I travelled down to the border," Longarm said. "But I figured things might've got better since I was here last."

"If you're looking to meet somebody, there's a westbound passenger train due in about seven o'clock, and the eastbound gets to town an hour or so later," the barkeep said.

"I guess I'll just have to wait, then," Longarm told the man. He drained his glass and put it on the bar, then pushed the dollar he'd placed there toward the barkeep. "I got some other business to tend to, so I'll mosey along and take care of it, and look in again later on."

Scooping up his sixty cents in change, Longarm left the saloon and remounted his horse. He rode through the warm afternoon sunshine along the railroad tracks until he reached

44

the hollow in which he'd seen the chuck wagon. It still stood where it had been when he first noticed it, but now an almost smokeless fire was burning nearby and several big cast-iron pots and a Dutch oven nestled on its coals.

There was no sign of the cook, and as Longarm drew closer to the wagon he shouted, "Hello, there!"

His call brought a reply from the little pond at the bottom of the vale. He reined over toward the water. A man sat in the pond a few feet from the bank, his half-bald head gleaming and water streaming from his matted chest and shoulders. He was not a youngster. Longarm put his age as being in the late fifties, for his week-old beard and shoulder-length hair were generously flecked with grey. Longarm reined in.

"I didn't believe what I was looking at when I seen your chuck wagon while I was passing by," he said. "From the look of things, you're waiting for a trail herd to get here sometime this evening."

"Along around sundown," the man in the pond replied. "And I guess I can't blame you for not believing it. This is the first drive I've cooked for in going on five or six years."

"Big herd?" Longarm asked.

"Sizeable. About two hundred head."

"Moving it to where?"

"Denver."

"That's a good piece to drive," Longarm observed.

"Sure is," the man agreed. He stood up and began rubbing his hands over his chest and down his sides and thighs to remove the streams of water running down his body. "It'll take a while, I guess, but we'll get there."

Keeping his tone carefully casual, Longarm asked, "Your trail boss wouldn't be looking for hands, would he?"

"Might be. Might not." The man in the pond was pulling on his underwear and inspecting Longarm at the same time. "You'd have to ask him."

"My name's Custis," Longarm said.

"I answer to Sam, or Cookie. But I like Sam better."

Longarm did not let his relief show. He understood from the older man's response and the changed tone of voice that he'd passed the preliminary sparring expected of old-time hands and that the time had come to get down to business. He said, "Some folks cuts my name down to 'cuss,' but I don't mind what they call me as long as they don't cuss me out and keep

45

on calling me when it's chow time."

By this time the other man had donned his shirt and pulled on his jeans and was shoving his still-wet feet into a battered pair of high-heeled boots. He did not smile at Longarm's remark, but started up the gentle slope that led from the pond. He had a pronounced limp, but Longarm followed the cowhand custom of ignoring it.

When he reached Longarm's side, Sam said casually, "If you're hungry, the stew ain't done yet, but I got some biscuits left from breakfast, and the coffee oughta be ready to drink. Let's go on over to the wagon."

Longarm breathed a bit more easily as he walked beside Sam to the chuck wagon. He'd learned during his cowhand days that if there was no hope of a job, the cook would have fed him a full meal and sent him on his way at once. That he'd been invited to stop and talk meant his chances of being hired as a hand ranged from good to excellent. He accepted a graniteware cup filled with steaming coffee and lighted a cigar while waiting for Sam to fill a cup for himself. Then he followed the cook's example and sat down on the chuck wagon's dropped tailgate.

Sam said nothing until he'd finished eyeing Longarm's horse and its scarred and well-used gear. Then he began. "The way your outfit looks, I'd say you ain't one of them Johnny-come-lately hands."

"Oh, I been here and there a while," Longarm replied.

"Sure," Sam nodded. "Me, too. But that's before I got my leg all busted up, eight, nine years ago on the Tumbling T up in Montana. So, ever since I found out I wasn't ever going to be fit to fork a horse no more, I been cooking."

"Beats not cowhanding at all," Longarm commented. His voice was flat, devoid of pity. He watched Sam's expression, and when it did not change, knew that he'd passed another test.

"Look here, Custis, you need a job right bad, don't you?" the cook asked.

"Not bad enough to hurt, but bad enough so's I wouldn't say no to hiring on."

"Even if you knowed it was gonna be a son of a bitch?"

"Now, Sam, when I hire on, I don't look for no pink tea party," Longarm replied. "But I'd like to know what you're getting at, if you feel like telling me."

"You've trailed before now, I reckon?"

"Some. Enough to know what herd dust tastes like."

"Ever work longhorns?"

"A time or two. Not lately."

"Mexican longhorns?"

"I seen a few here and there. I never trailed none."

"Don't unless you really need a job, Custis," Sam advised. "They're more'n a mite wilder than the Texas kind."

When he did not go on, Longarm remarked, "I hear they cut the critters in Mexico later'n they do in Texas, so their horns don't get so big."

"That's right. But a bull that ain't cut till he's damn near full-grown has got time to learn how a bull acts. Texas longhorns is a lot bigger, but they're tame when you put 'em up alongside them Mexican critters."

"I don't see that'd make no never mind to a trail hand."

"That's what some of the boys that signed on down along the Rio Grande figured. But it ain't been all that easy. Them damn Mexican steers still ain't settled down, and that country we just trailed over was pretty rough."

"Sounds like you stand to lose a hand or two here," Longarm said, keeping his voice casual.

"Well, there's three or four that's said they aim to draw down here in Abilene and hightail back home."

"So you figure was I to talk to the trail boss, he might hire me on?"

"I'd say he's gonna be wanting some fresh hands pretty bad."

"What's he like, Sam? This trail boss?"

"Why, he's a good enough ramrod. Expects a hand to work till his job's done, but he ain't mean-hearted. And I feed pretty good, if I do say so myself."

"If your grub's as good as your coffee, I'd say amen to that," Longarm replied.

"Well now, this is the way of it," Sam went on. "The herd oughta be getting here right at sundown. It'll be plumb dark before the boys get them feisty Mexican steers watered and bedded down. But the boss told me we'd be staying here a day or so, long enough to give the boys a chance to blow off steam and for me to buy what grub I need till we get to Tascosa."

"You're driving up the new Goodnight Trail, then?"

"Unless Tom—that's the ramrod— changes his mind. That make any difference to you?"

"Not a bit. I ain't on the dodge or anything like that."

Sam nodded. "Didn't figure you was. Now, was I standing in your boots, I'd stay clear of this place tonight, unless you're hurting for supper money."

"Oh, I ain't pushed that hard, Sam. I just want to hire on someplace before push turns into shove."

"Come out late tomorrow, then," Sam advised. "That'll give them fellows that's said they wanta quit a chance to pull down their pay, and Tom'll really be looking for hands."

"Sounds to me like good advice," Longarm nodded. "Think I'll just take it."

"You do that. I got an idea that about this time tomorrow, Tom'll be right glad to see you."

"And if we happen to run into each other when you come to town to buy your grub, the drinks are on me," Longarm said.

Sam shook his head. "My drinkin' days is all behind me, Custis. But thanks all the same. And good luck."

Longarm got the signal that his visit was over. He stood up and said, "Appreciate the coffee, Sam. And the advice. Now I guess I better get on back to town before that herd shows up."

Chapter 6

Though darkness had almost closed down by the time Longarm returned to Abilene, the town was still very much alive. There were no streetlights, even on Chestnut Street, but it needed none, for most of the stores were still open, and light spilling from their doors and windows brightened the night's gloom.

Longarm was hungry by now. He'd been so engrossed in his conversation with Sam that he'd lost track of time, but a glance at his watch told him that both the eastbound and westbound trains had passed through. Instead of looking for a restaurant he went first to the Delmonico, hoping Travis Morrison had arrived on one or the other of the trains.

In contrast to its midafternoon somnolence, the saloon was filled with patrons. Six barkeeps were on duty now behind the long stretch of polished mahogany, all of them working at top speed. Cowhands, farmers, and city dwellers, each easily identifiable by his clothing, stood two deep at the bar. Two and often three men occupied all the tables along the wall, with the exception of one at the back where a man sat drinking alone.

After his first cursory glance Longarm stopped just inside the doorway and lighted a cheroot while he studied the crowd. After a few minutes he gave up trying to sort out individual faces from the constantly shifting group bellied up to the mahogany and turned his attention to the tables.

His eyes were drawn first to the table where the solitary occupant sat, and he'd no more than turned his head in that direction when he saw the man sitting there give an almost imperceptible flick of the forefinger of the hand in which he held his drink. Longarm raised his eyebrows a fraction of an inch and the man at the table nodded.

Picking his way between the crowd at the bar and the chairs which stuck out from the tables along the wall, Longarm made his way slowly to the table where the solo drinker sat. He was a man Longarm judged to be pushing sixty, but he was still whipcord-wiry. Under a high-bridged hawk-beaked nose he had a bristly grey moustache that needed trimming, and his tall-crowned Stetson was pushed far back on his head, which was covered by a thinning growth of grey hair. He wore the Texas "city suit" of rusty black, a white shirt with a paper collar, and a thin black string necktie.

Longarm stopped beside the table and asked, "Was you maybe looking to meet somebody here?"

"If I recall Billy's description of that cigar you've got in your mouth, I've been sitting here waiting to meet you since my train got in a half-hour ago," the man replied.

"Then you'd be Travis Morrison?"

"Yes. And I don't need to ask your name, but I'm not sure it's the one you're travelling under now," Morrison replied.

"It ain't. My first name's Custis. Not many folks know I even got a first name, so that's what I'm calling myself on this case," Longarm replied.

"I'll try not to slip up and call you anything else where anybody's likely to hear us," Morrison nodded. "Sorta takes me back to my Ranger days. It's been a while since I was on a case."

"I imagine you and Billy could spin some tall tales about them days, Morrison."

"I guess we could, but you know yourself how hard it is to talk about what's happened to you," Morrison replied. "And, if you don't mind, I'd as soon you called me Travis or Trav."

"Sure. I answer to my nickname better'n I do to my own real one. I guess there's lots of us does."

"I guess," Morrison agreed. He nodded at the vacant chair and asked, "Aren't you going to sit down?"

Longarm glanced over at the crowded bar and said, "I was figuring I'd try to belly up and get me a drink before I set, and I guess that crowd ain't going to shrivel away none. Just a minute. I'll be right back."

Pushing up to the bar as politely as possible, Longarm got the eye of one of the barkeepers and ordered a tot of Tom Moore. He carried his glass back to the table and sat down across from Morrison. He said, "Sorry I was late getting here."

"That's not important. I can't catch a train back to Del Rio until tomorrow morning," Morrison said. "Hell of a note, having to travel more'n three hundred miles to get to a place that's not much more than a hundred miles from where I started out."

50

"I guess that's what they call progress these days," Longarm smiled. "I rode all around Robin Hood's barn to get here, too. I'd say Abilene's not exactly on what you'd call the beaten track."

"Well, there ain't much I wouldn't do for Billy Vail. When I got his wire that you wanted to talk to me, I didn't have to wait long to make up my mind you must've had a good reason."

"There's a lot of questions I got about this case Billy's sent me down here on, Trav. Too many things about it don't make much sense."

"They didn't to me, either," Morrison nodded. "That's why I smelled a great big rat travelling with that trail herd. But I'm damned if I can figure out what it is."

"Maybe we can do some figuring together," Longarm said. "It looks like I'm going to be able to pick up a job as a trail hand with the outfit moving them cattle, so I'll have plenty of time between here and Denver to see if I can figure out what's going on."

"I don't suppose you've had supper yet?" Morrison asked.

Longarm shook his head. "I was about to ask you the same thing. Soon as I down the rest of my drink, we'll go find ourselves a cafe and eat a bite."

He raised his glass and, while he was sipping his whiskey, saw Morrison's eyes flicking over the crowd of men at the bar. A frown grew suddenly on Morrison's face. Longarm gulped the rest of the Tom Moore quickly.

"Something wrong?" he asked.

"One of those fellows at the bar's been eyeing you since you come in," Morrison replied. "I figured at first it was because you're a stranger, but now he's watching you again. When that happens, in our business—"

Longarm broke in. "Don't pay no more attention to him, Trav," he said quietly. "I'll set my glass down like we was going to leave and grab a look at him when we stand up and turn around. Just tell me whereabouts he is, so I won't waste no time trying to spot him."

"He's up toward the front, maybe six feet from the door. Got on a Utah-creased blond Stetson and a fancy blue bandanna around his neck. Big man. Pig-eyed. Needs a shave."

"That don't mean much," Longarm said as he lowered his glass to the table. "Fits a lot of outlaws I might've had a brush with one time or another."

51

Morrison flicked a finger at the empty glass. "Whenever you're ready, then."

Longarm nodded and started to unfold his long legs from below the table. He'd just gotten both feet on the floor when Morrison said urgently, "If you wanta see him, look quick! He's heading for the door."

Longarm swivelled in his seat to look, but got only a glimpse of a light-colored hat and a shoulder-high flash of blue as the man pushed through the batwings. He stood up quickly, but by then the mysterious gazer was totally out of sight.

"If we hurry, we might catch up with him outside," Morrison suggested.

Longarm shook his head. "Not likely. All he's got to do is duck between this building and the next one and get lost in the dark. Judging by how fast he got moving after he seen I might catch sight of him, he'd be an old-timer that'd most likely know all the tricks."

"I'm sorry," Morrison apologized. "I guess it's been such a long time since I wore a Ranger's badge that I've got sorta slow. It's a habit a man loses when he don't use it."

"Why, it ain't your fault, Trav. Anyhow, whoever that fellow is will keep trying. If he's really after me, we'll run into him again sooner or later."

"But you might not have any advance warning next time."

"Shucks, if I let that worry me, I'd turn in my badge to Billy Vail in two shakes of a cow's tail," Longarm replied. "I put too many outlaws and the like behind bars to worry about what they might do to me after they was turned out. Now, let's go get that supper. It'll be a good chance for us to talk."

A short walk down Chestnut Street brought them to a building that displayed a cafe sign on a board hanging from its awning. A glance inside revealed that only two of its eight tables and fewer than half its counter stools were occupied. Longarm stepped inside the door. Two or three of the customers glanced up idly, showing no interest in him, and went back to their food. The oilcloth covering the tables and the counter seemed clean, and there was no smell of burned grease in the air. There was also a corner table which Longarm noted was almost invisible from the street.

Over his shoulder, he said to his companion, "I guess this place is as good as any, unless you got a hankering for something fancy."

"I'm a meat and potatoes man myself," Morrison replied. "Chile con carne and tamales is what I'd call fancy food, and I get all of that I can handle down on the Rio Grande."

Longarm and Morrison went in and sat down at the corner table where they could not be observed through the wide front windows. The waiter came ambling from behind the counter, carrying a menu card. Longarm spoke before the man could place the card on the table.

"I'll save you the time waiting while we look at your menu card," he said. "I want a piece of round steak fried till it's good and done and some fried potatoes, and that's all, except a good cup of coffee to go with along with 'em."

"That sounds good to me," Morrison agreed. "Make it two."

After the waiter had scribbled their orders on a pad and left for the kitchen, Morrison said, "Billy's wire said you had a few questions you wanted to ask me. I guess now's as good a time as any to start asking."

"Well, Trav, the first thing I'm curious about is how you got interested in that trail herd in the first place."

"All I can say is that the deal didn't smell right. First off, it struck me as being sorta strange that anybody'd bring Mexican longhorns across the border, when there's plenty of better cattle for sale on this side of the Rio Grande."

"I had a case a while back where there was a bunch of Mexican cattle being moved," Longarm nodded. "Except the crook was on this side of the border, cheating the Indian Bureau on steers bought for the Indian reservations."

"I don't see many big herds crossing," Morrison said. "Most of the movement is breeding stock. There's damned few big herds moved either way, these days, even if the *aftosa's* been pretty much wiped out."

"I guess you had to keep a pretty close eye on things as long as that hoof-and-mouth disease was so bad?"

"Real close," Morrison nodded. "And there's always a little bit of smuggling, rustled stock from one side or the other being moved, and little ranchers trying to get a herd across without paying a brand inspection fee."

"I'd guess your job's mostly cut and dried, though," Longarm suggested.

"Too much so to suit me," Morrison agreed. "When you come right down to it, what I do is lazy man's work, and I never did take much stock in being lazy. But I might not have

53

to worry about it much longer."

"How's that?"

"Oh, now that the *aftosa* panic is over, I've heard the government might try to get the states along the Mexican border to take over the brand inspection."

"And if that happens you might be out of a job?"

"Not exactly. I'd just transfer to the Customs Department. They're having a lot of trouble now with gold smuggling."

Their conversation was interrupted by the return of the waiter bringing their steaks. By wordless mutual consent, the two men ate without exchanging more than a few words about the quality of their food, which was satisfactory if not being really outstanding. When their plates were emptied and the waiter had removed them, Longarm lighted a cheroot and Morrison rolled a corn-husk cigarette to accompany their after-dinner coffee.

Leaning back in his chair, Longarm looked at Morrison through a cloud of blue smoke and said, "You was starting to tell me about gold smuggling when our grub got here. As far as I know, our outfit ain't heard anything about that yet."

"It's not likely you would, way up north in Denver. But what happened is that just a little while back, when Diaz was cutting up a lot, Congress slapped a twenty percent import tariff on gold from Mexico."

Longarm exhaled with a soft, low-pitched whistle. "I'd say that's a pretty stiff duty on something as expensive as gold."

"It is," Morrison nodded. "But gold's one of Mexico's chief exports to this country, and I guess they figured it was good politics to put a high duty on it to bring Diaz into line."

"I can sure see where it'd boost up smuggling, though."

"It has. And the smugglers are pretty much openly backed by Diaz and his political cronies. They're using some real tough customers, too. A lot of former *rurales* and soldiers, men that don't back off from a shootout if they get cornered."

"Well, I can see it'd be a lot more interesting for a man like you to chase gold smugglers instead of ranchers that're just trying to cheat on a few head of rustled cattle," Longarm said. "But my job right now ain't gold, Trav. It's cattle. We better get back to them Mexican longhorns."

"Like I'd started to tell you," Morrison began, "I got to wondering why anybody'd take the time and trouble to drive a herd that size almost six hundred miles, pay a trail crew and

54

all the rest of it, when they could ship them cattle on the railroad for a lot less money."

"And that's when you wrote Billy Vail?"

Morrison nodded. "There wasn't anything I could do, in my job. But since the herd was heading for Denver, I figured Billy might be interested in looking into it."

"Which he was, of course." Longarm had long since finished his cheroot, and his coffee cup was empty, as was Morrison's. He beckoned the waiter and pointed to the empty cups and after they had been refilled lighted a fresh cigar and picked up the conversation where he'd interrupted it. "How far did you go trying to check out that herd, Trav?"

"There wasn't much I could do but go by the book when I was checking it. The trail boss had the right papers, bills of sale and all, and the numbers on them agreed with the brands and the size of the herd."

"I guess you'd've said something in your letter if you'd noticed any of the brands had been changed, like with a running iron?" Longarm asked.

"That's one of the reasons why we've got brand inspection stations along the border," Morrison replied. "There's a lot of ranches in Mexico that don't have branding irons like the ones American ranchers use, that burn in the same identical pattern every time. Some ranchers, especially them that don't have a big spread, they'll just put on the brands with a running iron, so there'll be a little difference between brands even in the same herd, depending on who was handling the iron."

"And besides that, you didn't notice anything at all out of line about 'em?" Longarm prodded.

"No. Just the difference between any brands that're put on freehand. But there wasn't any sign the brands had been changed, if that's what you're getting at."

"I don't rightly know what I'm getting at, Trav," Longarm said, with a puzzled smile that was almost a frown.

"I'd guarantee the brands was all right," Morrison insisted. "Hell's bells, I've looked at enough brands in my day to spot one that's been changed."

"I bet you have, at that," Longarm said. "So you checked the brands and the papers, and then what?"

"Well, all that business was handled by the brokers. I know both of them, and they're both good men that wouldn't get

55

caught up in any kind of deal they'd think was crooked."

"So after that there wasn't much you could do, was there?"

Morrison shook his head. "All the steers had passed *aftosa* inspection, and since everything else seemed all right, all I could do was wave 'em on their way."

"Them bills of sale, how was they made out?"

"All of 'em read the same way—sold to the Arapahoe Cattle Syndicate in Denver."

"You didn't happen to run onto the name Sterns in any of 'em?" Longarm asked.

Morrison frowned thoughtfully before saying, "All the bills of sale were made out exactly the same, like I just said. Who is this fellow Sterns?"

"That's what me and Billy Vail'd both like to know. Billy run into the name when he was trying to check out the syndicate up in Denver, but he couldn't find out anything about him."

"If there was anything to be found out, I'd put my money on Billy to find it," Morrison said.

"Sure. Me, too," Longarm agreed. He sat silently for a moment, puffing his cheroot, then went on, "There's one thing I've found out since I been lawing, Trav, and I reckon you have, too. You can't always tell about something till you look at it more'n once."

"It is easy to be fooled unless you're careful," Morrison nodded. "I've made my share of mistakes, like we all have."

"It's like when you see a duck dive under water and then come up," Longarm went on. "It don't look like a duck at first because its feathers is all wet, but if it swims like a duck and quacks like a duck, you know damned well it is a duck."

"Well, this business of the Mexican longhorns has got that kind of crooked smell," Morrison said soberly. "Even if I haven't been able to trace it to where it starts."

"Tell me about the trail hands that's bringing them steers north," Longarm suggested. "Did you know any of 'em?"

Morrison shook his head. "Not even one that I saw while they were forming up the herd after they'd took the steers out of the inspection corrals. But that don't mean much. Hands change jobs these days a lot faster'n they change their socks."

Longarm hid his disappointment as well as his regret for having brought Morrison all the way up from the Rio Grande on a hunch that hadn't proved out. He said, "Well, our supper's settled down enough to where I'd like a drink, now. Let's mosey back over to the Delmonico and get one, and talk a little bit more. It might be you'll think of something else, or I will, and we'll come up with that fresh lead I'm looking for. And supper's on me. You go on while I settle up."

After paying the bill, Longarm stepped out into the cool night air. The street was almost deserted now. Morrison was standing on the board sidewalk, and turned as though to say something when from a dark slit between two buildings across the street a revolver barked. The slug whistled past Longarm's head, missing him by inches, and shattering the window of the cafe behind him.

In lightning-like reflex response, Longarm dropped flat, dragging Morrison with him. He drew as he fell, and stared at the black opening, but could see no target. A second shot blasted from the black aperture, raising a puff of dirt from the street. Longarm let off two quick shots at the point where he'd seen the muzzle-flash.

Morrison had his revolver in his hand by now, and he triggered a shot on the heels of the two Longarm had fired. A third shot came from the hidden sniper, and the boards in front of Longarm splintered as the slug tore into them.

Longarm rolled in one direction, Morrison in the other. They let off their shots at almost the same time, but there was no answering fire from the black opening.

"You take the side you're on," Longarm told his companion. "I'll go the other way."

In the instant communion that sometimes exists between men who have devoted most of their lives to upholding the law, no more conversation was required. Morrison rose to a crouch and began running, angling across the street away from the source of the gunfire.

Longarm waited until Morrison had a half-dozen steps start, then he crouched and ran in a zigzag pattern in the opposite direction. In the middle of the street they changed their course and began converging on the black space where the hidden attacker was holed up.

Chapter 7

When no more shots came from the black void between the two buildings, Longarm's experience and instinct told him the concealed gunman had fled. He called to Morrison, "Stay where you are, Trav! I'll go around this building and if he's still in there, I'll flush him out!"

Without waiting for his companion's reply, Longarm wheeled and started running along the facade of the building in front of which he'd stopped. The gap between it and the adjoining store was narrower than that which had provided shelter for the ambusher, and he was forced to turn sideways and squeeze along between the two walls. He was halfway through when he saw the flicker of a shadow cross the gap at the rear of the buildings.

Since he had already fired three shots and had only two left in the Colt's cylinder, he held his fire rather than wasting one of them on a vanished shadow. Instead, he raised his voice and shouted, "Trav! He's heading down the alley away from us! Come on, we got to catch up with him before he gets away!"

Sidling along the narrow gap to the end of the building, Longarm waited in its cover until he heard Morrison's footsteps pounding down the alley toward him. He called, "Hold your fire, Trav! I'm gonna step into the alley."

Morrison came puffing up and asked, "Is he still running along the alley?"

"Far as I can tell, he ain't stopped or turned off. I'd guess he's headed for the street at the end of the alley. If we move fast, maybe we can catch up to him."

By now the eyes of both men had adjusted to the darkness. They began running down the alley in the direction the would-be killer had taken. Longarm and Morrison caught sight of the fleeing man at almost the same time. He was still running fast, but he was only a few yards ahead of them now, keeping in close to the backs of the buildings where the darkness was blackest.

They got only a few fleeting glimpses of the shadowy figure ahead as they kept up their pursuit, and the soft earth of the alley smothered the sounds of the fugitive's footsteps. Longarm raised his Colt several times, hoping for a running shot, but each time the lack of light defeated his intention. He had no intention of wasting shells on an unseen target.

"I sure hope we ain't chasing the wrong man," he said as they continued their pursuit.

"That's got to be him," Morrison exclaimed. "I'd've seen him and cut him down if he'd tried to double back and come past me."

"I did see him," Longarm replied without breaking his stride. "But he'd already passed by me before I could let off a shot at him."

While they ran, Longarm slid his hand into his vest pocket and took out three fresh shells. Working by feel, his Colt and its shells familiar to his fingers, he reloaded without slowing or stopping, and though they were not gaining on their quarry they managed to keep the shadowy form of the running man in sight.

"He'll be getting to a cross street in a minute or so," Longarm said as they pounded along in the darkness. "Chances are he'll turn into it."

"Don't worry," Morrison gasped. "We're bound to catch up with him in a minute or so."

For the first time, Longarm realized that his companion, unaccustomed to strenuous activity, was getting winded. He asked, "You all right, Trav?"

"I got enough breath left to go a while yet," Morrison panted. "But if you can run faster, go to it. I won't be but a step or so behind you!"

Longarm put on a burst of speed as their quarry reached the cross street and turned into it, heading away from the center of town. He reached the street himself and swung around, running in the tighest arc possible to reduce the distance between himself and the man they were chasing.

A few yards ahead of the running man, a lantern glowed on the front porch of one of the houses facing the street. Longarm began angling to the side of the street opposite the arc of pale light shed by the lantern, planning to catch his quarry when he got close enough to be silhouetted against it.

He was slowing down, raising his gun hand and preparing

to shoot, when he realized that the fugitive ahead had seen the danger in time to avoid it. The man in front of him veered away from the lighted area to the same side of the street Longarm had taken, where the lantern light's glow did not quite reach.

Longarm saw that he was going to be forced to shoot in spite of the dimness. He skidded to a halt and braced himself, his Colt raised and ready. Before he could fire, the running man dived out of the street into the yard of a house, where the lantern's light did not reach at all. Longarm tried to catch a glimpse of him, but failed. Realizing that he would now have no chance for a shot at a visible target, and that if he kept up his present pace in pursuit he would become a target himself when he reached the lighted area, he did not start running again.

This ain't the first time that fellow's dodged bullets, old son, he told himself as he tried unsuccessfully to catch a glimpse of movement at the edge of the arc of light cast by the distant lantern. *And seeing that he's a cagy customer, you just better figure to be a mite cagier.*

Following his thoughts with action, Longarm edged away from the lighted area into the yard of the nearest house. He could hear Morrison's footsteps now, and realized that his companion was catching up to him and could probably see him outlined in the lantern light.

"He's holed up just ahead of me here, Trav!" Longarm called over his shoulder. "Circle around the back of them two houses up there and cut him off from behind!"

Red muzzle-blast cut through the darkness in the area where the fugitive had taken cover. Longarm hit the dirt for the second time during the chase, certain that the other man's shot would be wild, but taking no chance that a second one might be on its target. Morrison's footsteps had faded out now, and Longarm felt a surge of relief. He was sure that he, not Morrison, was the hidden shootist's target.

Peering through the night again, trying to find the fugitive in his sights in the dark area beyond the lantern's glow, Longarm strained his eyes, but could still see nothing. He'd heard no sound since his quarry's last shot, and was certain that the unknown man was holding his position, keeping the scanty edge of advantage that he'd gained, waiting for a certain shot. Then the idea he'd been searching for struck him.

Sliding his fingers into his vest pocket, he took out two

wooden matches. For a moment, he racked his brain trying to think of something in his pockets with which he could weight them and hold them together, and finally realized that he could push them into one of his cheroots with their heads protruding. He fished out one of the long slim cigars and shoved the ends of the matchsticks into its tip.

Holding the match-studded cigar in his left hand, Longarm twisted his leg until he'd brought his foot within reach of his hand. He dragged the match-heads along his boot sole and as they rasped on the rough leather he flipped the cigar off to one side in a single fluid motion.

In the instant the sputtering matches shot away from his foot, Longarm fixed his eyes on the darkness ahead. The matches sparked in a fair imitation of muzzle-blast from a pistol as they flew through the air. As Longarm had hoped, the fugitive's nerves were so taut that he fell for the ruse in spite of its clumsiness. When the matches fizzled into flame as Longarm tossed them out, the nerve-taut gunman fired.

Longarm was ready. With the muzzle-blast from the unseen shootist's gun pinpointing the man's position, he triggered off two quick shots. A gargled gasp sounded through the darkness ahead. Longarm began belly-crawling toward the sound, moving as quietly as he could over the rough ground.

As he drew closer the rasping, gargled sound faded into silence, but Longarm was close enough now to make out the figure of a man silhouetted in the dim glow of the distant lantern. He was sprawled face down, and lay limp and motionless.

From the darkness beyond he heard footsteps grating on the hard soil and called quickly, "Hold your fire, Trav! I'm right sure I got him!"

In spite of his certainty, Longarm kept his Colt ready as he drew closer to the recumbent body of the man who'd tried to ambush him from the darkness. When he was close enough to reach out and grasp the barrel of the revolver that the unknown man still held, and pull the weapon away, the man did not move.

Morrison, who had evidently been watching a short distance away, asked, "Is he dead?"

"Deader'n a doornail," Longarm replied, getting to his feet. "But I still don't know who he is."

Morrison had come up to join him by the time Longarm

finished talking. The dead man was lying face down and, after holstering their guns, the two of them turned the limp body face up, only to find that Longarm's slug had gone into the crown of the man's hat, pushing it down over his face. Longarm pulled the hat away, but even their darkness-adjusted eyes could not make out details of his features in the dim light.

Morrison said, "I don't imagine the people across the street'd mind if we borrowed that lantern on their porch to take a closer look. It don't look like they're home, anyhow; there's not any lights on inside the house."

He went across the street and returned with the lantern. As he drew close enough for the light to reveal the features of the dead man he exclaimed, "Hell's bells! That's the fellow who was eyeing you in Delmonico's! If your slug hadn't've knocked his hat outa shape, I'd've recognized him right off."

Longarm said, "I can see who he is now, Trav. He's called himself Clete Day as long as I've known him, but I don't guess that's his real name."

"Somebody you arrested a while back?" Morrison asked.

Longarm nodded. "Twice. The first time he drew ten years for robbing a stage in Arizona Territory. He busted outa the old prison—that was before they built their new one down at Yuma. The second time I pulled him in was for murdering a mail clerk during a train holdup in South Dakota. He was part of a gang there, and his pals raided the little city jail where he was being kept till he went on trial. They busted him out and he ain't been seen since. There's a Wanted flier out on him."

"Damned if Billy Vail ain't right about you," Morrison said.

"Right? How's that?"

"Why, in the letter he wrote me saying he was going to send you down to look into that trail herd, he said you draw trouble like honey draws ants."

"I suppose I do get into more'n my share of scrapes," Longarm admitted. "But I'll guarantee you, I don't go outa my way looking for 'em."

"I don't suppose this Clete Day's the only outlaw that's out to get you," Morrison suggested.

"Oh, he ain't the first one that's tried, and I don't guess he'll be the last one, either," Longarm said matter-of-factly.

Both men turned to look up the street then, as the buzzing

of excited voices reached their ears. They saw two or three lanterns bobbing, and in their light a score or more men hurrying toward them.

"I guess my luck's sorta mixed up tonight," Longarm told Morrison. "Now I got to tell the town marshal who I am, so he'll understand how this shooting happened."

"He'll likely understand and keep quiet, if you ask him to," Morrison said.

"If I could talk to him in private, I guess he would. But it's a dollars to doughnuts bet that some of the hands from that trail herd is in the crowd, so my scheme to go along with the herd as a trail hand is going to be busted plumb to hell."

"Wait a minute, now," Morrison said thoughtfully. "We don't have to tell the town marshal which one of us shot that fellow."

"If he don't know I got a federal marshal's badge, we could both be charged with murder," Longarm pointed out.

"Not if I flash my old Texas Ranger badge on him," Morrison replied. He produced a battered leather wallet from his hip pocket and flipped it open to show Longarm a silver star pinned inside its fold. "They give me my badge when I left the force, and I still carry it around, sorta like a souvenir."

"I ain't so sure I like the idea," Longarm said slowly. "I don't lie worth a damn, Trav."

"You don't need to. Just keep quiet. Where corraling crooks is concerned, I don't mind stretching the truth a mite."

"Suppose he was to wire Austin to check up on you?"

"I bet I can talk him outa doing that."

"It's worth a try," Longarm said thoughtfully. "But how're we going to account for me being along?"

"You jumped in to help me when you seen I was in trouble," Morrison said. "And there ain't any way they can tell which one of us shot Day."

"It's worth a try," Longarm nodded. "I'll keep my mouth shut as much as I can, if you're willing to go along."

"I had the idea to start with!" Morrison said. "You just possum along and let me do the talking. Hell's bells, this is just like the old days to me!"

By this time the crowd had reached the scene. The man in front wore a town marshal's star on his shirt pocket and carried a sawed-off double-barreled shotgun. He did not level the gun threateningly at Longarm and Morrison, but swung the muzzle back and forth at a low angle as he stopped and gazed coldly at them.

"What in hell's this all about?" he asked.

Morrison opened the wallet to show the Ranger badge. He said, "My name's Travis Morrison, Marshal. If you'll get that fellow by you to lift his lantern up, you can read it on this badge."

Bending forward, the marshal scrutinized the badge. Then, his voice no longer gratingly harsh, he said, "If you're here on a case, how come you didn't stop in to see me when you hit town?"

"Because I didn't want to show my face anyplace I didn't have to," Morrison replied. He gestured toward the body. "That's Clete Day laying there. He's a killer that busted outa prison up north before they could hang him. Likely you've got a flier on him in your office."

"I got so many fliers on my desk I can't catch up with all of 'em," the marshal said. "So you tracked him here and he resisted arrest? Is that the way of it?"

"Something like that." Morrison nodded.

"How about this fellow with you?" the local lawman asked, indicating Longarm.

"We was setting at the same table in that little restaurant on Chestnut Street and we walked outa the place together. Day taken a shot at me, and he— Well, I guess it'd be stretching the truth to say I deputized him, because there wasn't time to do much but shoot back. But he sure as hell helped me catch up and get Day corralled."

"You got a name, I guess?" the marshal asked Longarm.

"Sure. My name's Custis," Longarm replied truthfully. "And it happened just about like this Ranger fellow told you. I didn't see his badge till all the shooting was over, but we'd got to talking while we was eating supper, and I figured he had to be some kind of lawman. Then when this dead fellow began shooting, it just sorta come natural for me to help out."

"So you jumped into the fracas." The marshal nodded. He paused for a moment, then went on, "Well, as far as I can see, it's pretty much of a cut and dried case. I sure can't find no fault with either one of you for doing what you did."

Morrison nodded. "Thanks, Marshal. Now I'll ask a favor of you. It'll be a big help to me if you'll get this body moved and see it's buried. I guess Abilene's got arrangements with one of the undertaking parlors?"

"Sure," the marshal nodded. "I'll be glad to see to it for you, Morrison. You'll be reporting to Austin, I expect, so I don't even need to bother you by asking you to stop in and help me with my report."

"Thanks," Morrison replied. "Now, I wanta take this Custis fellow over to Delmonico's and buy him a drink or two, so if you'll excuse us—"

"I'd feel the same way, if it was me," the town lawman agreed. "You go right ahead. I'll see to whatever needs doing."

Longarm and Morrison skirted the crowd that had gathered and walked on toward Chestnut Street. After they'd gotten out of earshot of the onlookers, Morrison said, "Well, it worked just about like I figured it would. We're both free and clear, and nobody's in trouble."

"You might be," Longarm said, "when they hear about this thing in Austin. But if anybody starts a fuss, you know me and Billy will stand behind you."

"Oh, there'll be a report sent to Austin," Morrison said. "I know what'll happen to it, too. Some clerk will give it a quick look and tuck it away in a file. I never will hear about it."

"I hope not," Longarm told him. "And I sure thank you for what you done back there. Now, let's go on to Delmonico's and get that drink. Except it's me that'll be doing the buying."

Chapter 8

"Damned if I hadn't just about as soon be in jail as cooped up in any hotel room anyplace," Morrison growled, striding to the window and looking down on Chestnut Street.

He came back to the table where Longarm was sitting and dropped into a chair. A bottle of Tom Moore sat on the small square table; the night before, the two of them had reduced its level very substantially at Delmonico's, and Longarm had bought the remainder so they would have a pre-breakfast snort handy. Breakfast lay two hours behind them now, and both were ready to do something besides sitting and sipping.

Longarm said, "I ain't fond of hotels myself, Trav, but holing up's the safest thing to do. After last night, I'd just as soon not let anybody notice us together on the street or in a saloon. They might get a notion to start asking questions."

"Oh, I don't argue that," Morrison replied. "A man's got to do whatever his job makes him."

"It's getting on for the time when I better be riding out to that trail camp, anyhow. By this time, the hands that was going to quit has likely drawn down their pay, and the boss is going to be worried about finding men to take their places."

"You want me to wait here? I don't have a thing to do until my train pulls out this evening."

"There ain't much reason I can see for you to hole up as long as we ain't going to be out together."

"I'll mosey around after while, then," Morrison nodded. "You figure you'll be out there very long?"

"Depends on how bad the trail boss needs to hire on a hand, or if he needs one at all. From what the cook said yesterday, I'm pretty sure there'll be a job open, and if two or three of their men has quit, I might have to start work right away." He threw his saddlebags over his shoulder and picked up his rifle. "I'm taking all my gear, just in case."

"Well, Long, if I don't see you before my train leaves, I'll know you hit a lucky streak." Morrison extended his hand and they shook. Then he added, "I'll be writing to Billy Vail soon as I get back to Del Rio. Anything you want me to tell him?"

"Just say I'll see him in Denver when the herd gets there. Not that Billy'd be worried. I ain't much good about sending in reports, or so he keeps telling me. So if I don't get back, good luck to you, Trav."

At the livery stable down the street from the hotel, where he'd left his horse overnight, Longarm paid the twenty-cent boarding fee and saddled up. The morning was already warming up, and he toed the horse to a fast walk to make a breeze as he rode out to the trail camp. The blatting of cattle filled the air even before he mounted the rise that rimmed the saucer-like hollow where the herd was bedded.

Reining in at the rim of the ridge, Longarm looked down, taking in the vale in a single sweeping glance. He saw only four men, one of them riding herd, the others near the chuck wagon. One of these was Sam, the cook, who stood close to the wagon. One of the remaining two was stretched out on his blanket at the edge of the pond, and the other stood some distance away, scanning the scattered cattle.

Two hundred longhorns, even the small Mexican breed, left very little room in the hollow. There was barely enough open space for a picket line for the horses, the chuck wagon, and a grassy strip close to the pond for the men to spread their bed-rolls. The cattle were bunched on the near side of the pond, and most of them were grazing on the tall summer grass, not yet yellowed from lack of rain.

Longarm had seen no Mexican longhorns for quite some time, but those in the vale looked very like the ones he'd checked when he was trying to catch up with the swindler who called himself the Real McCoy. He frowned as he looked at the herd. These steers were quite a bit smaller than the Texas variety, but their horns seemed to Longarm to be much bigger than the ones on the other Mexican longhorns he'd seen.

He remembered the horns on those he'd encountered earlier as being smaller, not much longer than those on the new cross-breeds which were now beginning to dominate the western range. But, though bigger than usual, the horns on the herd at which he was now looking still lacked the impressive spread and sweep that had given the breed its name.

In color, the steers were largely tan, ranging from a reddish cream that was almost white to a rich chocolate brown which in some lights looked nearly black. There were a few with hides of bluish-purple, and even fewer of the mouse-grey hue called *grulla*. The hides of many of the lighter-colored steers were flecked with dark splotches that ranged in size from a dappling of dots no bigger than a pinto bean to large, irregular blotches that covered forequarters or hindquarters or their midsections.

All of them, though, showed the longhorn back stripe, a streak a shade or two lighter than their predominant coloration which ran from their rumps to their shoulders and usually extended down their forequarters on each side to form a cross.

While all the steers bore the breed's widespread horns, there were a few on which the horns grew low on their heads or set far up near the base of their skulls. A few, only three or four as nearly as Longarm could see, had the horns which in both Mexico and Texas were called *chongas*.

This was the name given by *vaqueros* of Old Mexico to steers with twisted horns. He saw one *chonga* steer that had horns which swept out corkscrew-style, while on another the deformed horns grew in odd curves that brought the tips around to the animal's nose. On still another, the uncharacteristic curve swept the tips of the horns in a downcurve to its neck-wattle. As he scanned the cattle, looking for more *chongas*, and finding none, Longarm noticed that the few twist-horned cattle seemed to carry their heads higher than did those with symmetrical horns.

After he'd looked his fill, Longarm toed his pony ahead and walked it downslope to the chuck wagon. Sam, the cook, looked up and recognized him from the day before, and greeted him with a wave. Longarm reined in, dismounted, and walked over to the chuck wagon.

"Well, I'm back, just like I said I'd be," he announced, swinging out of his saddle.

"Oh, I figured you'd show up, Custis," Sam replied. "And you got here just about the right time. Two of the hands that started out with the drive drew their pay and quit soon as the herd was bedded down last night."

"And the trail boss ain't found anybody else to hire on?"

"Well, he picked up one last night when he went to Abilene, but there was some kind of shooting scrape that roiled up the town, so nobody wanted to talk about much of anything else."

"That still leaves him a man short, then?"

"He said he'd talked to another one that promised to come out and look the herd over today. But whoever the fellow was, he hasn't showed up yet."

"You figure I got a pretty good chance to pick up a job?" Longarm asked.

"Don't worry, Custis, Just go on over and say you want to be hired on. He'll take you in a minute, no questions asked."

"Which one of them two fellows is he?"

"Tom's the one that's standing up looking at the steers," the cook replied, pointing. "Likely he's trying to figure out how he's going to trail out tomorrow, being two hands short of having enough to move the herd."

"Thanks, Sam. I'll go chin with him."

Longarm walked over to the trail boss, who was still standing facing away from him. He turned when he heard Longarm's footsteps, and Longarm frowned. He'd known the man somewhere before, at some time in the distant past, but for a moment he couldn't recall where or when. Then the trail boss spoke and gave him the answer.

"Well, I'll be damned!" he said. "Custis Long! It's been a good long spell, but you haven't changed all that much since the old days up on the Half-Moon!"

Longarm saw his carefully planned scheme going up in smoke when the other man called his name, and mention of the Half-Moon brought memory flooding back.

"Tom Greenhaw!" he said, taking the trail boss's extended hand and shaking it, his face breaking into a smile that hid his disappointment, as he recalled an earlier day and other places. "It's been a while, all right."

"I hate to think how long it's been," Greenhaw replied. "I don't guess I'll ever forget those days up in Montana, when we were both lard-ass greenhorns trying to act like cowpunchers!"

"Looks like you made it, all right," Longarm said. He waved his hand to encompass the trail camp and herd, stalling for time while he juggled in his mind the elements of the unexpected situation he'd encountered, trying to fit the changed circumstances into the plans he and Vail had made so carefully. "You always said you'd be a boss hand some day."

"Oh, I got to be a boss hand quite a while back," Greenhaw said. "And I'll tell you for a fact, it's not the way it looked to be when we were greenies."

Longarm fished a cheroot out of his pocket and flicked his thumbnail over a match. Through a cloud of tobacco smoke, he said, "Tom, you're about the last man I figured to run into down here."

Frowning, Greenhaw said, "Damn it, Custis, you act like you're not a bit glad to see me, after all these years. I don't recall we ever had any sort of quarrel, back on the Half-Moon."

"Oh, we didn't," Longarm replied quickly. He'd made up his mind about a new course of action that seemed the only answer to his predicament. "It ain't that, Tom. I think as much of you as I ever did. It's just that I . . . well, like you said a minute ago, you're about the last fellow I expected to see."

"I still don't understand what that's got to do with anything," Greenhaw replied, his face still bearing the puzzled frown that had formed on it a moment earlier.

"Let's walk around the pond a little ways, Tom," Longarm suggested. "There's something I got to talk about with you."

"Sure," Greenhaw agreed readily. "It'll probably do me good to get my mind off my troubles for a while."

They started walking slowly along the edge of the pond and when Longarm was sure they were out of earshot of the cook and the trail hand who was lounging on his bedroll, he said, "You know, I didn't stay with cowhanding but a little while, after I left the Half-Moon."

"You still look like a puncher to me," Greenhaw said.

"That's because I figured to," Longarm explained. "But the fact of it is, I'm in a different kind of work now. It ain't a thing I'd planned on, but I've switched jobs since we seen each other last."

"But you always said you were bound and determined to make a top cowhand."

"Oh, I was. But then I run into a sheriff over in Bozeman that taken a liking to me. He was in a tight with a bunch of outlaws when I run into him first, and I give him a hand, so he made me his deputy. Then he lost the next election and I got a job as city marshal in—"

"Wait a minute," Greenhaw broke in. "Are you telling me you're a lawman now?"

"That's what I was getting around to," Longarm admitted.

70

"Custis Long—Longarm!" Greenhaw exclaimed. "Hell and be damned! You know, just like almost everybody else, I've heard about Longarm for years, but I never did think of connecting him with you! But that's it, isn't it?"

"Folks calls me that sometime," Longarm admitted.

Greenhaw shook his head, surprise written on his face. He said, "I remember, now, you said more than once that there had to be easier jobs than punching cattle."

"Well, I don't say I was right about lawing being easier, but I like it more," Longarm told him.

"Let's see," Greenhaw frowned. "You being Longarm means that you're a—sure, a United States marshal. Is that right?"

Longarm nodded and said, "Deputy U.S. marshal. I work outa the Denver office."

"And Denver's where I'm delivering the herd," Greenhaw said. "Is that what's brought you out here?"

"Something like that," Longarm answered.

Greenhaw went on, "Are you after one of the trail hands with my outfit? One of them wanted for a crime? Because if you are, three of them quit on me when we got into Abilene, and I don't have any idea where they've gone."

"No, that ain't it," Longarm said. "Now, just listen to me for a minute, Tom. There's a few things I need to explain, and I wouldn't want you to get me wrong, us being old friends like we are."

"Go ahead." Greenhaw nodded.

"What's your tie-up with the outfit that owns these Mexican longhorns you're trailing up to Denver, Tom?" Longarm asked.

"Why, I'm just a hired trail boss. I was on the loose in San Antone when a fellow named Sterns looked me up and said a friend of his, a foreman at the stockyards there, had recommended me for the job."

"You never had seen this Sterns before?"

Greenhaw shook his head. "I haven't seen him since, either. We cut a deal, and he gave me the papers I needed to get the herd across the border, and some bank drafts I could cash along the way north, to pay the hands and buy grub and so on during the drive to Denver."

"Didn't that strike you as being a mite strange, Tom? A fellow you never saw before, a man that didn't know you from Adam's off ox, handing you a big job and a lot of money and then just dropping outa sight?"

71

"I'd be lying if I said I didn't wonder about it some," Greenhaw admitted. "But I've heard about cattlemen making deals like that before, so I just put it down to the recommendation I'd got from my friend at the San Antone stockyards."

"Sterns didn't tell you who owns the herd, I guess?"

"Sure he did. It's a syndicate. He's one of the men in it, and the way he talked there's three or four others."

"Now, look here, Tom," Longarm said sternly. "You been on ranches and around cattle for a long time. Can you tell me why anybody in their right minds would even buy the kind of runty steers you got over yonder, to say nothing of driving 'em more'n five hundred miles instead of shipping 'em on the rail-road?"

Again Greenhaw shook his head. "No. And I wondered about the insurance, too."

Longarm cocked his head, frowning. "What about insurance?"

"Why, Sterns explained that some of the men in the syndicate are from the East, and they're used to buying insurance on merchandise they ship from one place to the other. So they insisted that the cattle be insured."

"Insured against what?"

"Loss. If a steer dies or gets killed in an accident or something like that, the insurance company pays the syndicate whatever the critter'd be worth on the hoof."

"I never run into that before," Longarm said thoughtfully. "Back in the old days before the railroads could handle cattle cheaper than trailing 'em, a trail boss used to figure on losing maybe one critter out of every hundred from a herd on a long drive like this one."

Greenhaw nodded. "That's the way it was, all right. But Sterns told me that the insurance would pay two hundred dollars for every steer I lost, and then he said he'd pay me a nice bonus if I got the critters there without losing any of them."

"Now, that just don't make no sense at all!" Longarm objected, frowning.

"It didn't to me, either. But Sterns said the premium the syndicate was paying would be cut way down if I got the critters to Denver without losing any of them."

"Well, that'd stand to reason, I guess," Longarm said. "I don't know all that much about insurance, but it makes sense."

"That's what I thought, too. Then later on, it occurred to

me that if these steers are worth two hundred dollars a head dead, that's a hell of a lot more than they'd bring on the hoof."

"It just don't make sense," Longarm agreed.

"That was when I asked Sterns if these steers are so valuable, why he wanted to trail the herd instead of shipping it, but all he said was that with beef prices going up, him and his partners would make a good profit."

"I don't recall beef going up at all lately," Longarm frowned. "And it'd sure have to go real high for them critters I'm looking at to pay out."

"Well, I didn't see it, either," Greenhaw admitted. "I still don't, but I figured I'd be better off with a job that'd last three months instead of a couple of weeks, so I wasn't about to argue too much."

"Well, let's put that aside," Longarm said. "I know you been wondering why I come out here, so I'll set your mind at rest. My chief in Denver heard from one of his old Texas Ranger buddies about these Mexican longhorns, and sent me down here to find out if there's anything crooked going on."

"Now, hold up!" Greenhaw protested. "You don't think I'd be wound up in something that's on the wrong side of the law!"

"Simmer down, Tom," Longarm said quickly. "I didn't even know you was trail bossing the herd till I seen you just now. What I come out here for was to get a job as a hand and travel on up to Denver, and try to figure out what kind of scheme this fellow Sterns and his syndicate are trying to work."

"But you're not really sure they're crooks?"

Longarm shook his head. "I ain't sure about much of anything on this case, Tom. Hell, I ain't even sure I got a case to be on. But Billy Vail and his old Ranger partner can smell a crook a hundred miles away, and I got to admit I got a pretty sharp nose myself, after all the time I put in as a deputy marshal. And there's something wrong about this herd you're pushing. I'll bet my bottom dollar on that."

"Well, I hope you're wrong, but I don't want to be caught up in some kind of crooked scheme. What can I do to help?"

"I was hoping you'd ask me that," Longarm smiled. "The only thing I want right now is for you to give me a job as a trail hand and keep your mouth closed tight about who I am and what I'm after."

"If that's what you want, you've got it," Greenhaw replied unhesitatingly. "I'm short a man, so nobody's going to think anything about it if I hire you on. And I'll see that your job's a little bit easier than it might be if you really were just one of the hands."

"No, Tom," Longarm said, shaking his head. "If you was to ease up on me, it'd make trouble with the other hands. You just treat me like you would if I was a perfect stranger."

"Yes, I can see you're right about that," Greenhaw nodded.

"I'll hold up my share of the work," Longarm went on. "I ain't done any wrangling for quite a spell, but I can still throw a pretty good loop, and I ain't afraid to work."

"That's the way it'll be, then."

"Now, there's one other thing you got to keep in mind. Just forget my last name and forget all about my real job."

"What'll I call you, then?"

"Just what you did when me and you was buddies on the Half-Moon all them years ago."

"Custis?"

"That's right."

"It shouldn't be too hard for me to remember that."

"We got a deal, then, I guess," Longarm told Greenhaw. "And, seeing as how I'm here, and got all my gear, I might as well start work right now. And by the time we get to Denver, maybe me and you between us can figure out what's going on."

Chapter 9

A clatter as though the sky was falling while those watching
its collapse pounded an array of big brass gongs brought Longarm erect in his bedroll. As usual, he'd placed his Colt in his
bedroll, midway of his right thigh. As he sat up his hand shot
down to grasp the revolver's butt, and while the echoes of the
noise were still hanging in the air he was fully awake and alert
with the Colt in his grasp.

As suddenly as it had begun, the clatter ended, and around
him Longarm heard coughing and the raspy harking of throats
as the other men roused. He did not leave his bedroll at once,
but sat still and took stock of his surroundings.

A dozen yards away stood the chuck wagon, its white canvas
cover gleaming redly, reflecting the light of the dying cooking
fire. Sam had already stowed away all the utensils except the
coffee pot that was sitting at the edge of the firepit. Now, as
he saw the men were all awake, he put the dishpan and the
spoon he'd been using to beat on it into one of the shallow
drawers that rose in the wagon's bed just beyond the tailgate.

Longarm sat still, savoring the last few minutes of snug
warmth that remained in his disturbed bedding. The sky was
still dark, each star a brilliant pinpoint through the clear air.
An occasional bubbling sound of lowing and a few blats drifted
across the pond from the cattle herd, and even less frequently
the high-pitched nickering of one of the horses sounded from
the picket line.

"On your feet, you lazy waddies!" Sam called as he came
around the end of the chuck wagon. "If you want supper tonight, you better get your butts over here in a hurry and pick
up your biscuits and bacon and grab your lunch before I pull
out! Get a move on, now, because I haven't got time to wait
for you!"

With seeming slowness, but actually within the space of
only a few minutes, the camp came to life. Most of the men

pushed their feet into their waiting boots and stepped away from the area where the bedrolls were spread to relieve themselves. Then they straggled back to the edge of the pond, dipped their hands into the night-cooled water, and washed the sleep from their eyes. Most of them headed for the chuck wagon after washing, but one or two of them remained to roll up their blankets and cinch up the bedrolls against the time when they'd be riding out.

Sam took his place at the wagon's wide tailgate, which was still dropped flat. Stacks of saucer-sized biscuits, split through the center and stuffed with thick slices of fried bacon, took up half the tailgate's top shelf. The remaining space was filled by a pile of small cloth bags, each containing a lunch for one man. The graniteware coffee pot, big enough to hold almost two gallons, was at the edge of the dying fire, cups stacked beside it.

There was little or no conversation as the men went up and took the biscuit-and-bacon sandwiches and picked up one of the bags that held their noon meals. Most of them had come in late from Abilene the previous night. Those who hadn't yet gotten acquainted with Longarm and the other newly hired hand looked curiously at their new companions, and nodded a morning greeting, but other than a gruff grunt or two none of the men had much to say.

Longarm took his place in the line—hardly long enough to be called a line, as there were only two men ahead of him—and waited for his turn to reach the tailgate.

"You figure to make it through the day, Custis?" Sam asked as Longarm reached the wagon.

"Oh, I sorta hope I can," Longarm replied.

"First day's the worst," the cook went on, handing Longarm two of the bacon-stuffed biscuits. "If this don't fill you up, I always make up a few extras, so don't be bashful about coming back for seconds."

"Thanks," Longarm nodded.

He took the sandwiches and one of the lunch bags and went to the fire. The men who were already hunkered down eating acknowledged his arrival with nods. Longarm returned the greetings in kind, then bit into one of the biscuits. While he chewed, he eyed his companions without seeming to do so. They were all dressed in similar style: duck or drill trousers tucked into calf-high boots, and tan or blue cotton shirts. Longarm's plain grey flannel shirt fitted the uniform pattern.

With the exception of Longarm's low-crowned, wide-brimmed hat of snuff brown, the men had on high-crowned hats with brims curled up at the edge, each crown creased in a different style. Their scuffed boots showed the same original touch; no two of the stitchery patterns ornamenting them were alike. Longarm was again the exception, with his undecorated cavalry boots. He sat studying his companions, his mind busy matching faces with names.

He was sitting next to the other newly hired man. Longarm could recall only his last name, Grayson. He had the kind of face that was easy to forget, and was no more a stranger than the other hands were, but Longarm found it easy to separate the newcomer from the others because of the man's hands.

Grayson's hands were at variance with his face; by his tanned, unwrinkled features he was in his early thirties, but at least twice that many years should have been required to batter his hands into the condition they were. Longarm had seen the same effect of range work on the hands of many other veteran cowhands. The tip of one finger was missing from Grayson's left hand, and the finger itself was pretzel-twisted from having been caught in the holding loop of a lariat when the rope had suddenly been jerked taut by a recalcitrant steer. On his right hand, the thumb was deformed from having been disjointed in a fall.

Beyond Grayson sat Joe Bidler, one of the men who'd been with the drive from its start at the Rio Grande. Bidler was not a talkative man; beyond a nod when Greenhaw had introduced them, he'd paid no attention to Longarm. But Longarm had noticed that he gave others the same treatment, seeming to prefer his own company. He was a man in his early thirties, with a hard-muscled face that hinted at a life which had been as tough as his jagged features indicated. He sat further back from the fire than did the rest, and did not join the little conversation that was going on or pay attention to anything except his food.

Across the fire sat Slim—Longarm couldn't recall his name, since nobody used it in addressing him—who had earned his nickname by his build. A tall, lanky, and loose-jointed man, Slim had a long narrow face that matched his body in its scantily fleshed contours. His jaw bobbed down below his Adam's apple when he talked and, unlike Bidler, Slim had been amiable enough on the two or three occasions the previous evening when Longarm had chatted with him.

Lucky Karnes sat beside Slim. Longarm had already noted that the two were close buddies, and seemed to gravitate toward one another when they had a free moment. Karnes—though nobody called him by anything other than his nickname—was the youngest of the group, with fine features that were almost girlish and a skin that was clear and pink instead of being tanned, lined, and grizzled like the others'.

Completing the circle around the darkening coals were Parson and Doc. Longarm had guessed that Parson was a nickname earned by the man's use of grammatically correct English, his inclination toward frequent Biblical references in his conversation, and his habit of addressing others as "brother." Parson was the fat man of the crew, though anywhere except on the Western cattle range his tendency toward obesity would not have been considered remarkable. Among cowhands whose active life kept them lean and taut-muscled, Parson stood out because of the paunch which overflowed his trousers, a roll of belly fat that hid his belt when he sat down.

Doc, like Parson, was an educated man. Longarm had tagged him as also being a haunted one, an exile from a richer life that he'd once known. Doc was the oldest of the hands, a small-statured, wiry man in his late fifties or early sixties, with pale blue eyes and a seamed face darkened by a tan that emphasized each wrinkle. He said little, but when he spoke his voice carried traces of what must once have been a considerable amount of authority. His eyes were sleepy now, as he'd been riding night herd until relieved for breakfast by Greenhaw.

Grayson finally broke the silence. "What's it like ahead?" he asked of nobody in particular. "I never have been in this part of the country before."

"Oh, it ain't so bad," Slim said. "We've put the worst of it behind us till we get to the caprock; then there ain't always enough water to fill the steers' bellies."

"All we've got to do is keep the Almighty on our side," Parson said. "He'll see we get through all right."

"He didn't keep the Comanches off when I came up this trail fifteen years ago," Doc volunteered. "We didn't have to fight, but it cost the boss twenty steers to let us pass. But we ought not have to worry about Indians this trip. They're all on reservations in the Territory now, or ought to be."

78

"You've made this drive before, have you, Doc?" Longarm asked.

"Sure. That was before the Porter Trail was blazed. This was the only trail there was, then."

"Where does the Porter Trail go to?" Lucky asked.

"It swings west, to Montana and Utah and Idaho."

"I thought that was the Goodnight Trail," Lucky said.

"No. The Goodnight—Loving trail starts over in New Mexico Territory, from Fort Sumner," Parson volunteered.

"But Tom said we'd be on the Goodnight Trail after we'd come up this way," Lucky frowned.

"He'd've been talking about the new Goodnight Trail," Longarm told the youth. "That don't begin till we get way up north, after we cross the main fork of the Red River."

Lucky shook his head. "I didn't know there was so many trails going up north. Back where I came from, all I ever heard about was the Goodnight Trail and the Chisolm Trail."

"There's a lot more'n them two," Longarm said. "But they won't be used like they was before the railroads come West."

While they'd been eating and talking a streak of grey had formed in the east, outlining the jagged horizon that marked the ridge at the edge of the Edwards Plateau. The streak widened very quickly after its first appearance, the sky over the distant ridges coloring from silver to pale blue. The growing day was not yet bright enough to compete with the glow of the dying fire when Sam came up, carrying a pail in each hand.

He stepped over Slim's long legs and emptied the pails, one after another, on the blackening coals. The men jumped up and stepped away, one or two of them swearing, as thick clouds of steam billowed from the firepit. Within the next few moments, as the steam was swallowed by the cool, dry morning air, the sky seemed to have grown brighter and, though colors were not yet visible, the men around the firepit could see each other in shades of grey.

"Same thing every morning," the cook said cheerfully as he picked up the coffee pot. "You fellows'd do better chewing your breakfast than gabbing. Tom's going to be yelling at you to form up the herd in a few minutes. Now, hold out your cups and I'll fill 'em up before I empty out the pot. I got to get rolling, or your supper won't be waiting when you stop to-night."

Moving from one to the other, Sam filled their cups. When he reached Doc, he asked, "You sure you feel all right today?"

"Fine as can be," Doc replied quickly. "Not a bit of pain last night or this morning, either."

"That's good," the cook nodded, emptying the dregs left in the coffee pot on the ashes and coals in the still-smoking firepit. "Now, remember to put them cups in your saddlebags and bring 'em with you," he said to the group. "I'll be looking for your dust up the trail about sundown." Going back to the chuck wagon, Sam tossed the coffee pot and the pails into its low-slung bed, swung into the seat, and geed the two-horse team into motion.

With the fire no longer providing a center of attraction, the hands scattered to make their preparations for the day. The few who had finished lashing up their bedrolls before breakfast headed for the picket line, while the others began the job of readying their bedding for the trail.

Longarm had not formed up a bedroll for several months. His cases recently had all been centered in towns, and his fingers moved clumsily at first. By the time he was ready to go to the picket line for his horse, the other hands had finished, and when he reached the picket line they were busy saddling up. The remuda was a small one, only one spare horse for each man and two extras as a hedge against some unforeseen accident that might put a mount or two out of action.

By the time the hands were all in the saddle, the sky in the east was blushing pink with sunrise. Driving the remuda ahead of them, they started in a straggling line for the herd, and as they rounded the rim of the pond they saw Tom Greenhaw riding toward them. He signalled for them to stop, and they reined in and waited for him to reach them.

"I'll be riding left point for the morning," Greenhaw told them, his voice carrying authority despite its conversational pitch. "Parson, you take the right point. Doc, since you was nighthawk, you get the easy job. You start at right flanker, and Slim can take the left flank. Lucky, take care of the cavvie. Bidler, I'll put you out front to scout. Grayson, you and Custis are the new hands, so you'll be riding drag, and you two can settle up between you which side to take. In case nobody's bothered to tell you new men, we all move around one place at noon. Now, let's go roll 'em out."

"Well, it looks like me and you draw the dirty job today,

Custis," Grayson said, toeing his horse over to ride beside Longarm as the group started around the pond toward the herd. "I sure don't like the idea of eating dirt for half the day."

"Oh, I don't like it either," Longarm replied. "But it goes with the job, and we hired on for it without nobody pushing us. Anyhow, it'll only be for half the day."

"All day, if you draw the left side," Grayson said.

"You ride the right side, then," Longarm told him. "Then you'll be outa the dirt at noon when you move up to flanker."

"Now, I didn't start out to ask you to do me no favor!" Grayson bristled. "I'll swing my weight. Let's toss for the right-hand side."

"Fair enough," Longarm nodded. "You got a half-dollar or something to flip?"

"I guess." Grayson dug into his pocket and pulled out a coin. Extending it to Longarm, he asked. "You wanta toss?"

Longarm shook his head. "No. You go on."

His misshapen hand surprisingly flexible, Grayson tossed the coin, caught it as it came down, and slapped it onto the back of his left hand. He said, "I tossed, you call it."

"Tails is good enough for me," Longarm answered.

Grayson lifted his hand to expose the coin. It was heads, and he grinned. "Thanks, Custis. I always like a man that'll take a sporting chance."

"Oh, I figure a man's got to take a chance now and then," Longarm replied. "Life gets right dull if nothing ever happens."

"Not much chance of this drive getting dull," Grayson said. "I never drove Mexican longhorns before now, but I heard they're feisty as all git-out."

"Well, we'll see soon enough if they are," Longarm said. "The way the head honcho's waving, he wants us to get a move on and form up the herd."

During the hours of darkness, with only the night herder to keep an eye on them as best he could, the cattle had drifted. Some were high on the upslope of the basin, a few stood in the pond itself, and there were some stragglers far behind the pond close to the point where the trace to Abilene began.

Fanning out, making their own decisions except for an occasional shout or wave from Greenhaw, the hands circled behind the strays and started them moving toward the bulk of the herd, which was being compressed into a compact unit by Greenhaw and the two men he'd motioned to join him.

81

After a full day and night of resting, the Mexican longhorns lived up to their reputation. On the upslope behind the pond, Slim and Greenhaw were circling around to get behind a half-dozen drifted steers and haze them back to the herd.

Bidler had taken off toward the eastern rim, where by now the sky had brightened to pale blue as sunrise drew closer; a score of the steers were scattered between the rim and the pond, and Longarm kicked his horse up the slope to help Bidler gather them and bring them down the incline.

East of the pond, the main body of the herd had spread thin around its margin. Parson was circling around upslope to get behind the strung-out cattle. Doc had taken a position upslope to squeeze the cattle down when Bidler started them moving, and Grayson was in place to turn any of the animals that tried to bolt from their fellows.

Lucky was on the opposite side of the pond, checking the spare horses before forming them into the cavvie—short for "cavalcade"—that would follow the herd when it moved out. All the men worked as individuals, needing no instructions from Tom Greenhaw. As one of the riders saw he was needed elsewhere, to turn a bolting steer or haze a stray or two toward the slowly forming herd, he left whatever he was doing and tended to the stray before returning to his job.

Little by little, as the herd took shape on the slope north of the pond, the riders worked themselves into the positions they'd been assigned by Greenhaw. Doc rarely moved more than a few yards from his spot on the upslope; he would have only a short distance to cover to reach his flanker's position on the right-hand side when the herd moved out.

Bidler, after reaching the east rim and getting behind the strays on the slope, bunched them as he began moving them toward the pond. He glanced at Greenhaw, Slim, and Parson, who had finally collected the strays along the pond's south edge, and left the cattle he'd bunched for them to incorporate with those they were driving. Then Bidler moved upslope again to give Longarm a hand in heading off a pair of feisty bolting longhorns before riding around to reach the position he would hold ahead of the herd, as scout.

Grayson was riding slowly back and forth between the pond's edge and the rim of the hollow to act as a buffer and press the bulk of the steers into a compact herd. When he saw Bidler take a position in front of the cattle, Grayson skirted them to ride up the east slope and turn the steers being brought in by the three riders who had cleared the area to the south.

Once Grayson was in place, Longarm left the cleared eastern slope and circled the herd, pulling his horse to the edge of the pond between the cattle and the cavvie. Finally, the trio that had been working the south slope angled around the herd and each man took up the position assigned to him.

Bidler moved out, and soon disappeared over the north rim of the hollow. Tom Greenhaw stood up in his stirrups and looked over the undulating backs of the Mexican longhorns, checking the positions of the riders. He waved to Grayson, who was now at the right rear of the herd, and Grayson nudged his pony ahead, into the rear of the compacted mass of cattle. The longhorns in the back began jostling the rumps of those ahead of them. A ripple like a small ocean wave rising from a varicolored sea passed through the herd, followed by another.

Pressed from behind, the cattle at the front of the herd took a few steps forward. When the next ripple reached them, they moved a bit further, and as the pressure from behind continued, they began walking slowly ahead.

Parson reined his horse aside far enough to let the cattle in front move past him without spreading. Behind him, as the longhorns began flowing past, Doc started his horse moving beside their flanks. On the opposite side, Greenhaw had reached the front line of the cattle and was moving along in parallel to their forward course. Slim galloped up after having circled the west side of the pond and plugged the gap opened by Greenhaw's move, to keep the steers in the center from spreading.

Grayson waited until the steers had gotten a few yards' lead and moved to follow the tail-enders. Longarm had the longest wait. When Slim moved ahead he toed his horse forward a few yards and lighted a cigar while he waited for the herd to pass, then fell in at the rear. As the last of the steers topped the rim, he looked back and saw Lucky setting the cavvie into motion.

Ahead, the low-held heads and bobbing backs of the cattle made a roughly rectangular blotch that spread along a section of the green prairie, a quarter of a mile wide and half a mile long. The herd progressed with slow deliberation and the riders matched the pace of their horses to its speed as the Mexican longhorns started on the long trail north.

Chapter 10

Longarm touched the reins to slow down his horse and kept a closer watch on the surface of the Double Mountain Fork of the Brazos. After floundering around most of the day in the narrow strip of land between it and the Clear Fork, he knew the herd was now getting uncomfortably close to him, and he still had not found a place where the Double Mountain Fork could be easily reached. He looked back at the brush from which he'd so recently emerged and shook his head.

Old son, he told himself silently, *that country back there sure ain't no place to drive a herd as feisty as them Mexican longhorns is. Even if Tom was to form 'em up tight as can be, them wild steers would take to the brush and it'd take a whole damned army to scour 'em out of it. Now, there's got to be a trail along here someplace, and you better hyper along until you find it.*

Longarm's day had not been a good one. After the Mexican longhorns had been herded across the Clear Fork of the Brazos on the fourth day after leaving Abilene, the Western Trail had been swallowed up in a thicket of scrub oak and huisache and agarita, broken only by an occasional mile-wide patch of prickly pear.

Until then, the old trail had been easy to follow. The land had been clear, mostly small rolling hillocks covered with the short thick-growing grass that predominated on the high plateau. The cattle had been moving along at a fairly steady ten or twelve miles a day, and the old trail had been easy to follow, marked by the barren spots which had been used over a long period of time for the overnight camps of earlier drives. In some of the old campsites there had still been dead coals of the cooking fires of those older days.

Suddenly the old trail had petered out into half a dozen branches. During the years that had passed since shipping by railroad had almost totally replaced the cattle drives, the less-used trails had been overgrown, hidden by a fresh growth of grass and brush. For two days progress had been measured by inches instead of miles, as the cattle plodded along the course of the Clear Fork of the Brazos.

His face creased by a worried frown, the trail boss had taken Longarm aside and, after pulling a much-creased map from his saddlebag, had spread it on the ground.

"Longarm, I'm going to put you out scouting tomorrow," Greenhaw had said. With a work-rough forefinger, he'd traced the course of the Clear Fork, a shallow horseshoe bend with its curve to the north. "I figure we're about here," he went on, stopping his finger just below the point at which the stream began curving northward. He put his other forefinger above the first and went on, "Now, look here at the Brazos' Double Mountain Fork. See how it flows down toward the Clear Fork till there's just a few miles between 'em?"

"Sure," Longarm nodded, looking at the map. The Double Mountain Fork also curved in a horseshoe bend, but its curve was a mirror image of the bend in the Clear Fork. The two arcs, their curves the reverse of one another, were very close at the apex of each bend. Longarm went on, "I'd say there ain't more'n a half-day's drive between them two forks where they're closest together."

"That's how I figured it," Greenhaw agreed. "So what I want you to do is find a trail that'll get us from the Clear Fork to the Double Mountain Fork. Then we can follow the Double Mountain Fork upstream, and use the gap it flows through to get past the caprock. If we can do that, we won't have any more real rough country to worry about till we hit the foothills outside of Denver."

"Makes sense to me," Longarm told Greenhaw. "It's a sorta winding way to go, but anything's better'n trailing a herd across the mountains."

"You'd better figure on leaving earlier than usual tomorrow, then," Greenhaw went on. "Find the best way to get us to the Double Mountain Fork. And be sure to break some bushes as you go, so we'll have a clear trail to follow."

His eyes still fixed on the map, Longarm had nodded and said, "I don't reckon I'll have much trouble, Tom."

By midmorning, Longarm was ready to eat the words he'd spoken so confidently the evening before. He'd ridden upstream along the Clear Fork until the changed position of the sun told him he was now heading almost due west instead of northwest. As he'd travelled, the brush had grown thicker, and he'd begun to wonder if it was possible to get a herd of cattle through the densely brushed area without losing half the steers.

Old son, he told himself, *looks like you're out on a fool's chase. If there ever was a herd of cattle trailed through this thicket, there sure ain't no sign of it left by now.*

He looked for a rise in the ground which would give him a vantage point from which to survey the thickly wooded terrain, but there was none. Still, he had little choice. He turned the Tennessee gelding north and began zigzagging through the brush, scanning the ground carefully, looking for signs of a swathe of thin underbrush that might have grown up through the years and covered the ground beaten bare by a trail herd in years past.

Longarm had covered less than half a mile, a miserable half-mile of prodding the gelding with his booted toe to force the animal to keep moving through the snagging brush, when he saw what he had almost given up hope of finding. Ahead, the horizon line suddenly dropped away, and half a mile beyond the drop-off reappeared in the distance as a gently rising slope.

Pushing the gelding a bit harder, Longarm moved through the snagging brush until he reached the drop-off and dismounted. Dropping the reins over the gelding's head so the horse would stand, he walked up to the edge of the cliff and looked down. From the vantage point of the drop-off, he could see an old cattle trail very plainly beneath a shield of thinning growth.

Looks like this is what you been hunting, he told himself. *That's got to be the Double Mountain Fork down there. Now all you got to do is find a place where them Mexican longhorns can get to it and get across it.*

Reining his mount to the right, Longarm set out to follow the rim of the drop-off. He'd ridden only a mile or two when he found what he'd been seeking, a shallow canyon meandering to the south, the bed of a creek that had dried up long before. The floor of the canyon was wide, its walls sloped up in a gentle rise, and the brush covering them was not dense enough to make driving difficult. Where the brush thinned and stopped at the edge of the Double Mountain Fork, there was a wide stretch of mixed sand and gravel that extended into the water and promised easy footing for the cattle.

Longarm toed the gelding down the slope to let it drink and rest a few minutes before following the canyon back to cut across the trail of the herd. Dismounting, he walked a few steps upstream from the gelding while it drank and hunkered down at the edge of the creek to scoop up the clear water in his cupped palm. He'd swallowed one palmful and was leaning forward to get another when a clicking of the stones on the opposite bank brought his head up with a start.

Standing on the opposite bank, directly across from him, a bare-chested Indian stood, covering him with a rifle.

"You move, you die," the Indian said harshly.

Longarm swore silently for having failed to check his surroundings before drinking and for letting the redskin catch him in a position that made a swift draw of his Colt impossible. He did not reply, but held his uncomfortable squatting posture and remained motionless while he examined the bushwhacking Indian and his weapon.

From the evidence of the man's hair, features, and dress, Longarm placed him as a Lipan Apache. He wore no war paint, though his torso was bare, revealing well-muscled shoulders and arms. His coarse black hair was cut straight around his head above his ears; his nose and chin were pointed rather than blunt. In features and facial contours, he resembled a Kiowa or an Apache, in spite of the thinness of his lips. He had on a pair of baggy cloth trousers that ended at mid-calf. His moccasins were short; they did not cover his ankles as did those of the other Plains tribes.

His rifle was a short-barreled cavalry model Sharps carbine, and Longarm did not intend to try drawing his Colt with the muzzle of the weapon so close to him that if the Apache should shoot a miss would be almost impossible. Longarm had no illusions about his position. It was not his first encounter with Apaches; he'd fought against them and parleyed with them before, and he also remembered that of all the Apache tribes the Lipans were the deadliest, fiercest, and most merciless. Still, he decided to try talking to the man.

"I ain't carrying but a few dollars," he told the Indian. "You're welcome to what little money I got. But if you figure on taking my guns away from me, I reckon I'd put up a fight, so maybe you better tell me what you got in mind."

"You not fight. I kill you too easy before you get gun."

Longarm was not too surprised at the Apache's fluency in

English. Even the warlike tribes and the relatively isolated tribes such as the Lipans had been exposed to the missionaries and the Indian Bureau teachers, who had done their jobs well. He was sure that the Apache he was facing had an even better command of English than he was willing to show. It was commonplace for almost all Indians who spoke and understood English to conceal their true knowledge of the white man's tongue.

"Looks like we'd have to try that out to see whether or not you're right," he said calmly, still obeying the Apache's command not to move. "Suppose you tell me what you're after?"

"Beef," the Indian replied.

"Sure," Longarm nodded. "There's a little bit of jerky in my saddlebags. You're welcome to it, if you'll get that rifle outa my face."

Without changing expression, the Apache shook his head. "Not jerky. Two steers. Land you travel now belong my people. You pay steers for water, grass."

Longarm had half-expected the Apache's reply. Demanding tribute from cattlemen driving herds across land the tribes considered theirs by ancestral right was a custom of long standing, though until now it had not occurred to him that the drive might encounter it in such relatively long-settled country.

"What makes you think I got anything to do with a herd of steers?" he asked, stalling for time to think.

"We know. We watch."

There was a ring of truth in the Indian's tone, and Longarm accepted his statement. He said, "If you know as much as you say you do, you know I ain't the boss of that herd. I can't give you no steers."

"Boss can. You go tell him to."

Longarm had been watching the Apache very closely, hoping that he would forget to keep him covered with the rifle, but the gun he held had not wavered during their conversation, nor had the Indian shown any sign of anger. Instead, he had presented his demand with coolness, as a business proposition. Though by now he had little hope of persuading the Indian to drop his demand, Longarm was not yet ready to give up. He decided to stretch out their parley.

"You got a name, I guess?" he asked.

"Kiutate. Chief."

"I'm—" Longarm remembered in time to use the name he

was travelling under. "I'm Custis." When the Apache did not reply, he went on, "Look here, Kiutate, I talk a lot easier when I ain't looking down a gun barrel. How about you dropping that muzzle down and I'll stand up slow and we'll parley man to man."

Without changing expression, the Apache continued to stare at Longarm for several moments. Then he barked a few quick words in his own tongue. Within seconds a dozen or more other Indians appeared as if by magic; Longarm had no idea how they had stayed hidden from him in the thin brush-cover. The newcomers made their way silently to the water's edge and formed a rough semicircle behind their chief. Only then did Kiutate lower the butt of his rifle to the ground beside him.

"We talk," he nodded.

Longarm slowly levered himself to his feet, ignoring the twinges of his cramped thigh muscles. He'd managed to hide his surprise when the Indians called from the brush by Kiutate began to appear, and stared at each one in turn, counting them as he gazed at their stolid faces.

There were twenty-one of them, and fourteen were armed with rifles or pistols. The others had bows across their shoulders and all carried sheath-knives dangling from their belts. They did not have war paint on their faces and bare chests, which Longarm took to be an encouraging sign; they were obviously not a war party, but a group in search of food. In spite of his feeling of relief, Longarm kicked himself mentally for having failed to search the undergrowth with his eyes more thoroughly after their leader had appeared.

He did not look directly at Kiutate during the time when he was inspecting the Apache fighting men. To do so, or to speak first, would have caused him to lose face. When he had completed his inspection of the warriors arrayed behind their chief he met Kiutate's eyes and returned the Apache's stare, his face as expressionless as that of the Indian.

At last Kiutate broke the silence. "You say talk. Start."

Longarm felt that he'd gained a tiny edge by forcing the Apache to speak first. He took his time replying, then said, "I don't expect this is the first time you've tried to get a trail herd to pay for crossing what you claim is your land."

"Our land," Kiutate repeated, stressing the first word. "You pay."

"If you've pulled this stunt on other trail herds, you know

I'm just out scouting ahead," Longarm said. "I ain't the boss."

"I know. Chief with herd. You go tell."

Again Longarm took his time replying. He did not want to anger the Apaches, and when he saw Kiutate's lips compress into a thin line he asked, "You'll come along with me, I guess?"

It was Kiutate's turn now to make Longarm wait. Afer a long silence, the Apache shook his head. "You go. We wait."

Since he hadn't expected the Apache to agree to go with him, Longarm had no disappointment to conceal. After what he judged to be a suitably long delay he said, "My boss ain't going to believe me when I tell him there's a bunch of Apaches here."

"You tell him. He listen."

"He'd listen a lot better if you was there. He ain't going to just hand over no steers to you without seeing you," Longarm warned.

Kiutate repeated, "He listen. He pay. Not want fight."

"You ain't really serious about fighting, Kiutate!" Longarm remonstrated. "Not in this day and age!"

Kiutate spat expressively, then barked a few words of Apache without turning around. The men standing behind him who carried rifles raised their weapons and levelled them at Longarm. Just in time, Longarm halted the instinctive gesture the Apaches' threatening move had triggered. He kept his hands motionless at his sides, knowing what would happen if he drew his Colt.

Kiutate had not changed his expression. He said, "I wait here. You go now."

Although obeying the Apache went against Longarm's grain, he knew it was the only thing he could do. He mounted the Tennessee gelding and started south, hoping that he would be in time to intercept the herd before it got within earshot of the Apaches.

Keeping the sun at his right, Longarm pressed the gelding through the slapping, clinging brush at a faster pace than he liked, knowing that the ground hidden by the low growth could be treacherous. The wind was in his face as he rode, and he could smell the herd before he caught sight of it. The cattle had not yet reached the apex of the big horseshoe bend made by the Clear Fork of the Brazos.

He still hadn't sighted the herd when he saw Greenhaw's

head and shoulders bobbing above the low-growing brush. Longarm shouted and both men turned their horses to bring them together.

"I guess you found the trail you were looking for, or you wouldn't be heading back," Greenhaw said as they reined in.

"Oh, I found your trail all right, Tom," Longarm replied. "But I found some trouble, too."

"What kind of trouble?"

"Apaches."

"You got to be joshing!" the trail boss exclaimed. "There can't be any Apaches this far east of their reservation, and that's clear over in New Mexico Territory!"

"These ain't the New Mexico kind of Apaches, Tom. They're Lipans, and you've knocked around in this part of the country long enough to know what that means."

Greenhaw's face suddenly became very sober. He said, "I've heard enough about 'em to know they're supposed to be the meanest Apache tribe there is."

"You heard right," Longarm nodded. "Them Lipans is worse than the Mescaleros and the Kiowa Apaches stirred together."

"You'd better tell me about them," Greenhaw said. "Is it a big bunch?"

"Big enough to give a little more trouble than I'd like to think about. I counted twenty-one. Twenty-two, with the chief."

"Armed, I guess?"

"Hell, you know they are! The chief and fourteen of 'em got rifles; the others is carrying bows."

Greenhaw whistled softly. "Damn! They'd outgun us almost three to one even without counting those with bows and arrows!" Then his frown cleared. "But I don't guess they're looking for a fight, or you wouldn't look so cool. Am I right?"

"That depends. They ain't exactly asking for a fracas, but the chief says they'll take us on if we don't give 'em a couple of steers outa the herd."

"You mean you talked to them?" Greenhaw asked, his voice sliding up the scale in astonishment.

"Why, sure. Leastways, I talked to the chief. His name's Kiutate. Don't underrate him, either. The way I size him up, he's as smart as he is mean."

"How many steers is he asking for?"

"Two."

For a moment Greenhaw was silent. Then he said soberly, "I think if it was any other herd but this one, I'd give him two steers to save a fight."

Longarm frowned. "You mean you ain't going to—"

"You've forgotten something, Longarm," Greenhaw broke in. "Remember I told you these steers are all insured? Well, the man from the Arapahoe Syndicate that hired me said it doesn't matter how I come to lose a steer. If I don't account for every critter we left the border with, the insurance company's going to have to pay two hundred dollars a head and my bosses are going to have to pay a whopping big premium. Now, I can't let them down, Longarm. If we can't talk that Apache chief out of what he wants, it looks like we'll have to fight them!"

Chapter 11

For a moment Longarm stared in silent disbelief at the trail boss. Then he said quietly, "Now, Tom, you can't mean you'd have this outfit take on a bunch of wild Apaches just to save your bosses a few dollars."

"It's not a few dollars, damn it!" Greenhaw exclaimed. He fell silent, and Longarm waited for him to go on. At last the trail boss said, "I didn't tell you the whole story of the deal I made with the syndicate, Longarm. It's not that I'm ashamed of it, or anything, but—" He stopped again, a fresh frown growing on his face.

Longarm waited several minutes, then said, "I ain't one to pry into a man's private business, Tom, but if you got something bothering you, maybe it'd do you good to spit it out."

"I guess you're right," Greenhaw nodded. "Well, the whole story is that if I bring the herd into Denver without losing any of the steers, the syndicate's promised me a thousand dollars on top of the salary they're paying me to boss the drive."

"That's a good-sized chunk of money." Longarm frowned.

"Yes. I was surprised when they made the offer. To tell you the whole truth, I might not've taken on this job if it hadn't been for that extra money. I need that thousand dollars like a desert needs water."

"Sounds like you got money troubles," Longarm commented, his voice flat, neither questioning nor sympathizing, but indicating he was ready to listen further.

"I have." The trail boss's answer was curt and Longarm saw that Greenhaw was embarrassed.

"Well, Tom, I guess a man's got to work out his troubles for himself," Longarm said slowly. "But you never did strike me as being the kind that'd make other people pay for trouble they didn't have nothing to do with starting."

"You don't understand, Longarm!"

"No, I guess not. I just can't understand how a man could

be so hungry for money that he'd make men that works along-side of him pay for something he wants—maybe pay with their lives."

Stung by Longarm's cold, unsympathetic tone, Greenhaw exploded, "That's not the way it is, damn it!"

"I won't call you a liar, Tom, because that's a fighting word, and I don't want to fight you. But I don't cotton to the idea of fighting alongside you, either, just to fill your pockets with money."

"That money's not for me, Longarm!" Greenhaw blurted. It's for—" He stopped short, his face twisted with emotion.

"Hold on," Longarm said, his curiosity aroused. "If the money's not for you, who is it for?"

After another long silence, the trail boss told Longarm, "I guess I'd better explain."

"I'd take it as a favor if you did."

"I haven't mentioned it before, but I got married a good while back, when I was foreman at the Walking Y, up in Idaho. Lucy and me have a son, as fine a boy as she is a woman. But there's one thing—" Greenhaw stopped, and his face clouded. He swallowed hard and went on, "My boy's crippled, Long-arm."

"How'd it happen?" Longarm frowned.

"It wasn't an accident, if that's what you're thinking. He just took sick a few years ago with some kind of disease none of the doctors up in that country could figure out. Luke—we named him that, after the apostle—he had one fever right after another, and almost couldn't breathe sometimes. We had to help him get air by pumping on his chest."

"Nobody could tell you what was wrong?"

Greenhaw shook his head. "After a while, he begun to get better, but then his muscles started wasting away and twisting up. Lucy and me thought he was going to die, sure, but we did the best we could to look after him, so he pulled through. Except he can just manage to crawl around and talk a little. He's got days when he can't feed himself, things like that."

"And you or the doctors still don't know what's wrong?"

"No. But there's a new doctor, named McGee, who's come out from the East. He patched up a lot of soldiers after the war, and he says Luke's muscles have shrunk up. He doesn't know why, but he figures maybe he can fix Luke up so that he can talk and walk and use his hands at least a little bit. But he says it'll take a long time and he'll have to do a whole lot of operations."

"You think he can do it?"

"I don't know. What I do know is that a year or so ago, Dr. McGee fixed up a sheepherder that had his jaw just about shot off. He told me he had to do forty different operations to connect up all the herder's muscles and nerves and so on, but the man can chew and talk now."

"Then you wanted that thousand dollars to try to get your boy cured up?"

Greenhaw nodded. "Yes. And I blinked my eyes at why the syndicate's herding those Mexican longhorns to Denver. I just plain don't know, and I don't much care, as long as I get that extra money. So now you see why I've got to deliver every one of those steers on the hoof, without fail."

"Well, it answers a lot of questions that's been running around through my mind, Tom," Longarm replied.

"After talking this way, I can't ask those men with the herd to fight, maybe get killed, just on my account. Come on. Let's go get a couple of steers and drive them up and hand them over to the Apaches. Then we'll get the drive moving north again."

"Wait a minute, now!" Longarm told Greenhaw. "I've had a little more time to think about this snarl than you have, Tom. I got half of an idea that we might get them steers moving without having to give none of 'em away."

Greenhaw brightened at once. He said, "I've got plenty of money with me. I cashed one of the bank drafts the syndicate gave me to pay the expenses of the drive. Maybe the Apaches will settle for the price of a couple of steers."

"Maybe, but I wouldn't put down a bet on it," Longarm replied. "They're like all redskins, Tom. They don't set much store in money."

"I don't see why," Greenhaw frowned. "With money they can walk into a store and buy whatever food they want."

"There ain't all that many stores hereabouts," Longarm pointed out. "And such as there is don't generally like to sell to Indians. If they do, they'll likely try to cheat 'em."

"I suppose so. But I won't be satisfied unless I try to get them to settle for something besides cattle."

"Well, you're the boss. But when you start dickering with that Apache chief, don't give in too quick. And watch what you say to me, too. I got a hunch he understands a lot more English than he lets on to."

"I'll be careful," Greenhaw promised. "But I never saw a man yet, white or Indian, who'd turn down hard cold cash."

"If you're dead set on trying it, you can see if they'll settle for some money, but I don't imagine you'll have much luck getting 'em to take it."

"Money or whatever else they want, Longarm. A horse out of the remuda, maybe. We can get along with one less than we've got, and pick up a nag to replace it somewhere up ahead."

"They're used to stealing their own horses," Longarm said drily. "But we can try to get 'em to settle for one."

"Or anything else that's halfway reasonable," Greenhaw said. "Anything but the cattle."

"All right," Longarm nodded. "But I got a feeling we'll get back to this idea I got before we finish dickering."

"You're sure you don't want to tell me about it?"

"I ain't sure it'd work, Tom, or I'd tell you in a minute. But if you don't get noplace trying to buy 'em off, then you step aside and we'll give my idea a whirl."

"I've got a hunch you've got something dangerous in mind. I've heard too much about Longarm not to know that."

"Why, just about anything a man does can be dangerous, Tom," Longarm said. "If it is, that's my worry. And I won't even try unless you give me your solemn word you won't butt in."

"All right, you've got it," Greenhaw nodded. "Let's go see what we can do."

Backtracking along the trail Longarm had just broken, the two men made fast time in returning to the Double Mountain Fork. The noise they'd made pushing through the brush had alerted the Apaches by the time they reached the stream. Before Longarm and Greenhaw had dismounted, Kiutate was coming up to the bank, his warriors behind him.

Greenhaw studied the Apache warriors as he and Longarm walked to the riverbank. Despite the weapons they carried, the Indians looked like they'd dressed themselves from ragbags. One or two wore ill-fitting coats that had originally been U.S. Army issue, but most of them had on nothing more than tattered cotton trousers, baggy and ill-fitting, and a few sported nothing but breechclouts.

"They're sure a ragtag bunch," Greenhaw said under his breath to Longarm.

"They might not look like much, but don't misjudge 'em, Tom," Longarm said, also keeping his voice low. "They'll fight like that many devils if their chief tells 'em to."

He and Greenhaw walked up to the opposite bank and for a moment the Apache chief stared across the river at Greenhaw. Then he returned his gaze to Longarm, his lips compressing into a thin, angry line.

"You not bring steers," he said accusingly.

"I figured you'd get around to noticing that sooner or later, Kiutate," Longarm replied. "But this man here's the chief of our bunch. Maybe you and him can palaver and work out some kind of deal."

"We want two steers," Kiutate said. "Nothing else."

Greenhaw spoke for the first time. "Suppose I give you the price of a couple of steers. In gold. There's bound to be a ranch somewhere close by where you can buy cattle."

Kiutate shook his head. "Gold not good to eat. Give us two steers."

"We don't have any cattle to spare," Greenhaw told the Apache. "But we'll give you money. You can take it to a ranch and buy what you need."

"No good," Kiutate said. His voice was tight. "You not give us steers, we take them!"

"Wait a minute, now!" Longarm said. "There's got to be something you need besides steers, Kiutate."

Greenhaw spoke quickly. "We've got a spare horse we'll—"

"No horse!" the Apache snapped. "Got plenty."

"You can trade—"

Kiutate's growing anger had been apparent to Longarm for the past several minutes. Now it surfaced. The Apache raised his hand and gestured, and the warriors clustered behind him moved up to the edge of the stream. As they advanced, they brought up their weapons.

"Too much talk!" Kiutate growled. "You give us steers now, or we take!"

Longarm spoke up. "I never did think Apaches was cowards, Kiutate."

For a moment the chief stared at Longarm. Then he said, "Apaches good fighters. Never run. Always fight."

"Sure you do," Longarm said. "You'll fight when there's twenty of you against two of us. If there was twenty white men here, you'd be running for your reservation right now."

"Have you gone crazy?" Greenhaw whispered to Longarm. "We don't want to make them mad at us!"

"Hush, Tom," Longarm said, his voice also a whisper. "You had your chance, and it didn't work. We got to try my scheme now. It's all we got left, unless you want to give 'em the two steers they're after."

"I hope you know what you're doing!"

"If I didn't, I wouldn't be doing it," Longarm said. "Now keep quiet and don't butt in, regardless of what I say!"

Kiutate recovered from his surprise. He turned to his men and rasped out a command. Raising their rifles, they began moving up to the riverbank beside him.

Longarm said quickly, "You're just proving what I said, Kiutate! Go on, send your men over here to take on two of us and you stay there where you're safe!"

Kiutate raised a hand and motioned for his warriors to stop. He turned back to Longarm and said, "You talk much, white man."

"Maybe. But I'm ready to back up my talk, and you sure ain't."

"What do you mean?" the Apache asked.

"I mean you ain't warrior enough to fight me man to man!" Longarm challenged.

"Do you challenge me, white man?"

"Sure I do!" Longarm said mockingly. "I know you ain't man enough to fight me single-handed! If I lose, you get your steers. If I win, you take your men and go!"

Greenhaw whispered, "Stop it, Longarm! Two cattle or a thousand dollars aren't worth a man's life!"

"Shut up and leave me alone!" Longarm told him. "I got him backed in a corner."

Kiutate handed his rifle to the warrior next to him and took a step closer to the bank. He said, "I am a chief because I am not afraid to fight! Come, white man! I will fight you!"

Longarm slid off his vest and handed it to Greenhaw. For a moment the trail boss hesitated; then he took the vest. He said, "You tricked me as bad as you did the Apache, Longarm, making me promise I wouldn't butt in."

"I done what I set out to do," Longarm snapped, dropping

his hat on the ground and starting to unbuckle his pistol belt.

"If I could see any way to stop you, I would, but this thing's gone too far now," Greenhaw said.

"I figure it has, too."

"I can still stop it by giving them the steers."

"Damn it, Tom, I ain't doing this just to save two mangy Mexican longhorns! I'm doing it for that boy of yours!"

"Even so—" Greenhaw began.

"Shut up!" Longarm commanded, handing Greenhaw his pistol belt. "I don't think this'll get outa hand." He began levering off his boots. "Indians mostly live up to a promise like the one Kiutate made. But if they do get ugly, you got my Colt to back yours up."

Before Greenhaw could reply, Longarm turned and started for the river bank. Though the rock-strewn ground jabbed painfully into the tender soles of his bare feet, he knew that once in the water he would have a more secure foothold. He reached the end of the bank and began wadi.1g slowly ahead. The stones on the river bottom were slick and sharp, but Longarm found that he had been right; his bare feet gave him control of his movements.

Kiutate was still standing at the water's edge. Longarm stopped in mid-stream, the water almost waist-deep.

"What's the matter, Kiutate?" he taunted. "Afraid to get your feet wet?"

His moccasined feet splashing as he leaped forward, Kiutate ran into the river. Longarm did not move, but forced his foe to come to him. As the Apache reached him and spread his arms to grab him and throw him, Longarm launched a roundhouse right. His fist landed on Kiutate's jaw, sending him back and almost bringing him down.

When Longarm saw that the Indian was forced to spread his arms wide and was waving them wildly in order to keep his balance, he lunged forward and buried his fist in the red man's belly with a jab that brought a wide-mouthed, wheezing gasp from Kiutate. He staggered backward, doubling up from the force of Longarm's blow, then lost his balance and went down with a splash.

Longarm inched forward while Kiutate was still struggling to his feet. He'd gotten almost close enough to wind up for another telling punch when the Apache suddenly found his balance. He came up from the water with a forward leap and dropped his head as he neared Longarm.

There was no way for Longarm to fend off the lunging Apache. Kiutate's head rammed into his stomach like a battering ram, and this time it was Longarm who staggered backward and flailed his arms to keep from falling. He went down to one knee, the water lapping at his shoulders, and their momentary disengagement gave Kiutate time to recover. He tried to run forward, but the water slowed him down and gave Longarm time to regain his feet.

Waiting until the Apache spread his arms, Longarm tried for another chest hold, but the distance between the two combatants was too great. To keep from being caught in Kiutate's embrace, Longarm swerved away from the Apache's arms, and they closed on empty air.

Less than a yard separated the combatants now, and Longarm suddenly felt Kiutate's foot touch his leg. He tried to whirl away, but the Apache managed to lurch forward and slide his outstretched leg between Longarm's calves. He tried to kick upward, into Longarm's crotch, but the water's resistance made his effort ineffective.

Instead of repeating the kick, the Indian twisted his entire body, using his leg as a lever to lift one of Longarm's feet off the bottom. He hooked his foot into the back of Longarm's knee and completed his half-turn, and this time succeeded in pulling Longarm's leg high enough to upset him. Longarm fought to hold his position, kicking his leg free of Kiutate's foot, but the effort did what the Apache had not been able to do. Longarm fell forward, face down into the water.

Before his head went under, Longarm managed to fill his lungs with air with a quick, gasping inhalation. He opened his eyes as his face broke the surface, but the debris and silt on the bottom had been stirred up by the fight and he could see nothing through the murky water.

Before he could get his feet under him and stand up, Longarm suddenly felt Kiutate's hands close in a vicelike grip around his head. He grasped the Apache's wrists and wrestled with all the strength he could exert to pull them away. His head was ringing from the effort of holding his breath, but Kiutate stubbornly kept his hold until Longarm dislodged one hand and slipped free, thrust hard with his legs, and surfaced a split second before he would have been forced to gasp for breath.

Panting heavily, Longarm filled his lungs. His underwater

movements had separated him from his adversary, and he looked around with water-filmed eyes, trying to locate the Apache. He saw Kiutate at last, standing to one side of him, just out of reach, but moving toward him. Biding his time, Longarm let his arms hang limp as though he was exhausted and totally breathless from his struggle below the surface.

Kiutate closed in, but Longarm was ready for him. He swung a pair of roundhouse blows, putting all the force of his sinewy shoulder muscles and bulging biceps into them. His left fist landed on the Apache's high cheekbone, slipped on the Indian's wet skin, and slid up from his cheekbone into his eye.

As Kiutate recoiled from the blow, Longarm brought his right fist down on the top of his enemy's head. The bunched muscles of his well-exercised gun hand were as hard as steel. He drove down with all his considerable strength in a smashing blow that sent Kiutate to his knees, half-stunned, kneeling on the bottom, only his face above the surface, staring with glazed eyes at Longarm.

Seeing that he had the advantage, Longarm followed it up. Grabbing one of Kiutate's ears in each hand, he pulled the Apache's head underwater. After a second or two had passed, Kiutate began to struggle. He twisted his head and planted his hands on Longarm's thighs, trying to pull away, but Longarm held firm. He felt his enemy's struggles reach the panic point and still held on until Kiutate's efforts gradually waned, became feeble, and finally stopped.

When Longarm felt the Indian's hands slip from his legs, he shifted his hold to the semi-conscious man's armpits and lifted his head and shoulders from the water. He heard Tom Greenhaw's Colt bark, and looked up in time to see one of the Apache warriors drop his rifle and sag to the ground. Glancing over his shoulder, he saw Greenhaw levelling his weapon for a second shot.

"Hold your fire, Tom!" he called, and clamped his hands around Kiutate's throat. He lifted the Indian's limp form to shield his own body and shouted to the Apaches, "You men drop them guns or I'll kill your chief!"

Chapter 12

For a moment, Longarm thought the Apaches did not understand him. Then one of them called out in their own tongue to his companions and they slowly lowered their guns. Kiutate was beginning to stir now, and Longarm eased the pressure of his hands on the chief's throat to let him breathe more freely.

He called to the Indians, "If you want Kiutate alive, you do what I tell you to!" The Indians gazed at him with stolid faces and blank obsidian eyes, but made no move to obey. Longarm went on, "I know some of you understand me! Now drop them guns and get outa here, or Kiutate's a dead man!"

Again, one of the Apaches translated for the benefit of his companions, then put down his rifle and started slowly toward the brush that lined the bank. One by one, the others followed his example. Soon the shore was bare of movement, the Indians' rifles strewing the narrow strip of rocky soil, the body of the one Greenhaw had shot sprawled limply at the water's edge.

Kiutate was not yet fully conscious, but was beginning to gasp and spew out the water he'd inhaled. Longarm dragged the Apache to the bank where Greenhaw stood. He said, "This fellow ain't likely to give us trouble for a while, but you keep an eye on him till I get back."

"Back from where?" Greenhaw asked.

"From a little chore that just popped into my mind to do," Longarm replied over his shoulder as he started back toward the river.

Wading the stream, he got busy with the rifles dropped by the Apaches. Picking up two of the guns at a time, he carried them to the water's edge and thrust their muzzels several inches deep into the moist, sandy soil. He then pulled the weapons out and wiped away the residue that clung to the outside of their barrels before replacing them. After he'd treated each of the rifles, he waded the stream back to where Greenhaw stood on the bank keeping an eye on the reviving Kiutate.

"I figure them Apaches ain't going to feel real kindly toward us," he explained. "And I'd bet a dollar to be a dried-out shrivelled-up doughnut that they're likely just a little ways back in the brush. For all we know, they're watching us right now. So I fixed their guns so they can't use 'em till they've cleaned out the barrels real good."

"I got the idea, but it took me a while," Greenhaw said. "I guess you've thought about the chance of some of them trying to fire them before they're cleaned?"

"Well, Indians don't always look after guns the way they oughta," Longarm replied, straight faced. "But if any of 'em is fool enough to pull the trigger on a gun with a clogged barrel, he'll have a mighty sore shoulder and he won't have a gun till he can steal another one."

"Now, what're we going to do with this fellow?"

"Oh, we'll let him go back to his men. But we better have a little talk with him first, and make sure they don't bother us again before we get outa their territory."

Kiutate gargled and coughed again and sat up slowly. He looked at Longarm and Greenhaw standing over him, then gazed across the river. He saw the sprawled body of the man Greenhaw had shot and his lips compressed angrily, but when he turned to face Longarm and Greenhaw again his face was impassive.

"One of my warriors lies dead there," he said, nodding to the corpse across the river. "Where are the others?"

"I'd imagine they're hiding in the brush on the other side of the river," Longarm answered.

"You will let me sing my death song before you kill me?" he asked Longarm.

"Well now, I don't hanker to kill you, Kiutate," Longarm told him. "You give us your word you'll leave our steers alone, and we'll let you go find that scruffy bunch of heathens that you call warriors, even if they did scatter like scared chickens when they seen you wasn't going to finish me off."

"Maybe we'd better take him along with us," Greenhaw suggested. "I've got an idea he might dog after us if we let him get to that ragtag bunch he calls fighting men. We'd better take him and hand him over to the army."

Longarm saw what Greenhaw was getting at and picked up his part in the dialog. "Hell, we ain't got time to carry him with us, Tom. We'd have to go out of our way to take him to Fort Griffen. It's either cut his throat or turn him loose."

"Then let's put him out of his misery," Greenhaw said, his voice cold. He lifted his hand to the sheath knife on his belt and added, "If you're too squeamish to slit his gullet, I'll do the job."

"I say turn him loose," Longarm repeated. "I figure he'll think twice before he tangles with us again."

Kiutate had been looking from Greenhaw to Longarm as the two discussed his fate. His face remained expressionless, and he could not hide the hatred that showed in his obsidian eyes, but he said quickly, "We will let your steers pass. We will not fight you again."

"You think we can believe him?" Greenhaw asked Longarm.

"He's likely learned a lesson," Longarm replied.

"Have it your way, then," Greenhaw nodded. "Let him go."

Longarm looked back down at Kiutate. He indicated the corpse and guns across the stream and said in a voice as cold as a Texas norther, "Go find your men and clear away that mess. We'll be moving our herd across the river here in a little while, and I'll be out in front of it. If I see any of you redskins skulking around, I'll shoot to kill. You get that?"

Kiutate got to his feet. He said, "We will let you pass in peace. But do not come here again, white man!"

Longarm and Greenhaw watched Kiutate wade the river and disappear into the brush on the other bank. Greenhaw asked, "You think he'll keep his word?"

"I figure he will. He taken a right smart beating, and even if he don't, we'll have the herd across before them Apaches has got their guns in shooting shape."

"Let's don't waste time, then," Greenhaw said. "We've lost a good half-day, and Sam's going to be pushed to get the chuck wagon ahead of the herd and fix supper tonight."

"We can't move too soon," Longarm agreed. "And if you don't need me with the herd, I'd as soon start ahead and find a place where we can bed down."

"Go on, then," Greenhaw agreed. He hesitated a moment and then added, "I owe you for what you did, Longarm. I don't know how to say thank you, but—"

"Don't try, Tom," Longarm replied as he swung into his saddle. "Like I told you, I done it for that boy of yours. And even if I was a mind to collect, which I ain't, I'd rather wait till I've run up a bigger tab. Now get on back and swing them steers this way. The more room we put between us and that bunch of Apaches, the easier we'll sleep tonight."

Though all the hands slept uneasily after the herd had been moved across the Double Mountain Fork of the Brazos and bedded down, the Lipan Apache chief kept his promise. The tension that had been hanging in the air faded and vanished as the cattle plodded steadily ahead, following the meandering course of the river up to its juncture with the stream's North Fork.

Progress was slower after that, for the upward slope of the ground grew steadily steeper as the herd approached the wide cut that broke the caprock. Only two or three of the hands with the herd of Mexican longhorns had never seen the caprock before, but even those to whom the land was strange breathed more easily when the steers finally plodded over the last rise and they saw the vast green plain of the Llano Estacado stretching before them, a sea of grass that seemed to reach to infinity, broken only by the occasional darker green hump of a mesquite clump.

As they turned the herd north the ghost of the old Western Trail became visible again, a winding, mile-wide swathe of grass beside the narrowing bed of the Brazos' Double Mountain Fork that grew lower and less densely than that on the untouched prairie.

With the ground now table-top level and their route clearly marked, they added two or three miles to their daily progress. To their right the caprock rose to heights of as much as a thousand feet, humped like a line of the sleeping dinosaurs that had roamed the area when the great stone barrier was created by the shifts and shivers of a beginning world. Its face was broken in only a few places, and through many of these gaps small streams flowed.

"You've been through this country lately, ain't you?" the cook asked one evening when Longarm came back to the chuck wagon for a spoonful of beans to eat with the half-biscuit he had left from supper.

"I had a job over west of here a year or so back," Longarm replied. "But it's been a lot longer since I was this close to the caprock. Why?"

"Well, the last time I was on a drive here there was two or

three little hidetowns close to the trail where a man could buy grub, but I sure ain't seen none this trip."

"I'd noticed you were leaning pretty heavy on pinto beans," Longarm said. "But if I was you, I wouldn't figure on finding a real store till we get up to Tascosa. Of course, there's Goodnight's new spread up in Palo Duro Canyon. We'll hit it in about two more weeks, and I'd imagine the colonel would let you have enough to tide you over."

"Well, I ain't what you'd call scraping yet," Sam said thoughtfully. "But I'm getting closer to the bottom of the flour sack than I like to be, and I just got part of a side of bacon left. I guess I figured too much on picking up what I'd need from them hidetowns that ain't here any more."

"I don't think you're going to see any hidetowns up ahead, either," Longarm told the cook. "I guess a few lasted after the buffalo got killed off, but most of them just folded down."

"Oh, I'll make do somehow," Sam replied. "And I'd take it as a favor if you didn't say nothing to Tom about me running short. He's got enough to worry about."

"Sure," Longarm nodded. "But was I you, I'd skimp as much as you can from here on."

Though during the next few days the biscuits grew thinner and the hands' plates were no longer heaped as high when Sam dished up their supper, none of the men seemed to notice. They were finding their work easier, even though their days were a bit longer, for the Mexican longhorns had lost some of their feistiness as the drive moved on. They were covering greater distances now than had been the case over the broken country that lay behind them, and day after day of constant plodding from just past sunup until the blue dusk of evening darkened the sky had subdued the cattle.

Longarm was riding flanker on the left of the steadily moving herd, and the morning had passed uneventfully. One or two of the hands had commented at breakfast on the hardtack which Sam had served instead of biscuits, but the remarks had been half-joking rather than unhappy or discontented. Lighting one of his thin cheroots, Longarm watched its thin trail of blue smoke whirl briefly in the clear morning air before dissipating and vanishing.

He felt at peace with the world, though the nagging question

106

of the Arapahoe Syndicate's backers and their motive in trailing the steers instead of shipping them still took up a corner of his thoughts.

His mind was not really on the herd or the day when a *grulla* steer, inspired by some notion peculiar to the longhorn breed, took that moment to begin pushing up from the center of the herd to the front. It swung its horns as it began advancing, and one of its fellows challenged its progress. Before Longarm noticed what was happening, a mill got started.

As though they'd responded to a command, the steers started rearing and pushing from one side to the other, blatting excitedly, jostling their neighbors. Their excitement seemed to be infectious; soon half the herd was moving ahead and the other half had turned into a crisscross maze of jostling, rearing cattle, their nasal blats breaking the quiet day.

Joe Bidler was riding flank on the side opposite from Longarm; Lucky and Slim were in the drag positions. All four of them rode into the mass of milling cattle, forcing their ponies to force a path through the excited steers, bumping aside those that were in their path, ignoring the threat of the animals' sharp-pointed horns.

They shouted at the top of their lungs as they moved and used their lariats as quirts, picking out the most excited of the animals and lashing their sensitive noses with the coils of hard-braided rope. Most of the steers calmed down when the lariats struck them, but when one ignored the lariat's thumping blows a man would chouse the animal by wheeling his pony and charging into the longhorn's barreled side or its flank or rump. At times one of the riders spurred into a knot of agitated, heaving longhorns and broke up the rearing, blatting, excited animals by dancing between their tossing horns and dancing feet.

Suddenly the mill ended as quickly as it had begun. The steers stood quietly, their legs trembling, their sides heaving, their heads hanging low. Their blattings died away.

Longarm reined the Tennessee gelding to a slow walk and took out a cheroot. He flicked his iron-hard thumbnail across the head of a match, lighted the long slim cigar, and puffed it while he looked around. The gelding had not yet resumed its natural rhythm of breathing, and he kept it moving slowly in a zigzag through the scattered bunches of steers. During the mill, he'd worked his way through the herd and was now on its right flank. Parsons was in the drag position at the back of the scattered steers, Bidler at the front, Lucky on the left side.

They'd paid no attention to the remainder of the herd while they were breaking up the mill, and it was now a quarter of a mile ahead of them. Parson and Grayson were keeping it formed by riding tight semicircles around the steers while Greenhaw rode ahead, keeping the shrunken herd moving in the right direction. By holding the remuda back while the mill was working itself out, Doc had managed to keep the horses calm. He was well behind the scattered cattle, and Longarm waved to him to come up.

When the other hands who had quelled the excited cattle saw the horses start moving, they began riding to the rear of the longhorns. Longarm toed the gelding in their wake and they reached the clear ground behind the steers just as Doc arrived with the fresh mounts.

"I figured the best thing for me to do was to hold the horses back," Doc explained when he got into easy earshot. He dropped the reins of his cow pony to let it stand and swung out of his saddle. "Come on, I'll give you a hand switching."

"I don't imagine we'll turn you down," Longarm said.

"I sure won't," Parson chimed in.

"Me, neither," Lucky agreed. "I ain't moved so fast for quite a spell."

Bidler grunted agreement, but did not break his usual taciturnity.

With Doc's help, the men were quickly remounted on fresh horses and started to reform the herd. The Mexican longhorns were as docile now as they'd ever been, perhaps even tamer than usual. With four riders at work chousing the steers into a compact group, the portion of the herd that had bolted was soon moving placidly ahead to join those which had kept moving.

While they had worked, the men had regained their original positions, and after he was sure the cattle were calm again, Longarm took out the cloth bag containing his lunch and began eating. He was brushing the last bits of crumbly hardtack off his chin when he glanced ahead. The cattle that had not joined in the mill were still plodding placidly forward, but Greenhaw had left Grayson and Slim to handle them and was galloping back. He reached Longarm's side and reined his mount around to ride beside him.

"I'd've come back to help you with the mill, but I haven't seen enough of Grayson to be sure he'd be able to hold up his end if I'd left him alone with Slim," Greenhaw said apologetically.

"Oh, we done all right," Longarm said.

"Sure. But I was afraid that when the steers got to milling so bad, one of 'em might get hurt."

"We lucked out, I guess. Far as me and the boys could see, there wasn't a steer hurt."

"Do you have any idea what started them milling?"

"Not a notion, Tom. I was just riding along easy, puffing on a cigar and feeling peaceful as all get-out when I looked around and seen 'em start acting up."

"Well, at least we didn't lose any. I'd've hated to see that, after we came off free from that fracas with the Apaches."

Longarm looked at Greenhaw levelly for a moment, then said, "It ain't my affair, Tom, but was I you, I'd load these damn critters into cattle cars at the first railroad stop we hit."

Greenhaw shook his head. "You know what the syndicate told me to do. Drive all the way."

"I know. But there's gotta be a reason why they'd do a thing like this. There's something about that outfit harping on driving these steers all the way that just don't smell good. I got a hunch they're pulling some kinda stunt that'd put all of 'em in jail if it was dug out."

"I know," Greenhaw nodded. "I've tried my best to figure out what it could be, but I always run into a blank wall."

"It's the same with me," Longarm admitted. "But I don't cotton to mysteries, Tom. Before we drive these damn critters into the Denver stockyards, I'm going to find out why. And I still say, was it me, I'd load 'em into cattle cars and come up with some other way to make that thousand dollars you're so set on drawing down."

"Oh, I've thought the same thing, Longarm. But there's two things that keep me from doing it now."

Longarm frowned thoughtfully for a moment, then said, "One's your boy; I know about that. I can't come up with the other reason, though. Mind telling me what it is?"

"Judging from what I've heard about the way you get around, I'd've thought you could see it right off," Greenhaw smiled.

"Well, I can't," Longarm confessed. "So suppose you come out with it."

"Where's the next railroad line we run into? Not one of the little jerkwater Texas lines that doesn't start much of anywhere and goes ten miles before it stops."

"Why, I guess it'd be the Kansas Pacific, up at Dodge."

"That's right. And even the KP doesn't make a straight shoot to Denver."

"I see what you're getting at," Longarm nodded. "When we get as far as Dodge, we'll have a straight shoot to Denver over pretty much level ground, even if it is uphill."

"That's right," Greenhaw agreed. "When we get that far, we're just as well off driving the rest of the way. So, whether I like it or not, I'm going to do what I'm getting paid for. We'll give Dodge a miss. What we'll do is lay over at Tascosa a day or two, then push right on to Denver."

Chapter 13

Longarm was riding scout, a bit more than a mile ahead of the herd, on the day the drive reached the headwaters of the Brazos' Double Mountain Fork. The steers had settled down in the two days that had passed since the mill. They'd been no wilder than usual that morning when Longarm rode out in advance of their start, and he had moved a bit faster than was his habit along the bank of the stream that was growing progressively shallower and narrower.

He had the sun at his back, the afternoon a little more than halfway along, with another four or five hours of daylight left to the day, when he looked ahead and saw a streak of white breaking the uniform green of the tall waving grass. He blinked unbelievingly and had to take a second look to convince himself that he was seeing the canvas top of the chuck wagon rising above the downward curve of the horizon in front of him.

Something's got to be wrong, old son, he told himself. *Sam wouldn't stop this early if he wasn't in some kinda trouble.*

As he drew closer and topped the last rise in the uneven ground, Longarm saw that the wagon was standing in a long oval hollow perhaps half a mile wide and three-quarters of a mile long. The depression contained three gleaming blue ponds connected by a single thread of sparkling water which grew larger as it passed from one pool to the next and finally ran out of the depression and disappeared into a deep cut on one side.

Longarm could see Sam now. The cook had already unhitched the team after pulling up the chuck wagon beside the largest of the three ponds. Sam saw him approaching and waved. Longarm reached the wagon and reined in.

"Sorta soon for you to be pulling up, ain't it, Sam?" he asked. "I hope you ain't in trouble."

"Not a bit, Custis," the cook replied. "This is where we bed down tonight. I was telling Tom about these springs a few

111

nights back, and he said it sounded like a good place to make an early stop if things worked out right."

"If you knew all along you was going to stop up here, why didn't you tell me so I'd know where to look for you?"

"Oh, me and Tom decided we'd keep mum. He figured it'd be a pretty good surprise for you boys and give us all a chance to take a bath and rest a little bit."

"Well, you sure surprised me," Longarm said. "I didn't know there was a place like this inside of a hundred miles."

"That just shows you never hunted buffalo," Sam said. "This place is called Buffalo Springs, and it's changed a lot since I saw it last. Before the herds got killed off there was a good-sized hidetown on that rise over yonder past the ponds. I was figuring on stocking up my grub box when we got here."

"There sure ain't nothing there now," Longarm said, looking in the direction the cook indicated.

"Just a few rotted-out hides laying on the ground. I guess everybody that made camp here after the buffalo got killed off used the frames of the old shanties for firewood."

"You're really scraping the bottom of the grub box, I take it?" Longarm asked.

"I can make out another few days. After that, it's going to be beans three times a day and no coffee except at breakfast. And I've cooked for enough trail outfits to know the hands won't like that a bit."

"I can't say I cotton to it much myself, but I reckon we can make do on beans a while. And remember what I told you about Goodnight's JA. We oughta be hitting it in about a week."

"A week's too long to wait," Sam said, shaking his head. Then, talking to himself as much as to Longarm, he went on, "I don't suppose I could talk Tom into slaughtering a steer while we're here."

"No, I don't suppose you could. Besides, hot as it is, half the meat'd be maggoty before we got around to eating it."

"Oh, I could cook all of it before we left. And that's the only way we're going to have meat to tide us over. If there's any wild game on these prairies I haven't seen it."

"There ain't much but a few jackrabbits," Longarm said. "But the grass is so high a man can't get 'em in his sights."

"Well, if you see anything at all I can cook, you shoot it, Custis. Jackrabbits, antelope, deer, even a grizzly bear."

"I'll keep it in mind," Longarm promised. "But right now

I aim to unsaddle and go over there to that other little pond and take me a bath and a shave before the herd gets here and the water gets all muddied up."

"How far ahead of it are you?"

"Not far. The boys oughta be here in less'n an hour."

"Then I better start stirring," Sam said. "And you keep in mind what I told you about wild meat."

Tired of eating dirt in the drag position he had drawn for the afternoon, Longarm looked across through the dust motes hanging in the air and saw that Parson was holding his place on the opposite side of the herd. He toed the Tennessee gelding to one side of the mass of slowly moving steers and pulled down the bandana that he'd tied around his nose and mouth when he changed position at noon to ride in back of the longhorns. Doc was in the flanker spot just ahead of him, and Lucky was riding point, while Grayson trailed along a hundred yards with the horses.

Warm as the air was, breathing it without inhaling trail dust was an improvement, Longarm decided. He took out a cheroot and lighted it. The cigar's blue smoke wreathed his face under the wide brim of his hat for a moment before he drew away from it. He looked ahead, started to glance away, then took a second look and this time studied the horizon for several moments.

It was the third day after they'd left the Brazos headwaters and the steers were still fresh after their rest. Until today, the sky had stayed clear from sunup to sundown and the air clear and cool. This morning, though, the gentle dawn breeze had died as the sun climbed steadily up toward noon and the air had grown sultry and heavy. Longarm felt a thin film of perspiration creeping over his face as he tilted his head back to study the sky. Its hue had changed subtly as the day advanced. A greyish film was pushing across it now from the northwest, and far ahead the blue line where sky and earth met was broken by a ragged rim of white clouds.

Looks like a shower or two blowing up. Longarm told himself as he watched the cloudbanks rising slowly. *Might be a blessing if it did rain, old son. From the looks of Tom's map, there's bound to be some water holes that need filling up in the stretch we'll hit after we get past that big draw up ahead.*

Longarm turned and looked to his right, at the caprock. Tom

Greenhaw had decided to keep following the grassed-over trace of the Western Trail after they'd left the headwaters of the Double Mountain Fork, and they were now moving almost due north. At a distance of fifteen or twenty miles, the caprock no longer looked formidable. Its rugged face appeared to be smooth, the ledges and creases and sharp jagged crests that broke its stone face merged into invisibility.

Distance also showed the prairie in a false perspective. Its cover of waving grasses and thin light brush topped out into a deceptive smoothness that hid the rolling nature of the ground, which below the foliage was actually a series of long low humps, much like the waves of the ocean which had once covered the vast basin. The impression it gave when viewed from horseback at a distance, that the actual surface of the ground was as level as a billiard table, was an illusion and nothing more.

A shout from Parson drew Longarm's eyes back to the cattle. While he'd been riding to one side, the steers had missed the prodding of a rider behind them, and a *chonga* in the corner nearest Longarm had started to lag. With his boot toe, Longarm nudged the gelding to a faster pace and guided the horse behind the laggards. When he was in place, he closed in on them, shouting and waving his hat to speed them up and make them close the gap that now showed between the dozen or so lagging steers and the rest of the herd.

Slanting his horse to the outside edge after he'd choused the stragglers into place, Longarm glanced at the horizon again. This time he did not like what he saw. The veil of high thin grey haze was almost overhead, pushed fast by a towering bank of roiling clouds that were the color of lead. Beyond the front edge of clouds, the leaden shade darkened to an ominous purple, so dark it was almost black.

From the darkly threatening clouds, long thin streamers of a lighter hue trailed almost to the ground in several places. In the herd just ahead of him he saw that some of the longhorns were raising their heads, nostrils distended. A few scattered blats rose from the usually quiet cattle.

Now, that don't look too good, old son, Longarm told himself. *A sky like that generally means a big thunderstorm, and these damn steers is wild enough to spook easy.*

In a few moments, he saw that his opinion was shared, for Greenhaw appeared around the front end of the herd. He stopped briefly to talk to Lucky, and rode back along its sides until he reached Doc. He reined in and the two men rode side by side for a few moments, then Greenhaw wheeled and came toward Longarm. The trail boss stopped a few feet distant and waited for Longarm to catch up, then turned his mount and rode beside him.

"I don't like the looks of those clouds ahead," he said.

"No more do I, Tom. But a good rain'd settle the dust."

"What I'm afraid of is that there might be more than just rain in them clouds. Hail, maybe. Lightning, too." Then, echoing Longarm's thought of a moment earlier, he went on, "These damn Mexican critters are still half-wild. There's no telling how they'll act, so I want the herd held as tight as we can and still keep moving. I'm going on around and pass the word to the other boys, so give me time to tell them and we'll start squeezing the steers tighter."

Without waiting for a reply, Greenhaw kicked his horse into motion and galloped along the back of the herd to pass the word to Parson. Longarm kept the gelding moving at the same pace the cattle were holding until he judged Greenhaw had been able to complete his circuit of the herd. Then he took his looped lariat off its saddle-string and started for the steers.

Ahead, he saw Doc start moving, lariat in hand. A low rumble of thunder rolled from ahead. Longarm reached the corner of the herd and began swinging his coiled lariat and shouting. The steers along the outer flank angled away from him, pushing those next to them, forcing them to jostle the animals that were plodding along beyond them.

Longarm saw that the crowding had caused some of the trailing steers to fall back, and circled to get behind them and haze them ahead. Another peal of thunder split the air, louder and more resonant than the first. In the center of the herd, Longarm could see some of the steers rearing up as they were squeezed by the animals around them.

Thunder was rolling from the clouds almost constantly now, and the first big drops of rain started spattering down. Gaps began opening ahead of Longarm as the steers in front speeded up. He twisted in his saddle and reached for the strings holding his slicker, but before he had pulled the first one free the flank of the herd broke between him and Doc and the animals began running sideways, away from the others.

What had been a spatter of rain swelled quickly to a pelting

115

torrent. Longarm kicked his horse's belly with the stirrup, and the gelding moved faster. He reached the bulge and skirted the moving steers until he'd come abreast of the leaders. Turning his horse, waving his lariat and shouting, he began forcing the reluctant animals back to the body of the herd.

A quarter of a mile away a bolt of lightning hit the ground with a blinding flash and smoke started rising from the brush and grass. Though the fire was extinguished almost instantly by the rain, which was now pelting down heavily, the herd was still trying to get away from the area where the lightning flash had been brightest. As though they shared a single brain, the longhorns tried to bolt toward the caprock.

Longarm choused the animals at the back corner with shouts and his flailing lariat, but the willywawing wind was now sweeping the rain in swirls that sent the big drops swirling under his wide hat brim and half blinded him. Suddenly the rain stopped, as though someone in the clouds had turned off a faucet. There were no more bursts of lightning, and the air was suddenly glass-clear. Then Longarm heard an ominous roaring behind him and let the herd move on away from him as he turned to look.

Less than a mile away, heading directly for the cattle, the dark funnel-cloud of a cyclone was running along the ground. Longarm stared at the whirling cone for a moment before realizing that the cloud was heading for the herd. It was moving with express-train speed, leaving behind it a swathe of bare ground. The whirling cone had sagged and widened now and was pitch-black. The noise of its approach was deafening.

Longarm stared at the cyclone for a moment before realizing that he was directly in its path. The Tennessee gelding must have sensed danger at the same moment, for it reared up on its hindquarters and began pawing the air. Longarm dug his heels hard into the gelding's sides and seesawed the reins until the animal dropped to all fours again. Digging his heels into its flanks, Longarm yanked the reins hard to turn the horse and the gelding made a few leaps away from the herd.

Longarm looked away from the herd to the funnel. Its bottom was a yard or so above the ground, and as it progressed across the prairie clumps of grass and bits of brush were sucked up into its vortex. The bits of debris whirled up into the center of the funnel at an unbelievably high speed and kept going round and round inside it, moving upward as they swirled.

116

Dust and the grass lifted by the funnel's suction outlined its size; it looked like a moving cone of water. As it sped toward Longarm the bottom of the funnel tilted from side to side, into an opening big enough to swallow him and his horse as well.

He pounded the gelding's sides with his heels and the animal leaped forward with a high-pitched neigh. The wind created by the moving funnel battered Longarm as it swept past, and even the horse swayed from its swirling force. Watching the funnel cloud's progress along the ground, Longarm suddenly saw Grayson riding across its path, the cavvie strung out behind him. He shouted a warning, but his voice was lost in the thunderous roar the funnel-cloud was making.

Grayson noticed its approach just in time to speed up, but the first horse in the strung-out cavvie was not so lucky. The tip of the cone swooped over it and when it passed the animal had vanished. Through the funnel's semi-opaque sides Longarm saw the horse rising in its center, its legs churning frantically as it was turned on its back, then on its side; then he lost sight of the animal as the cyclone rushed onward.

After it had passed the air was suddenly quiet except for the loud splashes of rain which suddenly began pelting down again in drops that seemed as big as silver dollars. Through the suddenly silvered air Longarm could see the scattered longhorns, no longer a herd, but a strung-out bunch of frightened cattle plunging across the prairie. Greenhaw and Lucky and Doc had already started in pursuit. Longarm dug his heels into the gelding's sides and galloped to join them.

Riding at top speed on the flank of the strung-out steers, Greenhaw managed to turn his horse in front of them a few minutes after Longarm caught up with those in the rear. The rain was dwindling to a normal shower by now, and for the first time Longarm realized that he was soaking wet, his clothes clinging to him soppily, water streaming from the wide brim of his hat. He ignored the clinging garments and concentrated on getting the cattle stopped.

Ahead, Lucky and Doc were charging the herd, forcing the steers to turn and lose their momentum. Longarm followed their example, riding up to the cattle, bringing his lariat into play again, getting close enough to see the whites of the panicked animals' eyes as they whuffled and dodged the oncoming horse.

Their panic was subsiding now, perhaps because the longhorns found themselves trapped not only by the busy riders, but in a more effective trap, one set by nature itself. Brief as it had been, the torrential rain had turned the ground into a quagmire. It was soft and slick now, and the steers' hooves slipped when they tried to run or charge. The horses' shoes helped them to keep their footing and to stay in more or less controlled motion.

Though it seemed to Longarm that hours passed before the longhorns were again reasonably calm and could be allowed to stand while the riders moved back and forth along the sides of the re-formed herd, his common sense told him that the job had taken only a half-hour or less. He looked around for the others. A hundred yards away, Lucky was standing up in his stirrups, his head swivelling, looking over the backs of the steers. Longarm toed the gelding ahead and guided it to Lucky.

"Something wrong?" he asked.

"Doc's gone."

"Likely he rode around to the other side of the herd," Longarm suggested.

Lucky shook his head. "No. I seen him not three minutes ago, and he ain't had time to ride outa sight."

"Let me take a look." Longarm stood up in his stirrups. The added height enabled him to look across the backs of the cattle. He saw Greenhaw and Bidler, then located Slim and Parson, but Doc was nowhere in sight.

"Did you see him?" Lucky asked when Longarm settled back into his saddle.

"No. But I'm going to take another look, and see if I can spot his horse, this time."

Longarm brought himself to his feet and craned his neck. He did not look for Doc now, but concentrated on the herd. He saw the saddled horse almost at once, near the center of the packed mass of cattle. Taking note of the location, he lowered himself back into his saddle. Lucky looked at him with an unspoken question in his eyes.

"I seen Doc's horse in the middle of the herd," Longarm told the young hand. "I guess he got jostled outa the saddle and we just didn't see him topple."

"We've got to get him out!" Lucky exclaimed. He started to dismount.

"Hold on!" Longarm said quickly. "Don't let them steers get sight of you afoot! They won't charge a man on a horse, but if they see you walking around close, they sure as hell will."

"How're we going to get him, then?"

"You stay here. I'll go look," Longarm replied.

He toed the gelding toward the herd, holding the reins with just enough pressure to keep the horse at a slow walk. He got to the herd and tchk'd. The horse tossed its head, reluctant to move forward, but it responded to the firm, gentle pressure of Longarm's boot toe and pushed into the closely packed cattle. The longhorns moved aside reluctantly as the Tennessee gelding pushed between them, but it allowed the horse to pass.

Longarm concentrated on keeping Doc's horse in sight. He'd gotten within a dozen feet of the animal when he heard Doc call, "Custis! Down here!"

Longarm looked down. Doc lay on his back in the mud. The cloven forefoot of one steer was planted between his head and shoulder, another stood with its hind foot between his thighs.

"Just lay still, Doc," Longarm said. "I'm going to drop a loop to you. Grab it and I'll pull you up. Don't try to stand up; just flop across my pony and hang on."

Doc grabbed the lariat. Longarm bent down, got a firm grip on the rope, and lifted. Though Doc's weight tested even Longarm's muscles, necessity lent him strength, and Doc fell forward across the gelding's rump. Longarm heeled the horse's ribs. It pushed through the restlessly moving steers and emerged from the jostling herd.

"Hang on a minute or two longer," Longarm told Doc. "If you was to get off now, you'd likely get gored."

Lucky fell in behind Longarm and they rode a safe distance from the cattle before Longarm reined in and let Doc slide to the ground. Doc staggered a bit. He reached out to steady himself by grabbing the cantle of Longarm's saddle, but a grimace of pain twisted his face and he dropped his arm at once.

"You all right?" Longarm asked.

"Just got my arm twisted, I guess," Doc replied. "It'll be fine soon as I use it a little bit."

"You better get back up here," Longarm said. "We'll go get Grayson to give you a fresh horse outa the cavvie. Lucky can cover this side by himself till I get back."

When they had cleared the back of the herd and could see

the cavvie, it had stopped. The horses were standing, and Grayson was a hundred yards away, bending over peering at the ground through the tall grass. Longarm stopped beside the horses long enough to let Doc slide to the ground, and when Grayson made no move to join them rode over to him and reined in.

"I want you to take a look at this," Grayson said before Longarm could speak. "I never saw a thing like it in my life, and I bet you ain't, either."

Longarm swung off his horse and stepped up to look. The carcass of a horse lay on the ground, its body flattened and twisted, its four legs twisted together like a massive rope.

"That cyclone picked it up," Grayson said. "Just pulled it up in the funnel and tossed it around before it fell back down. I seen it drop and come to look."

Longarm stared at the contorted carcass for a moment, remembering how closely the mouth of the funnel had swept past him. He suppressed a shudder, then straightened up and said, "Too bad. But the nag's dead, and there's a lot of miles left to go before we get them longhorn steers to Denver. Come on and fix Doc up with another horse. We got work to do."

Chapter 14

For the past two or three miles Longarm had been looking for a level spot on the broken, rock-strewn ground. The Tennessee gelding had started breathing hard about midway of the treacherous trail that Longarm had somehow gotten onto, and needed to stop and rest.

Ahead, he saw a narrow ledge. It was barely wide enough to allow the horse to stand, but it was the best place the unstable terrain offered. He reined in when the horse stepped onto the ledge. The gelding whuffled as it halted, its sides heaving and its legs trembling. Longarm took out a cheroot and lighted it while he looked down at the multicolored layers of sandstone that slanted below, and shook his head.

It ain't no wonder you missed the trail, old son, he told himself. *There ain't no trail down there to miss. If you'd've been tending to your job you'd've spotted that rock slide when you come to it and maybe had sense enough to go around it.*

From his vantage point a hundred feet or more above the wide valley, Longarm could see for the first time details of the broken land below, details that had been hidden earlier when he'd reached the point where the Western Trail had suddenly vanished. Now the face of the caprock revealed the scooped-out hollow left when a half-mile section of the almost vertical escarpment had left the mother rock in a massive landslide.

Thousands, perhaps million of tons of rock and sandy soil had swept across the land below, spreading as it moved, erasing long-existing features, the odd-shaped crags and hollows and small watercourses which had served as landmarks along a section of trail that suddenly no longer existed. Far to the west he saw the white canvas top of the chuck wagon and realized that Sam, on his way ahead of the herd, had been forced to skirt the edge of the slide.

Looking to the north, Longarm caught a glimpse of water glistening from a stream or pond that had not shown on the map he and Tom Greenhaw had studied the evening before. He looked back at the white speck that was the chuck wagon, and to the west beyond the wagon. Where the huge slide had lost its momentum and stopped, there was green grass.

Longarm studied the vista, memorizing landmarks and the rise and fall of the land, then began the ticklish maneuver of getting the gelding turned around on the narrow ledge. With the cooperation of the Tennessee gelding, he finally completed it. Letting the horse pick its own way down the precipitous slope, he started back to the herd.

Less than a mile from the place where the first mass of the slide had obliterated all signs of the trail, he saw the shining horns of the Mexican cattle, and as he drew closer could see them moving slowly forward, heads down, high rumps see-sawing, as they plodded along. He spotted Greenhaw leaving his position at the right point and veered to meet up to him.

"You can forget about your map for the stretch up ahead," Longarm told the trail boss. "That water hole you was figuring to stop at tonight ain't there no more, and there ain't a trail to the next water I run onto."

A frown of surprise swept over Greenhaw's face. "I don't guess I follow you. Maybe you'd better explain."

"Landslide. A big one. It's wiped out the trail and looks like it blocked off the river, too. About all you can do is swing west. The next water's quite a ways from here. I'd say the steers couldn't make it there before it gets dark."

"Did you catch sight of Sam and the chuck wagon?" Greenhaw asked.

"I seen the wagon, but I was up on the side of the caprock, a long ways from it. Sam run into the slide just like I did, only I tried to ride across it at first. He turned the wagon; he's going around it, and that's what the herd'll have to do."

"I suppose so," the trail boss nodded. "It'll make a long day, but that last water hole was so near dry that the steers didn't get their bellies full. We need to bed down where they can drink all they can hold, tonight."

"That water hole I see looks like it's big enough for ten herds the size of ours, Tom. But it's a longer ways ahead than you're going to want to drive."

"How much longer?"

"Close as I can tell, it's going to put about two or three hours on the day's drive," Longarm replied. "It's a right smart ways on the far side of the slide, so you can figure it'll be past sundown by the time the herd gets to the water."

"That'd have to be some little creek that's not on the map," Greenhaw said. "But if the rest of the map's right, we'll hit the Prairie Dog Fork of the Red River about the day after tomorrow. Then we can drive the herd along the river right up Palo Duro Canyon till we get back on the prairie."

"I've rode over part of that country before," Longarm said. "As I recall, after we come outa the canyon, it ain't such a bad jump on up north to the Canadian. If you figure to stay on this trail, we'll have all the water we need right on into Tascosa."

"That's what I'm counting on," Greenhaw said. "And since it's been a long haul from Abilene, we'll stop a day at Tascosa and give the boys a chance to blow off steam."

"Now that I'm back, you want me to stay with the herd, or go on scouting?" Longarm asked.

"You'd better scout just a little way ahead, along the edge of that slide," Greenhaw told him after a moment's thought. "And I want you out in front tomorrow, too. Now, let's get on with it, before we slow the drive down while we're gabbing."

Following the shallow curve of the great landslide's edge, the weary longhorns got to the water hole an hour after nightfall. Their feistiness subdued by the extra hours of steady walking, the cattle settled in for the night quietly enough. The trail hands were even more exhausted than the steers, and stayed in their bedrolls until the sky above the caprock was bright with dawn light. Even Sam had gotten a late start, and Longarm, who had ridden out before the men began forming the herd, caught up with the chuck wagon about noon.

"Have you got any idea how far it still is to the river?" the cook asked after they'd exchanged greetings. "I looked to hit that Prairie Dog Fork of the Red that showed on Tom's map, but I haven't see hide nor hair of it yet."

"It can't be too much farther," Longarm replied. "I ain't been cutting a shuck since I left the herd, but I didn't stop along the way, either."

"If you're in a hurry, I guess you'll be pulling on ahead of me." Sam frowned. "So if you see a trail that looks like it might lead to Goodnight's headquarters house, I'd appreciate it if you'll pile up some rocks so I won't miss it."

"Sure," Longarm nodded. "From the grub we been getting

123

lately, I imagine you need to fill up that wagon pretty bad."

"Custis, these last three or four days I've dug out every smidgin I had squirreled away that was fit to eat. If I can't get Colonel Goodnight or his foreman to sell me some stuff, there just won't be any supper tonight."

"Well, I ain't been this far south since Goodnight left his spread over in New Mexico and moved to the canyon, so I don't know how far the JA ranch house is from whatever trail there is up ahead. But if I see anything that looks likely, I'll leave a marker."

Riding on, Longarm soon entered the broad valley through which the Prairie Dog Fork meandered. Now, in midsummer, the stream itself was small, a trickle only two or three yards wide winding through an expanse of sand which marked its course during flood time. The river was a sinuous one, weaving along horseshoe and crane-neck bends within the mile-wide stretch of sandy soil that showed its flood path.

After he'd ridden two or three miles, Longarm found a trail of sorts that followed the relatively gentle arc of the caprock. He took the trail, keeping the stream in sight on his left. The caprock jutted up on his right, a sheer high wall marked with colorful streaks of purple, lavender, orange, grey, blue-grey, deep yellow, and tan. The sun was tilting now toward the west and its rays brought the high cliff's colors into blazing light.

He'd covered two or three miles after leaving Sam and the chuck wagon when the wide streambed began to shrink, and a wall of cliffs lower than the high caprock started rising along its western bank. The valley became a gorge which curved, re-curved, and twisted as had the river, and the trail he'd been following narrowed to a deeply beaten trace at the bottom of a narrow canyon, a trail on which no more than three or four steers would be able to walk abreast.

Ahead he could see a sharp bend which hid the canyon beyond. He reined in, looked back, shook his head, and frowned as he began a silent colloquy.

Looks like you might've overshot, old son. If it's this narrow on up ahead very far, there ain't going to be room to bed a herd tonight. Maybe you better backtrack and stop Sam and wait for the herd someplace before this canyon narrows down so much. He turned and gazed ahead again, and after a moment of silent debate decided to go on past the bend to see if the canyon widened once more.

Toeing the gelding into a walk, he rounded the sharp bend. The canyon widened, but the trail he was following was blocked by a cowhand astride a pinto pony. The man had a rifle across his saddlehorn, and as Longarm gave no sign of reining up, he raised the rifle with the casual motion that Longarm recognized as indicating that he knew how to use the gun.

"If I was you, friend, I'd pull up right fast," the man said. His voice was not threatening, but flat and level.

Longarm reined in. He said, "If you're looking for money, you're wasting time. Trail hands don't carry none."

"Don't worry, I'm not a bandit," the man replied. He put a toe into his horse's side, and as the horse sidled around a step, Longarm saw that the animal was branded JA, the Goodnight brand.

"No offense meant, but anybody can ride a horse with any brand on it," Longarm pointed out mildly.

"It happens I got a right to ride this one," the cowhand said. "Now, I ain't out to hurt you nor nobody else, but I been setting up on the rim keeping an eye on you and that herd you're riding scout for, because I got orders from the colonel not to let no trail herds cross JA range."

"That'd be Colonel Goodnight you're talking about, then," Longarm nodded. His remark was as much a statement as a question in spite of its rising inflection.

"You must've knowed that already, seeing as you don't look to me like a tenderfoot," the JA hand said. "I've been on the range long enough to spot a softhander a mile off."

"Oh, I had a pretty good good idea whose range I was coming onto," Longarm replied. "But I didn't see no fences across the trail, so I just figured the way was open."

"Well, it ain't. At least, the JA range ain't."

"Mind telling me why?"

"Now, friend, I wouldn't mind setting here flap-jawing with you the rest of the day," the cowhand said. "But it's keeping me from doing what I'm supposed to, which is keeping that herd of yours from going any further onto the colonel's range. And I don't know where you're from or anything else about you, but if you ain't heard of Colonel Goodnight, you don't belong in that saddle you're straddling."

"Oh, I've heard of him, for sure. Matter of fact, I rode for him a long time ago, when he first begun ranching over in New Mexico Territory."

A smile quirked the JA rider's face and he broke in to say, "I don't guess I've ever met a saddle tramp that didn't work for the colonel a long time ago."

Longarm held his temper in check and replied, "If you're pointing a finger at me, I won't take offense, because I know there's a lot of waddies that plays fast and loose with the truth."

"Oh, I ain't calling you a liar," the rider said quickly. "If you say you rode for Colonel Goodnight, your word's good enough for me,"

"I said I wasn't taking offense," Longarm replied. "I was a greenhorn then, and just about knew one end of a saddle from the other. It didn't take the colonel long to find out I couldn't keep up with his regular hands, so I got my walking papers. But I know who you're talking about."

"Then you know when the colonel says frog, whoever he's talking to better jump."

"That was the first thing I learned about him."

"If you learned that much, you'll rein that nag of yours around and start back the way you come from, then."

"Now, wait a minute!" Longarm protested. "If you work for Goodnight, you're bound to know why he give you the orders he did. Seems to me the least you can do is tell me why he's closed off his range this way."

"I guess you've heard about hoof-and-mouth?"

"Aftosa?" Longarm nodded. "Sure."

Ranchers and stockmen in the southwest had garbled the Latin name of aphthous fever into a word that suggested its origin lay south of the Rio Grande, in Mexico. It had appeared first in south Texas, an insidious infection which got its name because the first symptoms of infection appeared in the form of sores on the hooves and mouths of infected cattle. Dipping, originally adopted to control the spread of cattle ticks, was ineffective against it, as were all the other remedies which had been tried.

"And your herd was formed down in south Texas, I'll bet," the JA hand went on.

"That's a pretty safe guess, seeing as we're driving north," Longarm replied.

"Then that's all the reason I need to turn you back."

"You mean Colonel Goodnight's put up his own quarantine?"

"If you wanta call it by a fancy name. He's just made up

his mind not to take chances by letting steers coming up from the south cross the JA range."

"How's a man going to drive a herd to market, then?" Longarm asked. "The best trail north goes right through here."

"Maybe you better say it did go through before the colonel said it stopped at his boundary line."

"I guess that's his right," Longarm said thoughtfully. "But it sure don't—"

A scraping of hooves sounded from the sharp bend in the trail behind Longarm. The JA hand broke in. "You better stay real still, mister, if whoever that is coming up on us belongs to your outfit. If I see you move, I'll shoot you first and then knock him down."

Longarm spread his hands wide from his sides, their palms down and his fingers outstretched. Had he been facing an outlaw instead of a cowhand carrying out orders, he would have drawn and fired when the JA rider's attention was first distracted by the approaching hoofbeats, but the situation he was now facing called for talk and persuasion, not gunplay.

"You don't have to worry," he told the JA hand mildly. "I ain't seen a herd of steers yet that I'd gamble my skin on." Keeping his arms outspread, he swivelled in the saddle to look back along the trail.

Tom Greenhaw appeared. He took in the situation, saw that Longarm was not in a contest with the JA rider, and reined in.

"So this is what's been keeping you from coming back," he said to Longarm. "I kept wondering why you didn't ride back to tell me whether or not we had a trail, and when the team caught up with Sam and the chuck wagon, and he said you'd passed him and pushed on, I figured I'd better come and try to find you."

"Well, you found me, all right," Longarm said drily. "And you found that fellow ahead of me. He's one of Goodnight's hands and he says the colonel's closed his range to trail herds."

"Damn it, he can't do that!" the usually mild Greenhaw exploded.

"Mister, I got a full magazine of .30-.30 shells in this Winchester that says the colonel can do whatever the hell he wants to on his own land!" the JA man said. His voice was hard, and when they heard his tone neither Longarm nor Greenhaw doubted that the rider would carry out his orders.

"Simmer down, Tom," Longarm advised. "This fellow ain't

127

mad at us; he's just carrying out the colonel's orders."

"I'm not out to pick a fight," Greenhaw said, his voice once more its normal pitch. "But I'd sure like to know why."

"I was just getting around to telling your man why," the JA rider broke in. "Everybody knows that a herd carrying hoof-and-mouth leaves the infection on any range it crosses."

"Nobody's proved that's right yet," Greenhaw said.

"Maybe not," Goodnight's man retorted. "But nobody's proved it ain't, either. So the colonel's playing safe."

"What do you expect a man trailing a herd to do, then?" Greenhaw asked. "Backtrack clear to the Rio Grande?"

"Now, don't get your dander up, friend," the JA rider said. "The JA covers a good-sized piece of prairie, but it ain't so big you can't drive your herd around it."

"I'm damned if I will!" Greenhaw snapped. "If you think you're man enough to stop us—"

Blast from the muzzle of the JA rider's Winchester stirred the still air inches from Longarm's face. He had his Colt in his hand before the slug from the gun thunked into the hard ground a few inches in front of the forefeet of Greenhaw's horse.

When the JA rider saw the Colt in Longarm's hand he raised the muzzle of the rifle and Longarm found himself looking down its barrel. He did not lower the pistol, and the JA man held the barrel of his rifle steady.

"Well, now," Longarm said, his voice purposely mild. "It looks to me like we got a Mexican standoff here."

"All you've got to do to bust it up is to holster that Colt and ride back the way you came from," the JA rider said.

His voice was still cool, and Longarm knew that the JA man presented a serious threat because of his unemotional tone. At that moment, Longarm wanted anything except a gunfight which would end all hope of getting permission to cross the JA Ranch.

He kept his eyes fixed on the JA hand as he replied. "We didn't come up this trail to find a fight," he told the JA rider, still holding the Colt levelled unwaveringly. "All we need is to get a herd of steers up the trail. Now, if you was to take me and Tom up to the ranch house and let us talk to the Colonel himself—"

A voice from behind Greenhaw broke into Longarm's request. "You won't have to go anywhere to talk to me, whoever in hell you are. You can turn around and say what's on your mind. But before you do, I want that pistol holstered, and, Jim, you can let your rifle down at the same time. Whatever this fuss is about, I'll handle it."

Chapter 15

Even before he looked, Longarm had a shrewd idea who the new arrival was. He held his Colt level until the JA hand let his rifle muzzle down, then slid the revolver into its holster. Swivelling in his saddle, he looked at the new arrival. Though years had passed since he'd last seen Colonel Charles Goodnight, the years had not altered the famous cattleman too greatly. Longarm recognized him instantly in spite of the fact that in his earlier days Goodnight had been clean-shaven, and now he wore a short, neatly trimmed black beard.

"We can cut this short and keep it peaceful," the colonel said. "I know what the fuss is all about. I've been listening to you for the past ten minutes, up on the caprock. My *segundo* is still there, covering you two with a rifle, and he won't hold back from using it any more than Jim, here, would."

"We're not looking for trouble, Colonel," Longarm said quickly. He decided after he'd spoken that it would be better to let Greenhaw do the talking and went on, "This here's Tom Greenhaw. He's trail boss of the herd I'm scouting for, I guess you better talk to him."

"I'll talk right to the point, Mr. Greenhaw," Goodnight said crisply. "You'd better understand right from the start that I'm not going to change my standing orders just to accommodate you. No south Texas or Mexican cattle sets foot on the JA."

"If you'll just let me explain, Colonel—" Greenhaw began.

Goodnight cut him short. "Mr. Greenhaw," he said, "I don't even let my best friends and neighbors trail south Texas cattle across my land. I have a firm policy against it, and if I bar my own neighbors from crossing with their trail herds, I'm certainly not going to let strangers do it."

"You mean you're going to make us backtrack?" Greenhaw asked, his voice showing his disbelief.

"I don't know any other way you can get your herd off the JA," Goodnight replied tartly.

"But the steers have already grazed away what little grass there was along the trail on the way up!" Greenhaw protested.

"That's unfortunate, sir, but I'll remind you that it's your problem, not mine," Goodnight said levelly. "Now, I'll thank you to go back to your herd and get it started off the JA range."

Longarm decided the time had come for him to take a hand in what was obviously a very one-sided discussion. Not wanting to risk revealing his identity to the JA rider, he said, "If you don't mind, Colonel, I'd like to have a private word with you."

Goodnight stared at him for a moment, then replied, "It's my policy to listen to everybody, even if my mind's already made up. Come on, sir. I'll listen to you."

Longarm swung out of the saddle and walked past Greenhaw to where Goodnight stood. He said, "I'll ask you as a favor to take a step or two away from your man, Colonel."

Goodnight frowned, staring at Longarm curiously, then nodded curtly. He turned and walked a few paces down the trail, Longarm following him. Goodnight stopped and faced him.

"Well? What've you got to say, sir?" he asked.

"You wouldn't remember me, Colonel," Longarm began, "but when you was ranching over in the Cross Timbers, I handed for you about two weeks before you fired me because I couldn't cut the mustard."

"I've fired several hundred men for one reason or another," Goodnight replied. "No, I don't remember you, sir, but if you've got something important to say, I'd appreciate you getting to the point."

"My name's Long, and I'm a deputy U.S. marshal, Colonel Goodnight, outa the Denver office."

"Wait a minute," Goodnight frowned. "Long, you say? You wouldn't be the one they call Longarm, would you?"

"Some of my friends call me that," Longarm admitted.

"I've heard about you," Goodnight nodded. "You've made quite a reputation for yourself."

"Oh, I don't set much store by what folks say about me," Longarm told Goodnight. "I just go along and try to do my job."

"You do something more than your job, from what I've been told," Goodnight said. A smile flitted across his face as he added, "I hate to admit I'm wrong about anything—both my friends and my enemies will tell you that—but maybe I made a mistake firing you all those years ago."

Longarm shook his head. "No, Colonel. I got to admit, in them days I wasn't much of a hand. I sure don't blame you for what you done back then."

"If you're a U.S. marshal now, what're you doing riding with a trail herd?"

"My chief sent me to ride undercover with this one. He's got a tip the men that owns it is into to some kinda crooked deal."

"Who owns the herd?"

"A bunch of Denver men. They call themselves the Arapahoe Cattle Syndicate. We only know the name of one of 'em. It's Sterns."

Goodnight shook his head. "I never heard of an Arapahoe Syndicate or a cattleman called Sterns, and I know just about every cattleman for a thousand miles around. What's the federal government's interest, Long?"

"I don't rightly know, yet, Colonel. That's what I was sent to find out, but I ain't made much headway yet. All I know for sure is the herd crossed the Rio Grande at Del Rio and I been riding with it since Abilene, but I still ain't got a notion of what's crooked about it."

More to himself than to Longarm, Goodnight said, "I was sure those were Mexican steers from the glimpse I got of them. And that makes it more important to get them off the JA range as soon as possible. Mexico's as bad a source of hoof-and-mouth as Texas is. Now, what else did you want to tell me, Long?"

"Why, I was hoping you'd do the government a favor and let the steers go on across your land to pick up the trail on up to Tascosa. It's the shortest way, and we been having a lot of trouble on the drive."

"There never was a cattle drive made that didn't have a lot of trouble," Goodnight replied, half-smiling for the first time. Then the smile disappeared and he went on, "But I won't change my policy, even for the federal government. I don't notice they change policies to do *me* a favor, so I don't figure that I owe the government a damned thing, except my taxes, which I pay promptly and in full."

Longarm knew that argument or further pleading would get him nowhere. He nodded and said, "I sorta figured I'd be whistling in the wind. But I'll ask you not to repeat what I told you—my name or about my job."

"Don't worry, Long. Your devotion to your job does you credit as far as I'm concerned. And I know how to keep my mouth shut, even if some of my enemies don't think so."

"There is one more thing, Colonel," Longarm said, remembering Sam's plight. "Our cook's run out of grub, and he was hoping you'd have enough spare supplies on your place to sell him some flour and coffee and other truck."

"Your cook's already been taken care of," Goodnight said. "He managed to find his way to my headquarters an hour or so ago. In fact, that's how I learned about your herd. And I'm sure he's on his way back to the herd now, with enough food to see you through to Mobeetie."

"Mobeetie?" Longarm frowned. "But we're headed—"

"For Tascosa?" Goodnight interrupted. "Yes, I know. But I intend to recommend to your trail boss that he change his plans. And if you've said your say, I'd like to get back to him and tell what I have in mind."

"Why, sure, Colonel Goodnight. And I thank you for listening to me, even if we didn't see eye to eye."

When they returned to where Greenhaw and the JA rider were waiting, Goodnight said, "Mr. Greenhaw, your man hasn't said anything that makes me change my mind about breaking my rule, but I'm inclined to modify it a little in your favor. Now, sir, I'd like for you to pay attention to me for a moment."

"Go ahead, Colonel," Greenhaw nodded. "I'm listening."

"I'm going to send Jim, here, along with you to guide your herd around JA range," Goodnight said. "He'll show you a way to an old trail that will get you to Mobeetie—"

"Now, hold up, Colonel!" Greenhaw began.

Goodnight stopped him with an upraised hand. "I don't know how well you're acquainted with the Texas Panhandle, Mr. Greenhaw, but I suppose you do realize that there aren't many towns up in these parts."

"To tell you the truth, Colonel, I've only heard the names of two towns, Tascosa and Mobeetie, and I can't say I've heard either one spoken very highly of."

"Nor have I," Goodnight agreed. He went on, "I know you planned to take the Tascosa trail, but I will not allow you to cross my range to reach it. But, since I settled down here on the JA several years ago, I've driven my market herds to the railroad at Dodge City over a new trail that I scouted myself."

When the cattleman paused, Longarm broke in to ask,

"That'd be the one folks calls the new Goodnight Trail, Colonel?"

"It's been called that," Goodnight nodded. "It takes off from the east boundary of the JA and goes right up to Dodge. There are two little towns just off the trail where you can get supplies. One's called Wheeler, the other's Mobeetie."

"I know Mobeetie," Longarm said when Goodnight paused again. "Right close to Fort Elliott, as I recall."

"You recall right," Goodnight told him. He turned to Greenhaw and went on, "If you're going to make a supply stop, I don't think your hands would thank you for stopping at Wheeler, though. It's a temperance town without any saloons where they can blow off steam. But that's up to you, of course,"

"Oh, if you say Mobeetie's the place to stop, I'd take your word in a minute, Colonel," Greenhaw said quickly.

Goodnight nodded and went on, "As I started to say, Jim will guide you to the trail. He'll tell you the landmarks that you need to find creeks when you want to water your steers, and see you on your way."

"We'll be pushing along as soon as we get back to the herd, then," Greenhaw said. "And I thank you for your help."

"One thing more before you leave," Goodnight said. His voice had been amiable, but now it turned icy. "I'll warn you not to trail cattle across the JA range again. In fact, I'll appreciate it if you'll spread the word that no hands with a trail herd that try to do so will pass here in good health. Do I make myself clear, sir?"

Greenhaw smiled ruefully. "I don't suppose I've ever heard a man talk any clearer, Colonel. So, we'll follow your rider and do what he says. And I guess that's all, except I'll say thank you again for your help."

"No thanks expected, so none are needed," Goodnight said. "And I'll wish you good luck on the new Goodnight Trail."

"Tomorrow we'll be heading up into country I know, Tom," Longarm told Greenhaw as the hands sat around the supper fire.

After leaving the JA range late in the day, they'd taken the advice of Goodnight's rider and made their first night camp at the headwaters of Spiller's Creek.

"That just might be a help," Greenhaw said. "But if the rest of this new Goodnight Trail's as easy to follow as the little bit we saw today, I don't look for any trouble."

"It's been a while since I rode through these parts, but as far as I recall, it used to be just open prairie all the way, and I don't reckon it's changed much," Longarm said.

"Oh, I don't think Colonel Goodnight would've steered us wrong," Greenhaw said. "And I can't say I blame him for feeling the way he does about the hoof-and-mouth."

"I ain't sure I'd be taking it so nicey-nice, Tom," Bidler put in. "Goodnight's just like all boss cowmen. Wants everything his own way, and damn the little man."

"Now, he didn't strike me that way," Sam objected. "When he heard about the pickle I was in, he told his cook to give me whatever grub I needed to tide us over, and he wouldn't take a penny from me when I offered to pay him."

"Oh, he can afford to do that," Bidler said. "It don't cost him much, and it makes him look like a big man."

"You know, Bidler, I don't think I'd bad-mouth a man when I was eating his grub," Longarm said quietly. Bidler glared at him, but made no reply. Longarm stood up and stretched. "I don't know about the rest of you, but I had a long day in rough country. I'm going to crawl into my bedroll."

Sunrise found the herd in motion again. The Mexican longhorns were still suffering from the scant feed and long drives of the past several days, and they moved slowly across the prairie. In late afternoon, when the brakes of the Red River's Salt Fork yawned ahead of them, Greenhaw spotted the chuck wagon sitting on the near bank and called a halt.

Longarm had been riding point, and he nudged the Tennessee gelding forward to join the trail boss. Greenhaw and Sam were talking as he reached the chuck wagon.

"So Bidler said he'd ride along the bank a ways to see could he find a better place to ford the river," Sam was saying. "We could see where the place the road cuts across the river must've been washed out when the water rose."

Greenhaw looked across the stream. It was small by any standards except those of the arid prairieland of the Texas Panhandle. He looked upstream and downstream for a few moments, and when he turned back to the others his face was glum as he shook his head. Longarm had been examining the river, too.

"It don't look no more inviting to me than it does to you, Tom," he told the trail boss.

Spread below them, the brakes of the river stretched for a quarter of a mile from bank to bank. The banks on both sides were steep, plunging down in a sharp angle fifteen or twenty feet to to the river's wide channel. The greenish water flowed sluggishly in a bed sixty to a hundred feet wide.

Also on both sides, the brakes stretched from the water's margin to the beginning of the channel's precipitous sides. They formed a miniature wilderness, a hummocky expanse of red sandy soil dotted with clumps of mesquite and patches of tangled sandplum bushes and a few cottonwood, pin oak, and salt cedar trees.

"I'm not as concerned about the river as I am about Bidler not coming back to tell me what it was like," Greenhaw said. "I never had fault to find with his scouting before, but he ought to have sense enough to know that I'd want him to warn me what to look for so I could figure out what to do."

"He crossed to the other side, and rode on ahead," Sam volunteered. "The last glimpse I had of him, he was rounding that bend downstream, to the west."

"Do you think he's run into trouble?" Greenhaw frowned. "An accident . . . maybe his horse threw him. Or we're so close to the Indian Nation here that a bunch of renegade redskins might've jumped him."

"Maybe and might don't answer no questions, Tom," Longarm said. "I can read trail sign pretty good. You want me to ride across and see if I can track him?"

Greenhaw looked at the western sky. The sun was hanging at the rim of the horizon. He said, "I'm sure not going to start the herd across tonight. We'll have to haze 'em over in bunches, fifteen or twenty at a time, and that'll take a while."

"Half a day, maybe more," Longarm agreed. "Well, there's still two hours or so of daylight left. Say the word and I'll go across and see where his trail leads on the other side."

"I guess you'd better," Greenhaw nodded. "Chances are he just lost track of the time, or maybe couldn't find any better place to cross and went to scout ahead against tomorrow. But if something has happened to him, we'd better find out."

Longarm toed the gelding up to the edge of the bank and rode along it for a few yards until he found a place where the sides were a little less precipitous than elsewhere. He urged the gelding off the edge, and the horse bunched its hindquarters

136

and stiffened its forelegs as it half-plunged, half-slid to the bottom of the steep slope.

In the bed of the river, Longarm let the gelding pick its own way through the dense undergrowth. As he moved ahead the sandy soil grew softer and soggier under its ground-cover of brush and creepers. He did not try to push the animal, but let it test its footing until it was satisfied to move. At the brink of the stream, the vegetation gave way to a narrow strip of clear bank beyond which the green water swirled murkily.

Longarm peered at the surface but could not see the bottom. It could have been ten feet deep, or only a few inches. He kept the gelding moving along the edge, using only the pressure of his knees to keep it advancing slowly while he searched for a shallow spot and at the same time for hoofprints that would show him where Bidler had crossed. He saw no hoofprints, but he did reach a place where the riverbed rose in a long hump over which the water ran in a wide sheet only inches deep.

This time he did not give the gelding a choice, but reined it into the water. The horse splashed across the river, which was not more than twenty or thirty yards wide at this point. Across the stream, Longarm found what he'd been looking for. The soil on this side was firmer, and he could see fresh hoofprints of a shod horse leading to the bank.

That's got to be Bidler's trail, old son, he told himself as he started following the prints along the water's edge. *And there ain't no sign so far that he's crossed back, so he's got to be someplace up ahead.*

Longarm's slow progress in crossing the river had taken time, and in the streambed the horizon line was the rim of the drop-off that lay beyond the water's edge. The hoofprints led him along the narrow, clear strip at the water's edge, and as Longarm set out to follow them the sun had already dropped below the tops of the trees that grew in the brakes, shading the ground in promise of twilight that was soon to come.

Even in the fading light, Longarm had no trouble following the hoofprints along the soft soil of the water's edge. He rode slowly, expecting the prints to turn and lead him through the thick foliage of the brakes to the prairie beyond. When he had covered the better part of a mile and saw the hoofprints still dotting the sandy strip of soft earth ahead, his sharply honed lawman's senses began sending him a nagging warning.

There's something smells real bad about this trail, old son, he told himself as he reined in and lighted a cheroot. *There was more'n one place since you crossed over where the brakes thinned out enough for the herd to cross through. Them was just the kinda places Bidler set out to find. There ain't no good reason why he'd've passed 'em by, and if he hadn't rode on he'd've been back to the chuck wagon by the time we got there with the herd. So all that makes sense is, he had some other reason to keep on pushing along on this side of the river.*

Flipping the smoked-down cigar butt into the stream, Longarm moved ahead. He took his time now, following the hoofprints along the bank, moving slowly through the failing daylight. He'd covered perhaps another quarter of a mile when the light breeze blowing upriver brought him the scent of woodsmoke. Longarm pulled up and dropped the reins on the horse's neck, knowing the Tennessee gelding had been trained to stand. He swung out of the saddle and slid his rifle from its scabbard. Then he moved ahead on foot, slowly and cautiously, toward the source of the smoke.

Chapter 16

Dodging through the brush, counting on the fading light to help conceal him, Longarm moved quickly. He had covered only a short distance when he saw the flicker of a campfire ahead. He stopped in his tracks and surveyed the terrain. The fire was plainly visible now, a hundred yards distant, in a small grove of live-oak trees. The brush thinned where the trees had shaded it from the sun, and Longarm pushed carefully through to the edge of the diminishing cover.

Between the trunks of the trees he could see the dark forms of several men silhouetted by the blaze. Because they were moving almost constantly and the tree trunks broke his line of sight, Longarm had to watch for a moment before he could be sure of their number. There were five. He edged as close as he dared and dropped to the ground, placing his rifle at his side. The last few yards of his advance had made it possible for him to hear them, but not as clearly as he would have liked.

One of the men was saying, "And it was a damn good thing I finally got tired of waiting for that herd to get to Tascosa. If it hadn't been for me taking the trail south to find it, we might not've got connected up at all."

"Oh, you played a good hunch," another replied. "But I'd've managed to get word to you, one way or another."

Longarm recognized the voice of the second man, and with that recognition came a sudden realization that trouble lay ahead. The second man who had spoken was Bidler.

Old son, he told himself, *that Bidler done a good job of fooling everybody, including you. He never did mean to come back when he said he'd go scout around. He come here to meet them other fellows, and whatever they got in mind, it sure ain't no Sunday-school picnic.*

A chain reaction of deductions was taking place in Longarm's sharply honed lawman's brain. From the brief exchange between the two men, it was obvious to him that Bidler had

139

arranged to meet the others in Tascosa, and failure of the herd to reach there had sent his cronies searching for it. Finding the herd would have been easy, for the old Western Trail and the new Goodnight Trail were the only two ways the herd could be moved.

Longarm now understood that Bidler's recent surliness had masked a growing worry. Because his years as a lawman had honed his perceptions almost to an instinct, he deduced quickly that the men in the grove with Bidler were carrying out a prearranged plan to steal the trail herd.

The reason why they considered a herd of scrawny Mexican longhorns worth the trouble of stealing was as much of a puzzle to him as the reasons for the Arapahoe Syndicate buying the steers and driving them to Denver. But Longarm had learned long ago that honest cowhands did not meet to make plans in camps that were hidden in the river brakes. He put his deductions aside for the moment as the men began talking again.

"Well, now that you and the herd's got here, we might as well make our move," said the man who had addressed Bidler first. "I sent word to the others, and they'll be waiting to meet us when we cross the line over to the Indian Nation."

"Hell, Blackie, give the trail hands time to settle the herd down and get to sleep," Bidler responded. "We don't need to be in a big hurry to move. We ain't got far to drive them steers before we're outa Texas."

Using the noise of their conversation to hide any sound he might make, Longarm moved on all fours from the cover of the tree trunk and shifted a few feet to one side. The time he'd spent in moving was enough to give the men a chance to settle down with their tin plates, and though he had no cover in his new position, now he could not only see the faces of Bidler and two others of the five men around the small campfire, but he could also hear their conversation more clearly. Longarm did not recognize the two men sitting beside Bidler, but their hard-bitten faces told their own story; it was the mark of criminality that he'd read in the countenances of scores of other lawless men.

Either of them would have been at home on a Wanted handbill. Both were badly in need of a shave, and their clothing was rough and travel-stained. They wore their revolvers low on their hips and kept their gun hands close to the butts. Their pistol belts and holsters were well worn but well cared for.

More telling than anything else, they had the constantly shifting eyes of men forced to keep looking for an enemy in anyone they encountered.

As Longarm settled into his new position, one of the men whose face he could not see was saying, "I'd a hell of a lot rather we started moving. If that trail boss gets to wondering where Jeeter got off to, he might send somebody out to scout around looking for him."

Longarm realized that he had just heard Bidler's real name— or perhaps the name he used more often than others—for the first time. "Jeeter" stirred some half-forgotten memory, but he did not try to follow his train of thought, because he wanted to give his full attention to the conversation in the grove.

"I don't figure we got too much to worry about, Snow," Jeeter–Bidler replied. "They'll be shorthanded without me. It ain't likely they can spare a man while they're bedding the herd for the night. They'll just figure I'm late getting back."

Longarm added Snow's name to his list, though he had yet to see the man's face. Almost at once the second outlaw whose face he had not seen said, "Just the same, the sooner we get supper cooked and douse the fire, the better I'm gonna feel."

"Cash is right," the man sitting on Jeeter's left agreed. He was the youngest of the group, his moustache a silky line of wispy blond hair. He went on, "I say we get to it as soon as we're done eating."

Longarm now had Cash's name on his list. Then Jeeter turned to the youth on his left and addressed him and all the voices were matched to names when Jeeter said, "Hell, Todie, we don't have to be in no hurry. It ain't gonna take long to wipe out that trail camp. They ain't looking for us to jump 'em."

Blackie resumed his urging. "Maybe so, but suppose they do send somebody looking for you. They'd see our fire for sure."

Bidler—or Jeeter, as Longarm thought of him now—said reassuringly, "Like I said, they're shorthanded. They won't be worrying about me."

Todie spoke again. "I stand with Blackie. We got a job to do. Let's do it and get it over with."

"Maybe Blackie and Todie's right," Cash put in. "We got a long night ahead anyhow. After we take care of the trail hands, it's gonna take us a while to drag them bodies into the

141

brakes and dig graves and all."

"Burying 'em won't take long, Cash," Jeeter said. "The ground's soft, and we don't have to dig real deep, just enough so they won't be found till we've got across the line into the Indian Nation."

"Trail camps bed down early," Cash went on. "So we don't need to put it off too long."

"That's what I been saying," Blackie agreed. "By the time we finish eating and slip on down to where they've stopped, there ain't likely to be nobody awake but the night herder."

Now Jeeter spoke again. "Like I said a while ago, there ain't but one of 'em that gives me much worry. That fellow Custis I told you about don't act like he's used to punching cattle, and I been a little bit edgy about him ever since he hired on at Abilene."

"We better be damned sure to get him when we jump 'em, then," Todie suggested.

"We better be sure we get all of 'em, the way we was told to," Jeeter said harshly. "You know the orders we got."

Longarm's interest quickened. He had wondered why the five men were planning to steal the scrawny Mexican longhorns, and now he had his answer. They were not acting on their own, but were carrying out orders from a boss who remained in the background and hired others to do his dirty work. His thoughts were diverted when the men resumed their conversation.

"Don't worry, Jeeter," Todie replied. "All of us knows what we got to do. The boss made it real clear."

"Why the hell ain't we doing what we're supposed to, then?" Cash demanded.

"Well, if you're in such an all-fired hurry to start, I guess the only way to shut you up is to get moving," Jeeter agreed. "Let's eat up and we'll hit the trail. Might be best, getting the job done early. Then we can all get some sleep before we start heading them steers to the Nation."

As the men fell silent and devoted their full attention to finishing their supper, Longarm considered his next move. Though he was sure that he could make prisoners of all five of the rustlers, Longarm knew that once he had captured them they would adhere to the outlaw code and refuse to talk.

Longarm was more interested in learning the identity of the man who gave the orders than in arresting his hired gunmen,

142

but he could think of no way to bring it off alone. He knew the nature of the men sitting around the little fire in the walnut grove. He knew they would fight to the death rather than surrender, and dead men are notoriously untalkative.

He was still debating the best course of action, his attention riveted on the men around the fire, when something cold and hard pressed into his back and a man's voice said, "Just in case you ain't figured it out, that's a .30-.30 Winchester poking into you, mister. It's loaded and on full cock and I got my finger on the trigger. Now, you just get up slow and easy, and we'll go on up there to my friends, and find out who the hell you are and what you're doing skulking around here."

"I won't argue with you," Longarm replied. While he spoke he was trying to control his anger at himself for allowing the newcomer to trap him. He went on, "Just don't let your finger get itchy while I'm getting up."

Moving slowly and carefully, Longarm got to his feet. He'd already calculated his chances. There were two aces in his hand. One was that the length of the rifle barrel prevented the man holding it from reaching forward and taking away his Colt. The other was his .44 derringer, tucked into his lower vest pocket and attached by a sturdy gold chain to his watch in the pocket on the other side.

When he was on his feet, his captor said, "Move on, now. Let's go see what my friends have got to say about you being here spying on 'em."

Longarm marched ahead, the rifle muzzle digging into his back with an unrelenting pressure. The outlaws around the small fire jumped to their feet when they heard the two men approaching. They started forward, staring, as Longarm stepped into the circle of light cast by the fire, then stopped and stood in a loose half-circle facing Longarm and his captor.

"Well, I'll be damned!" Jeeter–Bidler exclaimed. "You got yourself a real prize, Parker. That fellow's the nosy trail hand I was talking about just a few minutes ago, boys. His name's Custis."

"Like hell it is!" Cash snorted. "Maybe he's calling hisself that, but his name's Long, and he's a U.S. marshal!"

"Wait a minute!" Parker said "You mean he's the one they call Longarm?"

"Nobody else but," Cash replied. "I oughta know. He owes me five years that I done in Leavenworth when he tracked me down after I'd held up a post office to get travelling money."

"And I'm going to put you back in that Leavenworth pen real soon," Longarm said. Even though he realized that, as far as the gang of outlaws was concerned, Cash's recognition was his death warrant, his voice was calm and level. He added, "Or another jail just like it."

"Listen to him brag!" Cash snorted. "Why, if I—"

"Shut up, damn it!" Parker broke in, speaking to Cash over Longarm's shoulder. "Hold your gab till after you take his gun away! Can't you see it's still in his holster?"

"Well, now," Cash grinned, moving toward Longarm and his captor. "This is gonna be a real pleasure! There ain't many men has got Longarm to hand over his pistol." He reached Longarm and stopped a pace in front of him, extended his hand, and went on, "Just slip that Colt outa your holster and pass it to me now. I'd say you better move real slow and careful, or Parker'll put a slug through you."

As Cash stepped forward, Longarm saw the moment he'd been hoping for had arrived. He brought up his left hand, moving it with purposeful clumsiness, bending his elbow awkwardly to reach for the Colt in its cross-draw holster.

His eyes flicked over the men in front of him. As he'd expected, they were watching the movement of his left hand as it closed on the butt of the Colt. While he tugged at its grip, giving the appearance it was stuck in its holster, his right hand was creeping unnoticed toward the watch chain attached to the derringer in his vest pocket.

Longarm's left hand closed on the watch chain. At that instant he brought his elbow around and up, knocking the muzzle of Parker's rifle out of his back.

Parker triggered the rifle a split second too late. The gun cracked and its bullet knocked down Todie, who stood at the end of the loose arc.

Longarm had yanked his derringer out of the vest pocket before Parker fired. He'd already realized that Cash must be his first target. The derringer boomed and its heavy .44 slug sent Cash reeling a step backward before he toppled. He collided with Snow, who was drawing his pistol, and knocked the weapon to the ground before Snow could bring it play.

Snow staggered as Cash's weight sagged against him and fell heavily, the limp corpse weighting him down. Both his revolver and Cash's were beyond his reach. Longarm saw Snow start toppling as he wrestled with Cash's sagging weight and knew that he'd have nothing to worry about from him for a moment.

Pushing himself back with his booted toes, he spun, twisting his Colt free as he turned. Parker was trying to bring his rifle around, but the bullet from Longarm's Colt thudded into his chest while the Winchester's muzzle was still in the air.

Parker's finger closed in his dying reflex, and the muzzle blast from the rifle sent a fiery streak into the sky as the outlaw staggered back and collapsed on the ground.

Longarm had marked Jeeter as his next target. Out of the corner of his eye, he saw Blackie drawing as he let off the second barrel of the derringer. The stubby weapon's dull, flat boom was still echoing in the evening air when Jeeter buckled at the waist and crumpled.

Blackie had his revolver in his hand and was bringing it up when Longarm looked back at him. Because he was not quite as skilled with his left hand as with his right, Longarm loosed two shots with the Colt. The first slug slammed into Blackie's shoulder and spun him round; the second broke the spin and knocked the outlaw down.

Snow had finally worked free from Cash's dead weight and had scrambled within reach of his revolver. He had it in his hand and was bringing it up to blast Longarm, but Longarm turned in time to see Snow's movement. He triggered the pistol and Snow collapsed in a heap.

Suddenly the grove was quiet. The sharp, penetrating smell of burned powder hung in the air. Longarm stood motionless, his eyes sweeping the ground, looking for any sign of life in the motionless forms that were sprawled on the ground. When he was sure there would be no danger from any of the prone figures, he took a handful of shells from his pocket and reloaded both the Colt and the derringer.

He holstered the revolver and put the stubby derringer back in his vest pocket. Then he lighted a cheroot and started moving from one of the recumbent figures to the next. Cash and Snow were both dead; so were Parker and Blackie. Jeeter gasped out his last breath as Longarm bent over him, but when he moved on to Todie he saw the young outlaw looking up at him with a plea on his young face.

"Don't kill me, please!" Todie said. "This is just the second time I got mixed up with anything bad, and I didn't know what I was getting into at first."

"I ain't aiming to kill you, Todie," Longarm replied. "But I'll feel a lot more like helping you if you'll tell me what you and them others were supposed to do."

Todie coughed, his face contorting with pain, then recovered and said, "The way it started out, all they told me we'd be doing was stealing a trail herd. They didn't say nothing till later on about killing all the hands and burying 'em in the brakes. I tried to pull away, then, but they said I was in too deep, that they'd kill me if I didn't go along after I'd said I would. So I did."

"Who was it you talked to first?" Longarm asked.

"Blackie. I knew him from a while back when we was punching steers together up in Colorado," Todie replied.

"How'd he put things to you at first to get you to steal the herd?" Longarm asked.

"He just told me we'd knock out the night herd and drive the steers over to the Indian Nation to sell. Nothing about killing and all that." A grimace of pain twisted Todie's face. He shuddered and tried to cough, but only a thin, raspy whisper came from his throat.

Longarm had seen enough men shot to realize that the youth was mortally wounded, beyond any help he could give him. He put duty before sympathy and went on with his questioning.

"Who was supposed to buy 'em?" he asked.

"I don't know. Never did know. Then the steers didn't show up and Blackie went looking for 'em and found where we could cut across their trail. Then they got to talking real mean, about killing and all that." Todie coughed again, and a rasping rattle sounded in his throat.

Longarm suppressed his sympathy. He asked, "You're sure you never heard nobody's name mentioned?"

"Only Jeeter. And somebody named—named Sterns." Todie's chest heaved. He opened his mouth to say something more, but blood gushed from his lips and his head fell back. He tried to raise it, but could not. A shudder shook his body and he lay still.

Longarm looked down at the body of the young cowhand. He shook his head slowly as he fished a fresh cheroot from his pocket and lighted it from the butt of the one he'd now smoked to a stub. The blue smoke drifted around his face. He turned away and surveyed the bodies scattered around the live-oak grove.

It's sure a shame when they go wrong so young, he thought. *But that's the way the cards fall, and the deck don't need to be stacked for a fellow to draw a busted hand.*

He heard the distant sound of hoofbeats, and men yelling through the darkness. Picking up a handful of the dry, broken branches that lay on the ground beside the dying fire, he tossed them on the coals, took off his hat, and fanned the coals until they grew bright and the fresh wood burst into flame.

As the fire blazed into new brightness, fresh shouts rose from the approaching riders, and Longarm raised his voice in reply. In a few minutes Tom Greenhaw and Slim reined up just inside the circle of brightness.

"Gawdamighty!" Greenhaw exclaimed. "What happened, Custis? It looks like you've been fighting a war!"

"Oh, it wasn't such a much," Longarm replied. "This bunch was getting ready to jump our camp and kill you and all the rest, and then steal the herd. I was the only one around, so I sorta figured it was up to me to stop 'em."

"Well, you didn't leave much for the rest of us to do," Slim said drily. "But you sure left a mess, and I got a pretty good hunch who's going to have to clean it up."

"We'll clean it up, and glad to do it," Greenhaw said. He turned to Longarm. "I owe you, and I won't forget it."

"You don't owe me one thing, Tom," Longarm replied. "It was kill or be killed, and I just done what I had to, saving my own skin. But there's one thing pretty sure. We can drive on to Denver now and sleep sound at night. And that's more'n we been able to say up till now."

Chapter 17

Blatting and pushing at the flanks of the steers ahead of them, the final bunch of Mexican longhorns moved up to join the remainder of the herd at the water hole. The drive from the Salt Fork of the Red River to the headwaters of the big stream's Elm Fork had been a dry one, and the trail crew had been busy keeping the cattle from stampeding after they had gotten close enough to smell the water ahead.

Longarm settled back in his saddle and watched the animals as they crowded up along the bank, pushing and jostling one another. Some of the steers discovered the Elm's small tributaries, tiny creeks and rills that were scattered over a two-mile area from their juncture, and the cattle that were jostled aside from the bank of the shallow pond moved away from their fellows and dipped their noses in the little trickling streams.

Longarm waited while they drank their fill, and was getting ready to try to bunch them again when Tom Greenhaw rode up and reined in beside him.

"Let 'em spread out a little bit," the trail boss said. "I don't think we'll have any trouble gathering them in the morning. They won't move away from the water."

"I guess you're right, at that," Longarm agreed. "It ain't like being in the brakes. I'll let 'em scatter, then, and ride back to the chuck wagon with you, if that's the way you're heading."

"It is," Greenhaw nodded. "And we can talk as well riding back as we could sitting here."

"You got something special on your mind, Tom?"

"Nothing that can't wait, but now's as good a time to talk as any," the trail boss said as they started toward the chuck wagon. "It seems like I remember hearing you mention that you'd been over this part of the country before."

"I went through here one time when I was going from Dodge over to the Indian Nation," Longarm replied. "That was quite a spell back, of course."

148

"You had to ford the Red River's North Fork and the Canadian then, didn't you?" Greenhaw asked.

"Oh, sure. Why? Them river brakes got you worried, Tom?"

"Well, that Goodnight rider said we'd better be careful of both those rivers. He told me the North Fork of the Red and the Canadian both have some pretty bad stretches of quicksand, and that the bottoms of both riverbeds keep changing."

"Oh, he was right about that. I've crossed both of 'em before, and one time I had to pull a rider out of a quicksand sink on the Canadian. It was a new one that nobody'd found out about till then."

"I'm going to set you riding scout till we get past those two rivers," Greenhaw said. "I'll feel better if somebody who knows the country's out in front of the herd."

"You're the boss," Longarm answered. "But seeing as we're short a hand already, was I doing your job, I'd just do without a scout right now. We got Goodnight's trail to go by, and the country ain't all that rough."

"I've thought about that," Greenhaw nodded. "But those rivers bother me a little bit."

"Well, there ain't no law against me staying with the herd till we get close to 'em, and then pushing ahead to try the bottom before the herd gets there."

"I guess that would be the best answer," Greenhaw agreed. "And I intend to hire on another hand when we get to Mobeetie, if I can find one. It'll be about the last chance to pick up a man before we get to Denver."

"You ain't figuring to stop at Dodge, then?"

Greenhaw shook his head. "We'll stay a day at Mobeetie and rest the herd and give the boys a chance to blow off steam. Then, when we get across that strip of No Man's Land, we'll leave Goodnight's trail and head straight for Denver."

"That's about as good a plan as any," Longarm agreed. "And if you still want me to scout ahead—"

"No," Greenhaw broke in, "your idea's better. Stay with the herd until we're getting close to the rivers, then ride ahead and check the crossings."

In spite of Greenhaw's misgivings, the drive from the Red River's Elm Fork branch to the Red's wider and deeper North Fork was made without trouble. The character of the country began to change halfway between the two watercourses, flat prairie grassland giving way to a more broken terrain, one of low rolling hills, dotted with clumps of elm and live oak on the prairie and with spreads of low-growing sandplums and salt cedars along the rivers and creeks.

Late in the day after their start from the Elm Fork, Longarm rode ahead of the herd to find a bedding place for the night. They'd gotten an early start, and the sun was still hanging only three-quarters of the way from the noon zenith to the horizon when he reached the Red River's North Fork. Goodnight's trail led straight to the sun-silvered water, a swathe where the grass sprouting from ground beaten hard by the hooves of plodding steers grew more sparsely than elsewhere on the prairie.

Longarm reined in at the bank and lighted one of his long, slender cigars. The slanting sun rays dancing on the water's surface threw back a reflection that hid the bottom except for a narrow strip that extended a few yards from the shore. Longarm could see the fine-grained red bottom-sand quite clearly until the mirrored rays blocked his vision. There were no hoofprints in the sand, and he toed the Tennessee gelding into the stream.

After its first few tentative steps, the gelding accepted the feeling of the water lapping at its fetlocks and moved ahead steadily across the firm sand. A dozen yards from shore the bottom began slanting sharply downward, and the horse hesitated. Trusting to the animal's instincts with more confidence than he felt in his own, Longarm tightened the reins.

Squinting into the glare of sun's rays reflected from the water, Longarm could see nothing. He toed the gelding again and the horse tossed its head and balked. Then, as Longarm let the reins grow slack the gelding swung to the right and started moving slowly downstream.

Old son, Longarm reminded himself, *there's times when a critter's got more sense than a human. Just you keep a slack rein, now, and see what the pony does.*

Given its head, the gelding moved ahead at a deliberate walk. It went downstream for several minutes, then began veering toward the opposite bank. When it changed direction, the sun's angle on the water also changed, and Longarm could see what lay below below the surface on his upstream side. He looked into blackness, a deep hole in the bottom, scoured out by some unpredictable current. Scanning the downstream side, he saw shallow water, no deeper than the hock-deep stretch across which the gelding was now moving steadily toward the opposite bank.

Chuckling to himself, Longarm waited until he saw shallows on both sides. Then he reined the animal upstream again. The water's depth at the edge of the deep hole stayed reasonably constant, and the gelding waded steadily for a hundred yards or more until it balked again. Now Longarm had the sun at his back and could see the bottom easily from his vantage point in the saddle high above the surface. When he saw that the water was not too deep ahead, he dug his boot toe into the horse's ribs. The gelding stood stubbornly. Then, when Longarm nudged it for the second time, it started slowly forward.

Its progress upstream was brief. Only a few yards from the spot where it had stopped, the animals' forward forefoot began to sink rapidly into the sand. It whinnied, and Longarm turned it sharply. For a moment the gelding hunkered back, its head tossing. Then it pulled its forefoot free of the quicksand into which Longarm had urged it and stood quietly.

You better be glad you got a trail-smart horse, Longarm told himself as he turned the gelding's head and started it moving downstream. *Now let's see if this ridge is wide enough to give them longhorns room to cross.*

For the next half-hour, Longarm zigzagged the horse back and forth downstream from the vicinity of the drop-off and quicksand. When he'd discovered that the bottom was solid in an area wide enough to accommodate the longhorn herd and the riders who would work back and forth to keep the steers bunched and moving during the river crossing, he reined the horse toward the south bank.

As he guided the gelding out of the water and started for the chuck wagon, he told himself silently, *Yes, sir, you got a right smart horse here, old son. Hadn't been for him, you could've drowned or got sucked under. Now, you know just where that herd needs to cross, and chances are there won't be a single critter that'll even get its belly wet.*

From the north bank of the Red River's North Fork, Goodnight's new trail ran straight as a string toward Mobeetie over a series of wide, shallow vales. The depressions were not quite deep enough to be called valleys, nor were the tops of the ridges separating them high enough or steep enough for them to be described as hills.

151

It was easy country for a herd to cross, and the distance from the river to the town was not quite far enough to require a full day. Longarm was riding point on the right-hand side of the herd when the straight man-created lines of the ridgepoles of Mobeetie's houses broke the gentle humps of the skyline ahead. He circled the front of the herd and rode up to Greenhaw, who was holding down the left flank.

"Mobeetie's just ahead," Longarm announced as he reined in to ride beside the trail boss.

"I thought we must be getting close," Greenhaw replied. "And if my map's right, the only water close by is north of town, between Mobeetie and Fort Elliott."

"So there is," Longarm nodded. "Sweetwater Creek. And, if I recollect rightly from when I was here before, the creek forks off just beyond the town, about two miles this side of the fort. That'd be a good place to bed the herd, unless the place has changed a lot."

"Tell Lucky to move up from flanker to cover your point, and you ride on ahead, then," Greenhaw said. "If that fork is the way you remember it, wave your hat and we'll come ahead. If it's not, you can come on back when you've found another place."

Longarm pushed on, skirted the town, picked up the wagon road that ran north to Fort Elliott, and followed it three-quarters of a mile until he splashed across the ford at Sweetwater Creek. Turning west, he rode beside the stream a quarter of a mile to the forks and found that the terrain had changed very little since he'd been there last.

Wheeling south, he had reached only the second ridge past the creek before he saw the herd plodding toward him. Waving his hat to Greenhaw, he waited on the ridge for the herd to reach him. Turning in advance of the steers, he led the way across the south branch of the rippling creek, and joined the others in hazing the herd toward the vee formed by the forks. Then he went in search of Greenhaw.

"I reckon you can spare me till supper time, can't you, Tom?" he asked. "There's an army telegraph station at the fort, and they can get a message through to Denver on the government wire. I ain't had a chance to send a report to my chief since we left Abilene, and he's likely wondering what I been up to."

"Sure, go ahead," Greenhaw said. "We're going to stay here

through tomorrow. The boys need a chance to blow off steam. In this fork, one man can stay here and keep an eye on the herd, so I'll just leave your name off the watch list."

Longarm wasted no time heading for Fort Elliott. He rode along the wagon road until he saw the flagpole in front of the headquarters building, and in a few moments the sod walls of the buildings were in sight.

They were no longer as shipshape as he remembered them. Half the long stable had collapsed, the sally-port had disappeared, and only two mounds of earth rose where it had been. One corner of the barracks sagged, and the mess hall was half its former size, but there were horses in the corral beyond the stable. Men in cavalry blue and grey moved around between the buildings, and the posts supporting the military telegraph wire still stood, stretching across the flat terrain until they were lost to sight in the distance.

Longarm recalled the trim, businesslike appearance of the outpost on his earlier visit, and shook his head. *Seems like the army's gone to pot like most everything else, old son,* he told himself. *It sure don't look nice and neat, like it used to.*

Longarm's sight of the fort had rekindled an old memory. On his previous visit, he had been helped in more ways than one by the mistress of one of its officers. He had spent a memorable night with her in her small house in Mobeetie, and the recollection came flooding back to him.

This ain't no time to be thinking about what you done before, old son, he reproved himself. *There ain't a chance him or her either one's still here. Now stop moping about what's done finished and gone, and get on about your business.*

Reining in at the hitch rail in front of the headquarters building, Longarm went through the door into the outer office, where a solider wearing the stripes of a lance corporal sat at a desk, scribbling on a yellow foolscap tablet.

He looked up when Longarm came in. "Do something for you?" he asked.

In spite of the resolution he had made only moments earlier, Longarm asked, "I don't reckon there's a lieutenant named Hastings still on duty here, is there?"

"Hastings?" The soldier frowned and shook his head. "We haven't got a Hastings on the roster."

"I didn't much imagine you would have. I was just asking because he was on duty when I was here a few years ago."

"There'll be a record in the files of where he was transferred to," the soldier said. "If you want me to look—"

"It ain't all that important," Longarm told him. "It don't have a thing to do with what I come here for. My name's Long, and I got to have a little visit with your commanding officer."

"Colonel Foster? He's at the latrine right now, but he'll be back in a minute or so," the soldier replied.

"I'll wait," Longarm said.

He saw an empty chair against the wall across the room, sat down, and lighted a cigar. The lance corporal went back to his writing, and in a few minutes an officer wearing the silver leaf-shaped insigne of a lieutenant colonel on the shoulder straps of his shirt came in. He saw Longarm and frowned, but before he could speak Longarm was on his feet. He flipped open the wallet containing his badge.

"My name's Long, Colonel. Deputy U.S. marshal, outa the Denver office."

"Foster," the colonel said, extending his hand. "What brings you here, Marshal?"

"I need to send a message to my chief. If your telegrapher could handle that, I'd appreciate it," Longarm replied.

"I'm afraid you've got the wrong idea about our military telegraph system, Marshal," Foster frowned. "Our wires are for army use only. Civilians can't send messages over them."

"Begging your pardon, Colonel," Longarm said. "Maybe you never have run into it before, but the army and the Justice Department has fixed it up for us federal marshals to send messages over 'em when we need to."

"You're right," Foster replied. "I've never heard about it, but in this man's army there's always something new."

"All your telegraph operator's got to do is send the message to your corps headquarters," Longarm explained. "They send it on to Washington, and the War Department passes it over to the Justice Department. Then the Justice Department sends it on a direct wire to whichever chief marshal's office it goes to."

"You've used military telegraph wires for this before, I trust?" Colonel Foster asked.

"A few times. My chief don't like for me to butt into army business unless I got to, but I'm still a long way from Denver and I need to let him know about a few things I've dug up since I been travelling."

"Go ahead, then," Foster agreed. "Corporal Hall over there

is my post telegrapher as well as my clerk. Hall, you've heard what Marshal Long wants. See to it."

"Yes, sir!" the corporal replied.

Longarm said, "Thanks, Colonel. Now, I'll ask you one more thing. Don't let none of your men talk about me being here, or sending a message. My business is sorta secret."

"A spying mission, Marshal?" Foster asked, his eyebrows going up. "I didn't know such things existed outside the army."

"Well, I ain't exactly a spy, Colonel. I'm after some crooks, and I'd just as soon they don't find out about me."

"Don't worry," the colonel promised. "Aside from Hall, I'll be the only one who knows you were here."

"I thank you real kindly for your help, Colonel," Longarm said. "I won't take up no more of your time, now. I'll fix it up with the corporal to hold on to whatever answer I get till I can stop by and pick it up."

Borrowing a sheet of foolscap from the clerk, Longarm wrote a short message to Billy Vail. He confined it to giving the date when he estimated the Mexican longhorns would arrive in Denver, and asking him to try to find the mysterious Sterns.

"I'll look in tomorrow sometime and see if you got an answer from my chief," he told the clerk as he handed him the message. "His name's Vail; it's right on the paper there. If you get an answer, just tuck it away for me."

When he reached Sweetwater Creek on his way back from Fort Elliott, Longarm hesitated. In the distance he could see the chuck wagon's white top, and the trail crew still in the saddle, forming up the herd for the night. Even at a distance, he could see that they had almost finished the job, and needed no help from him. He rode on toward town.

Mobeetie had changed little since his last visit. It was still a mixture of sod and frame houses, sprawled along the south bank of Sweetwater Creek. Though there were a few more houses and several brick and cut-stone store buildings on the higgledy-piggledy streets, and on the main street saloons still predominated. Lights were beginning to shine through the store windows and stream from below the batwings of the saloons.

Longarm picked one of the saloons at random and dismounted. Wrapping the gelding's reins around the hitch rail, he pushed through the swinging doors and went to the bar. There were only a handful of customers at that early hour, and the barkeep came at once to serve him.

"I hope you got some Maryland rye," Longarm said. "Tom Moore, if I got a choice. I don't cotton to that sweet rye that comes outa Pennsylvania."

"You've got good taste, friend," the barkeep told him. "I like Tom Moore myself, so we've always got it on hand."

Turning to the backbar, the man selected a bottle and glass and placed them in front of Longarm. "If you want me to pour..."

"No, thanks," Longarm replied, placing a silver dollar on the mahogany. "I ain't too tired to pour my own."

Seeing that Longarm was in no mood for chatter, the barkeep nodded and moved away. Longarm tossed back a shot of the rye, tilted the bottle over his glass, and lighted a cigar. He sipped at his second drink, his thoughts again going back a few years, and when he'd emptied the glass, his mind was made up. Leaving the dollar on the bar, he mounted the gelding and rode off the main street toward the outskirts of town.

Longarm's memory guided him in the zigzag path he'd followed before, through the scattered maze of dwellings to the small frame house on the creek's banks. It still stood off by itself, and lights gleaming through the windows told him it was still occupied. He reined in at the front steps, swung out of his saddle, and tapped at the door.

"Yes? Who is it?" a woman called.

Longarm remembered the voice and the question. He replied, "Sarah? You're in for a big surprise when you open the door."

The door swung open, and Longarm blinked. The small, slim woman who stood silhouetted against the lamplight, her hair a nimbus of gold, was just as he'd remembered.

"Sarah?" he repeated. "I hope you ain't forgot me. Deputy U.S. Marshal Custis Long?"

"I haven't forgotten you because I've never met you, Marshal Long. Sarah's my older sister. I'm Sally, and I've heard so much about you that I'd like to know more. Won't you come in?"

Chapter 18

Longarm recovered quickly from his surprise. He stepped into the house and stood blinking for a moment while his eyes adjusted to the light. When he could see clearly, he discovered that Sally was a mirror image of Sarah. She had the same small stature, small waist, and generous swell of breasts and hips. There was the same evidence of half-Apache parentage in her midnight-black eyes, high cheekbones, wide nostrils, and square chin, the same full crimson lips, like small elongated pillows puffed poutingly over strong white teeth.

Even her taste in clothing reminded him of Sarah. Sally was wearing a clinging robe of rich yellow silk with a border of paler lace. The robe emphasized the contours of her full breasts and lushly svelte body. When she moved, he caught the familiar scent of the same heady perfume her sister had favored.

"Well?" she asked, obviously relishing Longarm's surprise as well as his attention. "Do you think I look like Sarah?"

"Enough like her to be her twin," he replied. "But I guess you better tell me what all's happened since I was here last, when I met your sister."

"Oh, of course," Sally nodded. "It's just that Sarah's mentioned you so many times, and seeing you here in Mobeetie is such a surprise that I can't think what to say."

"I wasn't aiming to surprise nobody," Longarm told her. "I had to come this way with a trail herd I got to keep an eye on, and I thought about your sister when the trail boss stopped the cattle here for the night, so I thought—"

"I'm glad you did," Sally said. "Even if I'm not Sarah. I hope you're not disappointed."

"Now, you know better than that. A pretty lady like you is a plumb treat to my eyes after such a while on the trail."

"Take off your hat and sit down, Marshal," she invited. "I've got another surprise for you that I think you'll like."

Longarm took off his hat and sat down in the easy chair

she indicated. Sally stepped over to the glass-fronted china cabinet that stood where Longarm recalled having seen it before. He looked around while she opened the cabinet and reached into it.

He saw that the room he remembered so well had not been changed. The Aladdin lamp with its white glass shade still stood on the round table in the center, and he also remembered the red-upholstered sofa and twin easy chairs, matching window curtains, and ornately figured Brussels carpet. Even if he had never seen it before, Longarm would have felt at home.

Sally came back from the cabinet carrying a tray on which there stood a bottle of Tom Moore, another of Otard brandy, and glasses. She put the tray on the table and smiled at Longarm.

"You can see that Sarah's told me about you. She said she always kept a bottle of Tom Moore's rye whiskey in case you might be riding this way again and drop in," she said, filling one of the glasses with Tom Moore and the other with brandy. As she handed Longarm his glass, she went on, "I feel like I know you, too, Marshal."

"Now, if you did know me as well as you figure you do, you'd be calling me by the same name your sister did," he told her.

"Oh, I remember that, too. Longarm. You're sure you don't mind?"

"I answer to it better'n I do my own, Sally. But what in tunket happened to Sarah?"

"She's Mrs. Wilford Hastings now. And she and Captain Hastings are up in Idaho at Fort Boise."

"So they got married, did they?"

"Just after Wilford got his promotion and a week before he was transferred," Sally said. "I'd come to help her get ready for their wedding. Then, when his orders to move came from Washington, Sarah asked me to stay and look after her house until they'd found a house they could settle into up in Idaho."

"Well I'm glad to hear they're both happy."

"They are. The only thing that bothers Sarah is trying to find a house. I've been here by myself for nearly eight months, now, waiting to pack up her things and send them to her, but houses seem awfully hard to find up there."

"That's pretty wild country yet," Longarm said. He took out a cheroot and held it up for Sally to see. She nodded permission, and he flicked a match into flame with his thumbnail and lighted the slim cigar. "But they'll get settled after while."

"Soon, I hope," Sally said. She looked at Longarm, one eyebrow raised, and added, "I'm getting restless."

Longarm was sure he read an invitation in her words and in the questioning look she was giving him. But he wanted to be sure, so he said, "You're wanting to go back home, then? I'd imagine you got a husband at home? Maybe some children?"

"Goodness, no!" she exclaimed. "Sarah and I have always been alike in more ways than one, Longarm. I was surprised when she wrote me that she was going to get married again. You see, I tried marrying once. It didn't work out, and I decided not to try it again. I guess I'm just not cut out to be a wife."

"Seems to me I recall hearing Sarah say that, too," Longarm told her. "But she changed her mind."

"I won't, though. When I said I was getting restless, I had an idea you would understand what I meant."

"Oh, I reckon I did, Sally. You're like Sarah, all right. But I wanted to be sure. I remember how she was. Me and her was in bed by the time I'd been here about as long as I have now."

"Sarah told me you're a man who doesn't waste much time," Sally smiled. She stood up and took a step toward him, saying, "I remember the rest of what she told me, too, Longarm. What're we waiting for? You've been here before; you know the way to the bedroom."

One long stride took Longarm to Sally's side. She held her arms out to him and he clasped his hands around her waist, lifted her up until he could find her lips with his. Her tongue darted into his mouth as their lips met, and Longarm met it with his. They held their embrace, tongues darting and twining. The door to the bedroom was only two steps away, and Longarm carried her through it. By the soft light that filtered in from the other room, he saw that the big high bed had been turned down for the night.

Since leaving Denver, Longarm had not encountered a woman who had caught his fancy. Now, not only his memory of Sarah, but Sally's willing embrace, the pressure of her body against him, and the hot, moist prodding of her tongue on his had already begun to bring him erect.

He felt her hand slip down between their close-pressed bodies and cradle the bulge that was growing in his crotch. She

159

gasped and broke their kiss to whisper, "Sarah told me you were big, but I didn't expect as much as I'm feeling now! Let's hurry, Longarm! I can't wait to get to bed with you!"

Longarm lowered her to her feet and said, "I'm as ready to get on that bed as you are, Sally. But boots and a gunbelt ain't very comfortable bedmates. Let's hold up for a minute till I can get rid of 'em."

"I'll help you," she volunteered, releasing her grip on his bulging groin. She began unbuckling his gunbelt.

Longarm slipped his derringer into the pocket with his watch and hung the vest over a chair. He took the gunbelt and put it over the chair-back and levered out of his boots while Sally's fingers danced with eagerness as she unbuttoned his shirt. By the time she reached the last button and pulled the shirt away from his shoulders, Longarm was stepping out of his tight-fitting twill pants and balbriggans. He freed one foot, but caught the other foot in a tangle of his trouser leg.

"Let me help," Sally said.

She dropped to her knees and tugged at the stiff folds of the twill trousers until they slid away. When their caresses had been broken by the mechanics of undressing, Longarm's still-incomplete erection had started to fade. She looked up at him now and smiled elfishly.

"Oh, my!" she said, her soft hands fondling him caressingly. "I'm going to have to give you a little more help than I'd expected."

"You don't need to—" Longarm began.

"I want to," she broke in. "And Sarah said you liked to have a woman love you this way."

"Sure I do, as long as it's pleasuring you, too."

"It is," Sally replied, bending her head to take him into her mouth.

Longarm stood quietly while Sally's soft, hot lips engulfed his shaft. Her tongue darted out in quick, flicking caresses, and Longarm began swelling at once. As his erection returned, Sally bobbed her head faster, and instead of an occasional fast flick kept her agile tongue in constant motion.

His erection returned quickly and Longarm moved as though to step away, but Sally grasped his slim hips and held him still. His long period of continence on the trail brought Longarm to a climax faster than usual. He did not hold back or try to step away, and when his pulsations began Sally pressed her face into his groin and held him engulfed while her mobile tongue rasped gently over his sensitized flesh. She did not release him until he stood quiet, then she leaned back without taking her caressing hands off his still-jutting erection.

"You had too fine an edge because you've been on the trail so long," Sally told him. "Now, hurry up and take me to bed!"

Rising to her feet, she twisted her shoulders and her robe fell open. Longarm slid his hand under the soft silk and began rubbing her swelling breasts with his palm, pressing their burgeoning tips with his horn-hard fingertips. Sally started gasping as his hands moved over her satiny skin, and her own hands clenched tightly on his erection.

Longarm stepped back and said, "If you been here by yourself a long time, you're ready for some special loving, too."

He slid the robe off Sally's shoulders and gazed at her in the soft filtered light. The rosettes of her firm high bulging breasts were pebbled, their dark pink tips thrust out. Below the inward curve of her waist, her hips flared and then tapered into full swelling thighs, accented by the dark golden vee of her pubic brush. Longarm lifted her and placed her on the bed.

For a moment he stood looking down at her, a golden-ivory figure on the white sheets. He bent over her and began caressing her full breasts with his lips, drawing first his tongue and then the stiff bristles of his sweeping moustache across their firm, protruding tips.

Sally sighed softly, and her body began twitching as Longarm continued his caresses. After a few moments he trailed his tongue tip down her thin waist, and buried his face in the wiry curls of her golden fleece. Sally moaned and spread her thighs wide as his tongue reached and then found the small, firm button of flesh at the tip of her lower lips. He rasped the button with his firmed tongue-tip until her sighs grew to moans and the moans increased to small, sharp cries of pleasure. Her hips began to rise and fall as though she had no control over them, and her entire body started to quiver.

Suddenly she cried, "I want you in me right now, Longarm! "Hurry! Oh, hurry! I've never wanted a man like I want you!"

Longarm responded quickly. He rose and bent over the bed and Sally pulled him down to her. She grasped his erection and brought up her knees, guiding him between her thighs. Longarm plunged. Sally shrieked as he drove into her with a single hard thrust that brought their bodies together with a soft, fleshy thump and held himself pressed hard against her while she writhed and shivered and cried out with wordless sounds of ecstasy. He held himself quiet until her cries faded and her shudders died away.

"Oh, Longarm," she sighed. "I never found a man who can fill me the way you do! You're not going to leave me now, are you? Because I want to keep feeling you in me!"

"Don't worry, Sally," he assured her. "I ain't in no more of a hurry than you are."

"Don't leave me, please! Not for a long, long time!"

"I ain't about to," he promised. "I got a lot of lost time to make up, too."

Sally lifted her face for his kiss, and while their lips were still clinging Longarm began thrusting. He set a slow, measured rhythm that went on and on until Sally began to moan softly once again. Longarm gradually increased the tempo of his strokes until he was lunging with triphammer speed and Sally's cries rang out in the dimly lighted room as her ecstasy mounted to its peak. She shrieked and shuddered as her body grew rigid and jerked into another spasm, and Longarm held himself pressed deeply into her again until her quivering passed.

"I didn't believe what Sarah told me about you," she whispered as Longarm once more began to stroke slowly. "And I'm glad I'm finally finding out for myself. But you must be getting tired. Let me get on top this time."

Longarm rose and picked Sally up. He turned on his knees and sank down on his back without breaking the bond of flesh that made them one. Sally twisted her hips from side to side, squirming down on his buried cylinder. She brought her body erect and rocked back and forth for a few moments, then leaned forward to support herself on all fours, and her firm, rounded buttocks began rising and falling.

Longarm lifted his hips each time Sally brought her body down on his rigid shaft, her full breasts swaying rhythmically as she moved. Longarm took one of the soft globes in each hand and began rubbing their protruding tips. Sally gasped and began to increase the tempo of her rhythm.

Minute after minute ticked off while Sally kept up the steady rise and fall that her smiling lips and tightly closed eyes indicated was giving her so much pleasure. After a while her breathing grew ragged, and she pressed her lips together in a grimace that mixed pleasure and pain.

162

Longarm said, "I been holding back for quite a spell, Sally. You can let go whenever you're ready."

Sally opened her eyes and looked down at him, and her grimace became a smile. "So have I," she confessed. "But I thought I'd wait for you."

She leaned forward and dropped on Longarm's chest, and began to rotate her hips while she continued to bounce them up and down. Her head was nestled amid the curls on Longarm's chest and she rubbed her soft cheeks against the wiry curls for a few moments. Then he felt her starting to quiver while her breath came in rasping gasps. He held himself back for a moment until Sally moaned, then began the small shrieks that he'd heard before as she entered her climax.

Longarm relaxed the control he'd been imposing on himself and felt himself jetting as Sally gave her last shriek and fell forward, limp and spent.

They lay in silence for several minutes before either of them stirred. Sally was the first to move. She raised her head and smiled down into Longarm's face.

"I can't believe you're real, Longarm," she said. "If I couldn't still feel you in me, I wouldn't believe it."

"You make a man feel right fine," Longarm told her. "I think we better have another drink and rest a while now, before we start up again."

"You mean you still have something left after all that?"

"Why, sure," he replied. "We've had a good sample of what both of us like, but the night ain't half over yet, and I don't have to go back to the trail camp till late tomorrow. Of course, if you don't want me to stay—"

"You know better than that!" Sally broke in. "If this is just a sample, I won't be satisfied until I've found out what the rest is like!"

Longarm returned to the trail camp late the next afternoon. In spite of, or perhaps because of, his extended stay with Sally and their mutual exertions, he felt rested and refreshed. He had ridden out to Fort Elliott before going back to the camp, to see if Billy Vail had replied to his telegram, and found a brief answer reading, "Will be waiting for herd to reach stockyards. No clue to Sterns."

Tom Greenhaw came over as Longarm dismounted. "I sorta looked to see you in Mobeetie when the rest of us went in," he said. "The boys must've made every saloon in town, but you wasn't in any of them."

"Oh, I went to visiting a relative of an old friend that used to live here," Longarm replied. "And I had a little business to take care of out at the fort. I guess that's why we didn't run into each other."

"Well, if all the others come back looking as rested as you do, we ought to get along fine for the rest of the drive," Greenhaw commented. "I'd say the worst of it's behind us now, anyhow."

"You sound real cheerful, Tom. I'd say resting a day done you as much good as it did the rest of us."

"Why shouldn't I feel good?" Greenhaw asked. "All we've got left to do is keep on Goodnight's trail until we get close to Dodge, then swing due north and keep on going."

"Well, there's a few little things you left out," Longarm said drily.

"Such as?"

"For one thing, we got No Man's Land to cross before we'll get to Dodge," Longarm replied thoughtfully. "And a lot of rivers to cross while we go around the Rockies. But them things don't bother me as much as one other one."

"What's that?" Greenhaw frowned.

"I guess you forgot the Canadian River," Longarm said. "If you was to roll all them other rivers up north into one, it'd make a stream five or six times as big the Canadian, but that's the one I hate to see us hit."

"There's no way to go around it, as I recall," Greenhaw said. "If there was—"

"No, there ain't no way to miss it," Longarm said. "It winds all across the Panhandle like a rattlesnake, only it's about three times as mean. We're lucky we'll all be fresh when we get to it, because that damn muddy river's swallowed more trail herds than you can shake a stick at. So wait till we get across it, Tom. Then I'll put in with you that the rest of the drive will be easy."

Chapter 19

"From the way you've been talking since we left Mobeetie, I sure looked to see more of a river than this," Tom Greenhaw told Longarm.

They had reined in after riding up from the little hollow where Sam had stopped with the chuck wagon and were sitting their horses on a low ridge overlooking the brakes of the Canadian River. The stream itself was still more than a mile away, but from the ridge they could see its rippling yellow surface.

Goodnight's new trail had angled northwest after leaving Mobeetie, and for the first day out they'd followed the south fork of Sweetwater Creek. The second day, a long, dry twelve hours, had brought the herd to the headwaters of Red Deer Creek. Then, for the past three days, they had been crossing a stretch of country where several small creeks angled into the river only a few miles apart. The little watercourses had cut shallow miniature canyons as they trickled across the corrugated slope that led to the Canadian. Now, a full week after stopping over in Mobeetie, they'd reached White Deer Creek and moved along its gently undulating banks to the river.

From the crest where Longarm and Greenhaw had reined in, the trail sloped gently to a wide cut in the steep bank that led down to the stream. Their height in the saddle gave them a clear view of the brakes, which were a good half-mile wide on each side of the river, a tangle of lacy-limbed mesquite brush and low-growing salt cedar rising above a scant cover of ground-hugging vines and bunch grass broken by expanses of orange-hued sand.

Zigzagging in torturous curves through the brakes, the river ran in a yellow thread through a channel that was three times as wide as the stream itself.

"Don't let the Canadian fool you, Tom," Longarm warned the trail boss. "There's quicksand sinks and deep holes all along this river that'll swallow a steer, or even a man and his pony."

"So I've heard," Greenhaw nodded. "But I don't aim to let a little spit of water like this one scare me. We've put the herd across bigger rivers before."

"Oh, sure," Longarm agreed. "And we got a lot of bigger ones ahead, like the Cimarron and the Arkansas. But this one is still the meanest."

"We won't tackle it till morning," the trail boss said. He glanced at the sky, a thin clear transparent blue, and went on, "We'll bring the herd up to that little dimple we just rode across and let 'em rest good. Then we'll be over the Canadian and on our way north by noon."

Longarm's eyes had followed Greenhaw's to the sky, and now he dropped his gaze to the horizon. He pointed to the bright, jagged line of shining brilliance marking the point where the light of the late afternoon sun was reflected from the rim of a cloudbank. Above the line the sky was clear; below it a curtain of midnight-blackness cut off the blue.

"We better get an early start, then," he said. "If that ain't a storm over to the west, I never seen one before."

Greenhaw looked where Longarm was pointing. "I guess it's a storm," he agreed. "A right good-sized one, too."

"And moving this way, near as I can tell," Longarm said.

"Looks like it is, for sure," Greenhaw nodded. "But, hell, it's a hundred miles away. It'll likely break up during the night, but even if it doesn't, it won't get here soon enough to bother us. Now, why don't you scout out the bottom while I get back to the chuck wagon. The boys will be bringing the herd up pretty soon."

Longarm rode on to the river and reined in. Despite its yellowish color, the water proved to be clear enough to let him judge the bottom. Here and there a gnarled root rose above the surface, marking an area where at some past time the stream had changed course and washed out a stand of the salt cedars that sprinkled its banks.

Dark splotches showed in places, warnings to the river-wise that where they were visible the bed had been scoured by its unpredictable currents, and a deep hole formed by the swirling water. Some of the dark areas were big enough to swallow a steer whole, and Longarm made a mental note of the largest.

After a quarter of an hour of studying the river from its banks, he had a picture in his mind of a path that the herd could follow, unless the route he had selected contained areas of quicksand. There was only one way to discover this, and Longarm toed the Tennessee gelding into the water.

Zigzagging between the holes, he discovered only one soft spot before he reached the Canadian's north bank. It was at a place where there were fewer holes than usual, and after a bit of study he decided that by stringing the cattle out a bit, the crossing could be made without too much difficulty. Splashing back across the yellow water, its surface always a safe foot or more below his stirrups, he rode back to the hollow.

During the time he'd spent crisscrossing the river, the sun had dropped below the distant cloudline and the sky had taken on a twilight hue. The herd had arrived and all the hands except Sam were hazing the cattle to the creek to drink before bedding them down. Their job was almost finished and Longarm saw that his help wasn't needed. He reined in at the chuck wagon.

"I guess you got some coffee in that pot by now?" he asked, indicating the graniteware coffee pot at the edge of the coals.

"Sure. Help yourself," Sam replied, handing him a cup.

Longarm filled the cup and strolled back to the wagon. Sam was preparing the lunch bags for the next day. He did not look away from his work, his hands busy pulling tall biscuits apart and tucking thick slices of fried bacon between the halves.

"I hope you found a crossing where I can get the wagon across in the morning without too much backing and filling," he said.

"You won't have no trouble," Longarm assured him. "There's a stump where lightning knocked down a big old pin-oak on the other bank. You can't miss it; what's left of the tree's still leaning off the stump. Just keep it dead ahead of you and you can roll right across."

"Sounds good," Sam replied. He put the last bag beside those he had already filled and glanced past Longarm toward the hollow. "Looks like the boys got the herd settled down. If you want your supper before they crowd up, you better grab a plate and go after it."

Longarm followed the cook's advice, and was hunkered down near the fire eating when the hands began trickling up. They were still high-spirited after their rest at Mobeetie, and with three-quarters of the drive behind them were already planning the blowout they would have after they drew down their pay in Denver.

"How about you, Custis?" Lucky asked Longarm. "Didn't

I hear you say one time that you'd spent some time up there?"

"Some," Longarm nodded. "It's a friendly town. Except you wanta be careful when you go down to the Lowers."

"That's where the saloons and the girls are, I guess?" Slim asked.

Longarm nodded. "Past Eighteenth Street. Don't let nobody sneak up behind you, though. It's pretty rough around there."

"It sure is," agreed Clete, the new hand Greenhaw had hired on at Mobeetie. "I still got a scar from a fight I got into down in the Lowers. I was a young buck then, and figured I was a lot tougher than I turned out to be."

"Maybe you and Custis can steer us around," Grayson suggested. "I aim to keep clear of trouble all I can."

"If that's what you want, then don't go to places like you find there at all," Parson said. "The Good Book advises a man to turn his back on evil."

"It's a lot easier to say than do, Parson," Doc observed. "At least until you get to be my age." He stood up. "Go on and figure on the fun you're going to have in Denver, boys. I'm going to crawl in my blankets. We've got a river to cross in the morning and a long drag afterwards."

"I don't mind the drag so much," Clete said. "But I sure don't like that damn Canadian River. I had my fill of that when I was handing on the Turkey Track a few years back."

Greenhaw came up to the fire in time to hear the remark and asked, "You know the river pretty well, do you, Clete?"

"Nobody knows the Canadian, Tom," Clete replied. "That bottom can change so fast that tomorrow your pony can fall in a sinkhole and founder where it crossed less'n belly-deep today."

"Maybe you'd better get out in the middle with Custis when we cross the herd tomorrow, then," Greenhaw said. "I guess the two of you are the only ones that's ever been in these parts before."

"Sure," Clete shrugged. "I won't get any wetter than anybody else." He stood up. "Doc had the right idea. I'm turning in now, too,"

When a light pattering of raindrops hit his blanket, Longarm woke at once. As usual, he was fully alert the instant his eyes opened. Beside the chuck wagon, the breakfast fire broke the darkness. The sky overhead was still dark, though false dawn was already showing on the eastern horizon.

Looking at the sky, Longarm felt better when he saw that only a few scattered spots of cloud obscured the stars. He sat up in his blankets and looked around. There was no sign of movement from the other bedrolls; the spate of raindrops had not roused the others. Sam appeared from behind the wagon and bent over the fire.

Another raindrop hit Longarm's face as he slid out of his blanket and reached for his boots. Like all the hands on the drive, he slept fully clothed except for the boots and his vest. Sliding his arms into his vest, he fished a cheroot out of his pocket and lighted it as he walked toward the fire. A low rumble of distant thunder broke the hush.

"Sounds to me like that storm me and Tom seen last night's working our way about now," Longarm said as he reached the fire.

"It was cutting up a mite when I woke up," Sam told him. "I saw a few lightning flashes over to the west when I first got up about an hour ago. But it's still a long ways off."

"There was some pretty heavy clouds over that way when Tom and me was down at the river last night before sundown," Longarm frowned. "I figured if it was a storm, it'd bust up before it got this far. Maybe you just seen the last of it."

"Maybe," Sam nodded. He stretched and went on, "Well, I'll go rouse the boys, now. I got all my gear stowed away, and soon as they get their breakfast, I'll be ready to roll."

"Rouse 'em, then," Longarm said. "I'll walk up that rise before I eat and take a look at the river."

By the time Longarm reached the rise and strode up its gently slanting side to the top, true dawn was spreading across the eastern sky. Though the western horizon and the sky in its direction were still dark, there was enough light for him to see the landmarks on the near bank. He'd noted their positions in relation to the water during his scout the evening before, and he could see that the river had not risen during the night. Feeeling better, Longarm stayed on the rise only long enough to drain his bladder before returning to the chuck wagon.

"I guess you felt them little raindrops a while ago," he said to Greenhaw as he took his biscuit-and-bacon sandwiches to the fire to get coffee.

"That wasn't anything but a stray cloud," Greenhaw replied.

"I figured it was, too. But it's mighty dark upriver."

"Sure. It's not sunup yet."

Longarm cocked his head upward and studied the sky. "The wind's blowing some clouds toward us. But if that storm we seen last night was going to get here, it'd be raining by now."

"We'll get a move on, just the same," Greenhaw said. "And I'm betting we'll get the herd across the river all right."

After Greenhaw's remarks at breakfast, the hands needed no more urging to move fast. They hurried through the meal and were ready to start the herd moving shortly after full daylight. Since Longarm had scouted the river, he was the first rider into the stream. He saw the parallel ruts made by the chuck wagon's wheels when it had crossed earlier, and followed them until the gelding's hooves roiled the water and hid the tracks. Clete was the next rider in. He followed Longarm across the stream and rode up on the bank while Longarm turned the gelding at the water's edge and rode back, reining in about a third of the distance across.

By the time Longarm was in position, the first steers had been hazed into the water by Doc and Greenhaw. As back flank and clean-up men, they would stay on the bank until the last steers were in the water. Lucky and Slim rode the points, one at each side of the lead steers. As the first line of longhorns emerged from the water, they took up positions on opposite sides of the moving cattle, keeping the herd bunched and moving while Clete waited a bit farther from the water's edge.

Parson and Grayson were the flankers, and like Longarm and Lucky and Slim, they stayed in the stream while the longhorns moved across it. Grayson was on the upstream flank of the herd, while Longarm and Parson divided the downstream side of the river between them. All three kept their mounts walking slowly back and forth, forming a loose, widely-spaced mobile picket line to turn the animals in a new direction when necessary and to haze back into the herd any of the longhorns that tried to leave it.

On the north bank, Clete waited for the cattle to cross. When the first of the steers splashed dripping from the river and started slowly up the sloping bank, they began trying to fan out and scatter. Clete began moving, keeping his cow pony in a shallow arc a dozen yards in front of the animals, letting the leaders advance, but squeezing back into the herd any of the steers that tried to leave the herd on either side.

Within three hours after they'd begun the crossing, all but

a score of the longhorns had left the bedding ground and were either on the north bank of the Canadian or in the stream, crossing. Only a dozen or so of the most stubborn steers had tried to break away while they were in the water. None of the flankers had been forced to chase the breakaways more than a few yards.

Longarm was walking the gelding back into position after having had to chase down one of these wild, bolting steers and haze it back to the herd. Since breakfast he as well as the others had been kept too busy to give any thought to the weather, but now he looked upriver to the west.

Beyond the cattle that were moving across the stream the river's surface was placid, and he saw that while the bank of ominous clouds had moved closer than it had been last night, it was still too far away to threaten them. Relieved, he was starting to turn away and take up his post when a burst of tiny, scintillating flashes above the water's surface caught his eye. He reined in and looked more closely, saw still other pinpoints of light flashing intermittently over the water.

Turning the gelding, Longarm rode beside the moving cattle and up on the sloping bank. Reining in, he stood erect in his stirrups and gazed upriver. The tiny bursts of flashing light were still appearing and disappearing above the surface. Longarm concentrated on the stream now. From the high bank he could see that the surface changed character where the flashes appeared most often. His eyes adjusted quickly to judging details at a distance, and Longarm whistled softly at what he saw.

Upriver, less than two miles from where the herd was crossing, the Canadian was not flowing in smooth, unruffled fashion. The water was a brownish-yellow now, and he could see that the rushing, roiling water formed a yard-high wall of froth and foam. The little flashing spots that had drawn his eyes were bubbles tossed above the water by the branches and tree trunks and other bits of debris that smashed together in the rushing current and sent a froth of bubbles high into the air to burst and reflect the sun's bright rays.

Longarm wasted no time. He wheeled the horse and kicked it into motion. At the water's edge he looked for Slim, but the flanker was high on the bank, turning a bolting longhorn back into the herd. Longarm turned the gelding into the river just before he reached the dripping steers emerging from the stream. Some of the longhorns shied and crowded those next to them, but his concern was not with the cattle already safe on the north bank. He splashed across and reined in when he reached Parson.

"Trouble's coming," he snapped. "There's a three-foot wall of water rushing at us. Ride up the bank and tell Slim to pass the word. I'm going to tell Greenhaw now."

Without waiting to answer any questions, Longarm moved on. He looked back once and saw Parson riding toward the north bank. When he reached the south bank, Longarm saw that there were only about twenty head waiting to cross. Doc was walking his pony slowly, moving along the side of the shrunken herd; Greenhaw was behind the last of the steers. Ignoring Doc's surprised shout, Longarm galloped up to Greenhaw.

"What's wrong?" the trail boss asked as soon as Longarm came within earshot.

"High water coming at us, Tom. That storm we been watching upriver must've been a wet one. There's a wall of water three feet high coming at us, hell-bent for election."

"How bad is it?"

"Bad enough. If we move fast and we're lucky we can maybe get what's left on this side across before it gets here."

"I guess you told the others?"

"Parson's getting word to Slim and Clete and Lucky. Doc and Grayson don't know yet, but Lucky or Slim's bound to tell Grayson, and here comes Doc now."

"Stay here and we'll start pushing," Greenhaw said. "We've got the herd this far. I'm damned if I'll let this river take any of 'em!"

With three riders crowding them from behind, the last steers pushed ahead, protesting blats rising from their throats and their wide, shining horns swaying as they jostled into their fellows. A rumble of thunder sounded as the last steers took to the water. Longarm glanced upstream. The bulge of debris and froth was visible now from the level of the stream, and he could see that his estimate of its height had been right. At this distance the wall of water looked like a dam stretching from bank to bank across the river. A low roar, neither a rumble nor a splashing, but a blending of both, was coming from upstream.

By now all the steers were in the river. The Canadian was crowded with cattle moving head to rump, jostling for room, but making little forward progress.

"Spook 'em!" Longarm shouted.

Greenhaw and Doc did not look around at his shout and he knew that his voice had been drowned by the blatting cattle and the increasingly loud noise of the onrushing torrent. Longarm did the only thing he could think of. He drew his Colt and fired in the air. The steers nearest him jumped forward at the sound of the shot, and both Greenhaw and Doc turned to look. In dumb show, Longarm raised his gun hand above his head and waved it, then fired again.

Greenhaw and Doc got the idea at the same time when they saw the hindmost steers jump forward as the revolver boomed. They drew their own pistols and followed Longarm's example, and the sound of their shots brought the same reaction from the longhorns nearest them that Longarm had created with his weapon.

With the rearmost steers bucking and shoving, those in front speeded up. The last of the cattle was just emerging from the stream when the current created by the onrushing crest swept into the shallow crossing. Within instants too brief to count the surface of the river bulged a foot higher, and before the riders could urge their mounts ahead the rising flood engulfed their feet and the rippling water was lapping at the horses' bellies.

Longarm felt the gelding falter as the brown water swirled around its legs. He kicked its belly and the horse responded with a short forward leap, found its footing when it landed, and splashed through the swiftly rising water to the safety of the bank. Greenhaw and Doc had already reached the shore and were urging their mounts up the slope. They got to the rim and joined the other hands seconds before the wall of water and debris swept past with a guttural, muted roar broken by the clashing of the debris it carried.

"We made it just in time," Greenhaw said quietly, looking down at the churning brown current less than a yard below the crest of the rim.

All of them were staring at the river. It had been less than two hundred feet wide that morning; now it filled the brakes from bank to bank. They saw a mile-wide stretch of ugly frothed and boiling water, covering the trunks of the trees in the brakes. Here and there an uprooted bush twirled swiftly as it was caught by the swirl of an invisible current and was drawn under the surface, then bobbed up again a dozen yards from the point where it had disappeared.

"It's a mean river, all right," Longarm observed. "A man

don't ever wanta misjudge what the Canadian can do."

A clap of thunder sounded and rain began to fall. Greenhaw did not give the men an order, but dug his heels into the flanks of his horse and started toward the scattered longhorns. The men followed him. Rain or no rain, there were steers to be gathered and started on their way to the next overnight camp.

Chapter 20

Rain was no stranger to the trail hands. All of them had been rained on before, but never with the fierce persistence of that carried by the storm to the banks of the Canadian. Huddled in slickers that did not quite protect them from the heavy swirling drops, they rode their stations during the daytime hours, and sweated through the steamy nights crowded bedroll to bedroll under a tarpaulin stretched from the wagon-bed's sideboard and pegged to the ground.

For three days and nights, while the Mexican longhorns plodded to the top of the Panhandle and entered No Man's Land, the rain stayed with them. The sky did not clear until soon after they crossed the outlaw-infested strip in a forced drive that began before daybreak and ended after dark. Ahead lay the last few miles of the new Goodnight Trail, but they did not follow the trail to its end. After crossing the summer-slack Cimarron River where Goodnight's new trail swung east to Dodge, Greenhaw set a fresh course.

With only Greenhaw's compass to guide them, the crew turned the Mexican longhorns to the northwest. They started across the vast plains that began at the foothills of the Rocky Mountains and stretched to the Missouri River. Driving was easy over the level terrain, and the trail-hardened steers picked up speed. They splashed across the narrow headwaters of Two Butte Creek and three days later forded the Purgatoire in the wide shallows below its juncture with the Arkansas.

To the last man, the drive hands felt that the worst was behind them now, and each day confirmed their feelings. They found the Arkansas as slack-watered as the Cimarron and the Purgatoire had been, and on the north side of the river picked up Horse Creek. The creek led them through the wide break in the foothills' spur east of Colorado Springs, and through the English ranchers who had made the area a virtual outpost of Great Britian favored fencing, the scouts found gaps through which the herd could be squeezed.

Once over the hump of the foothills' spur, the land sloped down again and the streams ran north instead of east. Longer days of driving became possible on the easy terrain, and two days of pushing the longhorns brought them to Boxelder Creek.

"I figure if we start moving soon as the sky's light enough to see by tomorrow, we'll make Denver by sundown," Greenhaw told Longarm as they hunkered down around the supper fire.

"Well, I ain't going to ask you to hold back," Longarm said. "Since I still ain't come up with a reason why that Arapahoe Syndicate made this fool drive, about all I can do is tell my chief his hunch wasn't no good."

"I don't have any new ideas, either," Greenhaw said. "But if you're planning to make one last stab at finding out, I'll sure do whatever I can to help you."

"It rubs my back the wrong way to get buffaloed on a case," Longarm confessed. "The only shot I got left is if my chief's dug up something. I ain't had a chance to wire him since we left Mobeetie, so he just might have."

"It'll be too late after we hit Denver, I guess? Because as soon as we get to the stockyards, I'll send a messenger to the syndicate's office and somebody'll bring out the money to pay off the hands. Then the syndicate will take over the herd and I won't have much to say about anything."

"All that's going to take some time," Longarm said thoughtfully. "Maybe it won't be too late, if you'll go along with a fool notion I just got."

"I told you I'll do whatever I can. I meant it, too."

"Oh, I know that, Tom. Now, all I can think of is if you don't need me tomorrow, I'll start for Denver right now. If I push my horse, I can get there in time to talk to my chief first thing in the morning. If he's found out anything we can make a case on, I'll be waiting at the stockyards when you get in."

"If that's what you want to do, go to it," Greenhaw nodded.

"It ain't so much what I want to do," Longarm told him. "I just get mule-stubborn sometimes, and this is one of 'em."

When Bill Vail rounded the corner of the corridor and saw Longarm hunkered down at the office door, his jaw dropped a full inch. He stopped and stared and then recovered his poise.

"Well, it's a change to see you reporting for work on time," he said. "But I'd like it better if you'd taken a minute to get a shave and some fresh clothes."

"This ain't no time for joshing, Billy," Longarm told the chief marshal as he stood up and stretched. "I got until about sundown to close up this case you put me on, and I still ain't sure there's a case at all."

As he unlocked the office door, Vail said to Longarm over his shoulder, "You smell something wrong about that longhorn herd. Travis Morrison did, too. So do I. There's a case, all right, even if we still can't grab hold of anything. Come on in the office and tell me what you've found since you wired me."

After he had heard Longarm's scanty and inconclusive report, Vail summed things up, saying, "What it boils down to is this: You haven't found any reason why this Arapahoe Syndicate wanted those Mexican longhorns, why they insured them for three times what they're worth, why they're paying the trail boss a big bonus for getting them here without losing any of them, or why they've had them driven here instead of shipping them."

"That's about the size of it, Billy," Longarm agreed. "If you got anything else, it's time to trot it out."

Vail said thoughtfully, "All I've got besides the way the thing smells is that this fellow Sterns doesn't seem to exist, and nobody in the financial district has ever heard of the Arapahoe Syndicate. That means somebody's covering a lot of tracks, and the whole thing smells like crooks at work."

"Oh, I grant you that, Billy," Longarm nodded. "But what you and me smell don't make a case in court."

"Give it one last shot, then," Vail said resignedly. "Meet the herd at the stockyards when it comes in and see if Sterns shows up. I can't give you any official instructions—not that you ever seem to need any."

Longarm nodded. "Fair enough. I'll play out my hand, even if it ain't got a high card in it, and see if I can bluff things to some sorta showdown."

It was a different-looking Longarm who showed up at the Denver stockyards in the late afternoon than the one who'd ridden into town in the pre-dawn darkness. He'd started after leaving Billy Vail by soaking for a full hour in a hot tub at his rooming house with a newly opened bottle of Tom Moore and a supply of his long, thin cigars within easy reach.

Then came fresh balbriggans and a clean grey flannel shirt, followed by a careful brushing of his wide-brimmed snuff-colored hat. Finally there'd been a shave at George Master's barbershop, and a late lunch or early supper—Longarm couldn't decide which—at a restaurant that had white linen cloths on its tables.

Between indulging in the luxuries he'd missed on the long drive up Goodnight's new trail, Longarm had also found time to take care of necessities. His Colt in its cross-draw holster was freshly cleaned and oiled, and the derringer in his vest pocket had also been cleaned and, like the Colt, loaded with shells from a new box. He swung off the Tennessee gelding in front of the office and went inside.

"There's a herd of Mexican longhorns due in sometime today," he told the clerk. "Would you know if it's got here yet?"

"Funny," the clerk said, "you're the second fellow in ten minutes to ask about that herd. It's not here yet, and I've no way of knowing when it will be in. All I can do is tell you what I told him—you'll have to wait."

"I guess he went over to Henry's place for a drink while he was waiting?" Longarm asked.

"He said that's where he was heading," the clerk replied.

"Well, I'll wander over and have a little sip myself. Might be him and me oughta get aquainted," Longarm said thoughtfully.

Henry's Stockyards Saloon was almost deserted at that hour of the day, but Longarm knew that, like any saloon, the place would come to life at dusk. That was when the hands who'd driven herds in from the ranches near Denver finished their day's work and stopped in for a snort before heading home. He stepped across the narrow room to the bar and ordered a glass of Tom Moore while he covertly inspected the patrons.

There were only half a dozen men in the bar; three of them were Mexicans, judging by their clothing, hats, and faces too dark to be suntanned, but Mexican hands were commonplace on Colorado cattle ranches. One man sat alone at a table, his head swaying as he battled his liquor trying to keep awake, and two others in neat business suits sat with their heads together at a back table.

While Longarm was still glancing around, the barkeep set a shot glass and a bottle of Tom Moore in front of Longarm.

He poured and Longarm picked up the glass. It felt odd in his hand and he looked at it. He saw that it had been molded in the shape of a steer horn. Now, for the first time, he noticed that the beer steins on the backbar were made in the same shape. Not wanting to be too obvious, after his first quick look at the patrons Longarm watched them in the backbar's long mirror while pretending to inspect the saloon's decorated walls.

As befitted its name and location, the long, narrow interior walls of Henry's Stockyards Saloon were crowded with mounted heads of steers that had grown unusual horns, and the longhorn breed was well-represented. There were horns which resembled a taut-strung bow and others that looked like a bow unstrung; horns that recurved in a tight arc that brought their points down level with the steers eyes. *Chongos* made up a sizeable part of the longhorn display. There were horns which had corkscrew twists, reverse spirals, and those which grew unicorn-fashion and protruded from the head in a forward sweep above the animal's nose.

There was one set of normal horns which was unquestionably the prize of the saloon's collection, for it occupied the center of the backbar. Longarm had never seen such massive horns on a live longhorn steer. At the base they were the diameter of a strong man's thigh, and they swept symmetrically in a long curve that he judged spanned eight feet from one needle-pointed tip to the other. Looking for a way to open a conversation with the men in whom he was interested, Longarm lighted a cheroot and puffed it for a moment before turning to face them.

"I'd guess you men are in the cattle business, being in a place like this," he said. "And I'd just like to know if you ever seen a set of horns like that on a live critter."

With startled expressions, the pair looked up from their low-voiced conversation. They stared at Longarm for a moment, then the younger of the two replied, "No, friend, I can't say I have. They're big, all right."

To keep the conversation going, Longarm took a step toward their table to get a better look at the two and went on, "How big would you say a steer'd have to be to carry horns that big? Seems to me he'd be a real monster."

"Well, now," the young man said thoughtfully, "I wouldn't think he'd have to be such a large size."

"You mean he wouldn't have no more meat on him than

one with horns that wasn't so heavy?" Longarm frowned, keeping up his role as an innocent information-seeker, using the time to evaluate the pair.

"Maybe he'd be bigger, at that," the young fellow began, when one of the Mexicans interrupted.

"Dispense mi, señores," he said. "Would not be good meat on esteer thees beeg. Ees get *los musculos rigidos* wheen mus' carry beeg horn like so; meat ees be tough."

"I see," Longarm said impatiently, wanting to get on with his job of questioning the men he'd been talking to. He started to turn away, but the cowhand stood up, staggered for a moment, then stepped between Longarm and the others.

"I tal you, *señor,"* he said. "Een *los ranchos Americanos* ees cut *lost cojones* when bull ees calf. Een *Mexico* we are wait teel bull ees grow, then cut *cojones*. So ees have leetle *cuerno;* meat ees more tender."

"Hold on there, now!" the drunk at the side table broke in. "I ain't gonna let nobody run down Texas longhorns! They got as good meat as them damn little Mexican kind!"

No es verdad! Ees not so!" the Mexican cowhand exclaimed.

"Don't call me a liar!" the drunk snarled. "Any damn fool knows a steer's horns is hollow! They ain't so heavy a critter gets tough muscles just holding his head up!"

"Ees hollow, *verdad,"* the Mexican agreed quickly. "But ees *verdad egualamente* ees heavy!"

"I told you not to call me a liar!" the drunk growled. He whipped a Bowie knife out of his boottop and flourished it. "No greaser kin do that! I'm gonna cut you up in little pieces and stuff you inside them horns hangin' up over yonder!"

Longarm saw that to uphold his lawman's oath he'd have to stop the drunk. He started away from the bar, but before he'd taken a second step the barkeep dashed across the narrow room carrying a short, sturdy billy-club. He brought it down on the drunk's wrist, the Bowie knife fell to the floor, and while it was still clattering the barkeep tapped the drunk on the head with the billy.

As the drunk sagged and slumped, the barkeep turned and said, "Now, I hope you gents ain't upset by this little fracas. To settle your nerves if you are, I'm going to draw you a beer on the house. It's a new kind, a real fine beer, made up north of here in Golden."

Dragging the drunk to the rear of the saloon, the barkeep

was gone before anyone could speak. Longarm turned back to the bar, saw his unfinished drink in the horn-shaped glass, the Tom Moore glowing amber in the reflection of the mirrored backbar. He glanced from the glass up to the mounted steer-horns, an idea forming in his mind. It was still too nebulous to grasp firmly when the batwings swung open and the clerk from the stockyard office pushed in.

"Thought I might find you men here," he said. "That herd of Mexican longhorns just got in; the hands are driving 'em down to pen nine."

Longarm swallowed the rest of his drink and turned away from the bar. As he moved, he jostled against the two men with whom he'd been talking when the fracas between the Mexican cowhand and the drunk broke out. When he turned to face the pair he saw that the younger of them was now carrying a small satchel.

"Beg pardon," he said. "I wasn't sure you men was the ones that's interested in that longhorn herd. I'll just walk along with you to the pen. There's a few—"

Before Longarm could finish, the older of the two men slid his hand up under his coat. Longarm had not seen the outline of the shoulder holster the man was wearing, but he saw it now in time to whip out his Colt and fire before his unexpected adversary had his gun hand in position to let off a shot.

Longarm swivelled toward the second man, but he'd been so close to the pair when the unexpected gunplay erupted that the sagging body of the man he'd been forced to shoot lurched into him and threw him off balance. His shot went wild and the younger man swung his satchel around and smashed it down onto Longarm's gun hand. The Colt was jarred from Longarm's grasp, but he twisted his hand, grabbed the small valise, and hung on.

While Longarm struggled against the weight of the inert body pressing on him to bring up his left hand and reach the derringer in his vest pocket, the younger man's frantic tugging broke the handle off the satchel. Tossing the handle aside, he spurted for the batwings and dived through them.

Longarm had freed himself of the body's dead weight by now, and he scooped his Colt up and ran after the escaping man. Just as the fleeing man had done, Longarm dashed through the swinging doors, only to collide with Billy Vail, who was trying to enter the saloon. Swinging Vail aside, Longarm ran into the long passage between the stockpens, but the fugitive was nowhere to be seen. Smothering his frustration, he turned back to face Vail.

"Damn it, Billy! I could've got that fellow if you hadn't decided to go in the saloon just when I needed to get out in a hurry!" Longarm complained.

"Simmer down, Long!" Billy snapped. "How the devil was I to know you were in trouble? I heard a shot and started in."

Longarm had regained his poise by now. He said, "Well, I wasn't in no trouble. A fellow tried to kill me inside there, but I got my Colt out first. That'll wait, though. The fellow that got away was the one we want to close up that case I'm on."

"Soapy Smith?" Vail frowned. "What's he got to do with your case?"

"You mean you know him?" Longarm asked, his jaw dropping.

"Of course. I just got a glimpse of him, but I recognized him before he dodged into the stockpens."

"And you didn't try to stop him?"

"I didn't have any reason to. Besides, he's not the kind of crook that gets into federal cases. He's a small-time grifter the Denver police are after, but Soapy's crookedness isn't in our jurisdiction."

"What kind of crook is he, then?" Longarm asked.

"Oh, he's a small-time swindler, a con man, a grifter. He got his name selling bars of soap on street corners. He makes a spiel to draw a crowd and wraps twenty-dollar bills around some of them, then wraps plain paper over the bar and mixes them up with some other bars he had all ready in a basket. Then—"

"You don't need to finish, Billy," Longarm broke in. "I know the scheme. He sells the soap for ten dollars a bar, but nobody that buys one ever finds any money under that outside wrapper, because Soapy palmed the twenty while he was putting the second wrapper on."

"That's it," Vail nodded. "One of the oldest swindles in the world. But the Denver police never could pin it on him."

"Well, I hate to tell you this, Billy, but if I'm right he's moved up from street corners now."

"You're trying to tell me he's the man behind the Arapahoe Syndicate?" Vail asked incredulously. "I'll have a hard time believing that."

182

"Walk along with me down to pen number nine, Billy. I got a pretty good idea now what's behind this Mexican longhorn herd. If I'm right, we'll be wanting Soapy Smith bad as the Denver police force does."

At Pen #9, Greenhaw and the trail drive crew was waiting. The Mexican longhorns were packed into the pen, jostling and blatting in their unaccustomed confinement.

"Custis!" Greenhaw said. "I wondered when you'd show up."

"I'd've been here before now, Tom, but I run into Billy and we— Well, I'm here, anyhow. And you don't have to call me Custis any longer. My case is closed; you can use my last name."

"Wait, now!" Vail broke in. "You still haven't closed your case until I say so. And I want it explained, Long!"

"Sure," Longarm replied. He turned to Greenhaw. "Tom, I got to kill one of them steers, but don't worry. You'll get the money you was promised and the rest of the boys will get every penny they got coming." He handed Vail the satchel he'd been carrying since Soapy Smith's unsuccessful effort to wrench it away. "I guess you better hold on to this, Billy."

"You know what's inside?" Vail asked.

"I'd bet a bottle of Tom Moore I do. There's money to pay off Tom and his men, and I'd imagine some papers that'll tell us all about the Arapahoe Syndicate. Except I got a hunch it's the Soapy Smith syndicate. We'll see right quick if I'm right."

Vaulting over the top bar of the stockpen, Longarm drew his Colt and shot the closest steer between the eyes. The animal dropped instantly, dead before it reached the ground.

Taking a freshly folded bandanna from his pocket, he spread it under one of the dead steer's horns. He fired a second round into the base of the horn. The brittle horn shattered and Longarm wrenched it free. A dozen or more small pouches made from fine, thin leather dropped onto the handkerchief.

Picking up one of the pouches, Longarm opened the pouch and upended it. A pile of gold dust trickled into his palm. He held the dust out for the others to see.

"Mexican gold," he said. "They sawed off the horns these critters grew and fastened some bigger ones over 'em with some kinda waterproof glue after they put in these bags of gold. Soapy Smith was trying to cheat the U.S. government by bringing it over the border without paying duty on it."

"Now, how the hell did you come up with that answer?" Vail asked. "You said this morning—"

"I know, Billy. And I told you the truth. Then I seen a set of big horns off a Texas steer in that saloon a little while ago, and a couple of cowboys had a fracas over how heavy they was. One of 'em remarked that the horns was hollow and didn't weigh all that much, and I recalled how these steers walked with their heads down. About that time the barkeep said something about a beer brewed up in Golden, and everything come together. So I guess our case ain't quite closed yet, Billy. We ain't found Sterns, but you know how crooks is when they take a false name. Generally they'll take one starting the same letter as theirs. I'd guess we'll have our hands on Sterns just as soon as we catch up with Soapy Smith."

Watch for

LONGARM AND THE FRONTIER DUCHESS

eighty-first novel in the bold
LONGARM series from Jove

coming in September!

LONGARM

Explore the exciting Old West with one of the men who made it wild!

__08099-3	LONGARM AND THE OUTLAW LAWMAN #56	$2.50
__07859-X	LONGARM AND THE BOUNTY HUNTERS #57	$2.50
__07858-1	LONGARM IN NO MAN'S LAND #58	$2.50
__07886-7	LONGARM AND THE BIG OUTFIT #59	$2.50
__08259-7	LONGARM AND SANTA ANNA'S GOLD #60	$2.50
__08388-7	LONGARM AND THE CUSTER COUNTY WAR #61	$2.50
__08161-2	LONGARM IN VIRGINIA CITY #62	$2.50
__08369-0	LONGARM AND THE JAMES COUNTY WAR #63	$2.50
__06265-0	LONGARM AND THE CATTLE BARON #64	$2.50
__06266-9	LONGARM AND THE STEER SWINDLER #65	$2.50
__06267-7	LONGARM AND THE HANGMAN'S NOOSE #66	$2.50
__08304-6	LONGARM AND THE OMAHA TINHORNS #67	$2.50
__08369-0	LONGARM AND THE DESERT DUCHESS #68	$2.50
__08374-7	LONGARM AND THE PAINTED DESERT #69	$2.50
__06271-5	LONGARM ON THE OGALLALA TRAIL #70	$2.50
__07915-4	LONGARM ON THE ARKANSAS DIVIDE #71	$2.50
__06273-1	LONGARM AND THE BLIND MAN'S VENGEANCE #72	$2.50
__06274-X	LONGARM AT FORT RENO #73	$2.50
__08109-4	LONGARM AND THE DURANGO PAYROLL #74	$2.50
__08042-X	LONGARM WEST OF THE PECOS #75	$2.50
__08173-6	LONGARM ON THE NEVADA LINE #76	$2.50
__08190-6	LONGARM AND THE BLACKFOOT GUNS #77	$2.50
__08254-6	LONGARM ON THE SANTA CRUZ #78	$2.50
__08232-5	LONGARM AND THE COWBOY'S REVENGE #79	$2.50

Prices may be slightly higher in Canada.

Available at your local bookstore or return this form to:

JOVE
Book Mailing Service
P.O. Box 690, Rockville Centre, NY 11571

Please send me the titles checked above. I enclose _____. Include 75¢ for postage and handling if one book is ordered; 25¢ per book for two or more not to exceed $1.75. California, Illinois, New York and Tennessee residents please add sales tax.

NAME _____

ADDRESS _____

CITY _____ STATE/ZIP _____

(allow six weeks for delivery)   6

☆ From the Creators of LONGARM ☆

The Wild West will never be the same!

LONE ★ STAR

LONE STAR features the extraordinary and beautiful Jessica Starbuck and her loyal half-American, half-Japanese martial arts sidekick, Ki.

_ LONE STAR AND THE TEXAS GAMBLER #22   07628-7/$2.50
_ LONE STAR AND THE HANGROPE HERITAGE #23   07734-8/$2.50
_ LONE STAR AND THE MONTANA TROUBLES #24   07748-8/$2.50
_ LONE STAR AND THE MOUNTAIN MAN #25   07880-8/$2.50
_ LONE STAR AND   07920-0/$2.50
   THE STOCKYARD SHOWDOWN #26
_ LONE STAR AND   07916-2/$2.50
   THE RIVERBOAT GAMBLERS #27
_ LONE STAR AND   08055-1/$2.50
   THE MESCALERO OUTLAWS #28
_ LONE STAR AND THE AMARILLO RIFLES #29   08082-9/$2.50
_ LONE STAR AND   08110-8/$2.50
   THE SCHOOL FOR OUTLAWS #30
_ LONE STAR ON THE TREASURE RIVER #31   08043-8/$2.50
_ LONE STAR AND THE MOON TRAIL FEUD #32   08174-4/$2.50
_ LONE STAR AND THE GOLDEN MESA #33   08191-4/$2.50
_ LONE STAR AND THE RIO GRANDE BANDITS #34 08255-4/$2.50
_ LONE STAR AND THE BUFFALO HUNTERS #35   08233-3/$2.50

Prices may be slightly higher in Canada.

Available at your local bookstore or return this form to: ·

 JOVE
Book Mailing Service
P.O. Box 690, Rockville Centre, NY 11571

Please send me the titles checked above. I enclose _____ Include 75¢ for postage and handling if one book is ordered; 25¢ per book for two or more not to exceed $1.75. California, Illinois, New York and Tennessee residents please add sales tax.

NAME_____

ADDRESS_____

CITY_____ STATE/ZIP_____

(Allow six weeks for delivery.)   54